The Second Chance

"No one pulls her readers in like Reding."
—Catherine Coulter

"Powerful and immensely moving. . . . I can't wait to get my hands on her other books."
—*The Romance Reader*

"An author who knows what readers are seeking. Her stories will quickly wrap themselves around your own life and become a permanent fixture in your heart. The life she breathes into her characters is so heartwarming it will bring tears to your eyes."
—MyShelf.com

"I thoroughly enjoyed my time on the Massachusetts shore and feel that other readers will as well."
—Romance Reviews Today

The Secret Gift

"Reding is at her very best with this deftly written story of the heart and soul of Scotland and the man and woman who find each other there. An elegant and moving story." —Catherine Coulter

"A delicious contemporary debut . . . pure romantic fun!" —Mary Jo Putney

"A compelling contemporary romance that warms the heart and satisfies the soul." —Patricia Rice

"A deliciously detailed story of an inheritance lost and found." —*Booklist*

continued . . .

The Adventurer

"Wonderful. Don't miss it!" —Catherine Coulter

"A fine Scottish plaid expertly woven of romance, history, and legends, the second book in Reding's *Highland Heroes* . . . is sheer magic. Readers who enjoy such books as Connie Brockway's *McClairen's Isle* series and Diana Gabaldon's *Outlander* won't want to put this one down." —*Booklist*

"Jaclyn Reding does a wonderful job with this novel . . . marvelous character development." —*Romantic Times*

"One to read and remember. Don't miss it!" —Romance Fiction Forum

The Pretender

"A hero who is a heartbreaker—ruthless, dangerous, and so sexy you'll want him for yourself." —Catherine Coulter

"A fast-paced read. . . . Ms. Reding sketches a touching love story against the backdrop of turbulent political times." —*Romantic Times*

"[A] delicious blend of humor, history, and adventure—a story readers will truly savor." —*Booklist*

"The tables are turned on an unconventional heroine. . . . Colored with drama and humor, this one is a winner." —*Rendezvous*

White Mist

"The queen of Regency-era Scottish romance enticingly portrays a compellingly evoked wild landscape and its resilient denizens." —*Booklist*

"This is an exceptional book, one that ranks high . . . a truly wonderful tale." —*Rendezvous*

White Knight

"I'd be a damsel in distress any day if this white knight was in the vicinity. Don't miss Reding's latest goodie." —Catherine Coulter

"Jaclyn Reding spins a tale of love like no other! Highly recommended!"
—Under the Covers Reviews

White Magic

"With her superb knowledge and admirable skill, Reding captures the romance and grace of Regency England." —*The Literary Times*

"This very satisfying historical romance runs the gamut of emotions; it also leaves just enough unsaid to make you want to read the next book in the quartet." —*Rendezvous*

White Heather

"Captivated me from the start . . . a charming combination of mystery, murder, romance, intrigue, and legend . . . a magical journey to romance."
—Scottish Radiance

"Rich in historical detail, endearing characters, compelling stories—Jaclyn Reding has it all. This is a writer to watch." —Linda Lael Miller

Spellstruck

JACLYN REDING

A SIGNET ECLIPSE BOOK

SIGNET ECLIPSE
Published by New American Library, a division of
Penguin Group (USA) Inc., 375 Hudson Street,
New York, New York 10014, USA
Penguin Group (Canada), 90 Eglinton Avenue East, Suite 700, Toronto,
Ontario M4P 2Y3, Canada (a division of Pearson Penguin Canada Inc.)
Penguin Books Ltd., 80 Strand, London WC2R 0RL, England
Penguin Ireland, 25 St. Stephen's Green, Dublin 2,
Ireland (a division of Penguin Books Ltd.)
enguin Group (Australia), 250 Camberwell Road, Camberwell, Victoria 3124,
Australia (a division of Pearson Australia Group Pty. Ltd.)
Penguin Books India Pvt. Ltd., 11 Community Centre, Panchsheel Park,
New Delhi - 110 017, India
Penguin Group (NZ), cnr Airborne and Rosedale Roads, Albany,
Auckland 1310, New Zealand (a division of Pearson New Zealand Ltd.)
Penguin Books (South Africa) (Pty.) Ltd., 24 Sturdee Avenue,
Rosebank, Johannesburg 2196, South Africa

Penguin Books Ltd., Registered Offices:
80 Strand, London WC2R 0RL, England

First published by Signet Eclipse, an imprint of New American Library,
a division of Penguin Group (USA) Inc.

First Printing, February 2007
10 9 8 7 6 5 4 3 2 1

Dedicated in loving memory of
Patricia Adamowicz

You had a mother's heart,
a grandmother's grace,
and you filled the lives of those
you touched with laughter and joy.

I was blessed with the honor of calling you
Mom.

Wherever you are,
know that we love you,
and we're missing you so very much.

Chapter One

"Cut it off, Jen. I mean it this time. Cut it all off."

Jenna smiled at Hannah Greer's reflection in her salon mirror. It was oval-shaped—the mirror, that is, not Hannah Greer—topped by soft white lights that were neither too harsh nor too dim and otherwise framed by a photograph collage of Jenna's kids, a favorite *Calvin and Hobbes* comic strip, and the postcard her friend Flora had sent the last time she'd gone to Scotland. It depicted a herd of sheep crowding down a narrow country road with the words *Rush Hour in Scotland* printed in plaid beneath it. Jenna still found it funny enough to crack a smile whenever she noticed it.

"You know you don't really want me to do that," Jenna said to Hannah, wishing she had a dollar for every time she'd heard one of her clients say those same words. Whenever drastic times called for drastic measures, more often than not women seemed to take aim at their hair.

Not that Jenna was complaining. After all, if not for those drastic measures, she'd be unemployed.

"Yes, I do want you to do it," Hannah insisted. "I want you to cut it off."

Jenna slanted her a shrewd glance. "No, you don't."

"I do."

"You don't. And you know it."

A blow-dryer clicked on and started humming somewhere behind them, but Hannah only huffed louder. An attractive woman in her mid-thirties, she uncrossed and then recrossed her shapely legs, the result of, she always assured Jenna, *countless* hours spent trudging on the stair stepper. She kicked at the cotton skirt she wore for added effect.

Hannah Greer wanted to make certain everyone knew she was perturbed. Jenna smiled to herself. Hannah could always be counted on to add a bit of drama to a typical busy Saturday at IpSnips Salon. And that drama almost always had to do with whatever ill-advised thing her husband, Jim, had recently done.

Once he had "fertilized" her prized rose bushes with something that turned them brown and as brittle as winter twigs.

Another time he'd tried to "help" with the laundry. By the end of the spin cycle, all of Hannah's Victoria's Secret lingerie had turned a drab and mottled shade of green-gray, victim to the old army fatigues he'd tossed into the washing machine as well.

Men.

Who else would wash lace-trimmed tangas and push-up bras with dingy hunting camouflage?

Although Hannah had yet to reveal Jim's latest venture, Jenna knew it was only a matter of time before the whole tragic tale came pouring past that perfect Mary Kay pout.

But first Hannah had to decide just what she was going to do to punish him.

She seemed to deliberate for a moment, but in the end, stuck with her original plan. Her hair, and the removal thereof. She grabbed a handful of the honey blond stuff that currently fell to the middle of her back. With a tortured sigh, she held it up in a gesture of sacrifice to Jenna's styling shears.

"No, I mean it. Cut. It. Off. All of it. Make it as short as Sam's."

Jenna glanced across the salon to where her eleven-year-old son was hunched in front of the salon's computer, doing battle against the Internet army of his friend, Tim, from across the World Wide Web—or rather from just across the street since Tim lived three houses down on the corner. The crew cut Sam typically sported throughout the summer months had only just begun to grow out for fall.

"Hannah Greer," Jenna said, tucking her own straight, just-below-the-chin bob of black hair behind one silver-hooped ear. "I will not cut off your hair simply because you're angry at your husband, and do you want to know why? Because you'll go home. He'll apologize for whatever it is he did this time. He'll bring home flowers. Take you out to dinner. Probably buy you that new dishwasher down at Wilson's Appliances that you've had your eye on. And you know what will happen then?"

Hannah's shell pink lips puckered into a frown. "What?"

"You'll look at yourself in the mirror, see your hair—or the lack thereof—and all that anger you feel right now for Jim will be redirected. At me. I've been through this enough times before with other angry wives to have learned by now. No,

Hannah, I'm not cutting off your hair to help you get back at Jim."

Hannah simply stared at Jenna.

Emma, the stylist working in the adjacent booth, shot Jenna a sympathetic glance in the mirror over Mrs. Chambers' foil-topped head. Emma was young, barely twenty-three, and newly certified. She was tall and slender with a fall of shoulder-length dark blond hair and a face that was freckled from the summer sun. Both she and Mrs. Chambers, who was about as ancient as Emma was young, were listening raptly to the conversation between Jenna and Hannah, waiting to see what resulted from the apparent impasse.

"But what I will do," Jenna went on, crossing her arms over her aqua-colored smock, "is this. First, I will get you a pot of my special 'Husbands Can Be Such Idiots' tea . . ."

Apple blossom, Jenna noted to herself. *Yes, definitely tea made from apple blossom and a hint of lily of the valley tossed in for peace and harmony, too.*

"After the tea," she went on, "when you're feeling more yourself again, I will *trim* your hair and style it. Then we'll finish up with 'The Works'—a facial, manicure, makeup, you name it—so that when you go out with Jim for dinner tonight, you'll turn the head of every man there."

That, Jenna thought, along with the added little damiana amulet she would include for good measure, ought to have more than a few of the locals looking at Hannah Greer through appreciative male eyes—and that was sure to make Jim behave into the new year.

As Jenna had hoped, the prospect of making her husband jealous held much more appeal than ruining her beloved hair. Hannah smiled in wicked delight.

"Let me have it then, 'The Works,' and spare nothing. I'll even have my toes done. Paint them poppy red so they'll really stand out in that sweet little pair of open-toe slingbacks I saw in the shop next door. Spotted them in the window on my way here, but I wasn't going to buy them because they're far too pricey. You know, the kind of shoes you wear only once a year, with that *oh so* special outfit? But you know what? I am going to buy them. And I'll leave the receipt in the bag so he can see just how much they cost, too. That man deserves it for what he did."

Hannah fumed through a silent moment. Had Jenna not known better, she'd have sworn she could see smoke coming out of the woman's ears. And then . . .

"Well?" Hannah finally asked. "Don't you want to know what it was that he did?"

Before Jenna could respond, Hannah launched into a litany of the most recent marital catastrophe that had brought her to the tidy little red saltbox at Number Eight Elm Street.

Jenna Wren's salon was the place most of the women in Ipswich-by-the-Sea came to at times when they found themselves in need of a "healing touch." Healing was something the women in Jenna's family had been doing in one way or another for generations. Back in the earliest times, many of her relatives had practiced as midwives and village wise women, dispensing their knowledge of herbs to heal the sick or ease the suffering of their neighbors. Others, such as her mother, had turned their talents to baking, or what some might call modern-day *brewing*. Jenna's gift was in helping women to feel attractive, boosting their confidence so that they could feel empowered and rejuvenated both inside and out.

Jenna knew specific herbs that would make hair glisten and others that soothed frazzled, over-worked nerves. Some, when used properly, could even help melt away unwanted pounds. She knew of plants that when used in a certain combination could virtually erase the dreaded crow's feet, firming sagging skin more safely than Botox. Jenna could even cast the occasional spell when it was called for.

But the most important part of dispensing with any of her "magic" was in being a good listener first. Jenna smiled and nodded sympathetically, throwing in an "Oh!" and a "He didn't!" whenever Hannah paused to draw breath, all while she sham-pooed Hannah's hair with a calming chamomile and lavender concoction.

Behind the buzz of the blow-dryer and the mur-mur of conversation, the earthy strains of Enya soothed their way through the salon in surround sound. The teapot was always ready and a soft fire crackled in the corner hearth next to cushy arm-chairs and a selection of the latest romance novels from Mrs. Evanson's bookshop. Here at IpSnips women could forget about the carpool, the hockey practices, the groceries that needed buying. Through that simple wooden door, they could step into a place where their bosses and their husbands were a world away, where that urgent fax couldn't possibly reach them, where ruined lingerie no longer seemed to matter. Cell phones were strictly forbidden and there were no clocks ticking away on any of the walls. Whether it took twenty minutes or

two hours, each client left IpSnips feeling physi-
cally, spiritually, emotionally reborn . . .

. . . as if by *magic*.

If only Jenna could find a way to treat herself to
some of her own brand of healing. Then maybe,
just maybe, as she wrung the water from Hannah
Greer's wet hair, she wouldn't be imagining herself
wringing her ex-husband's neck as well.

Jack was late.

Again.

Damn him.

And she didn't need a clock to know it. Because
Jack Gabriele was *always* late.

As she massaged a rosemary-scented conditioning treatment into Hannah's hair, Jenna glanced
over at Sam again and caught sight of his backpack
stuffed with his weekend clothes waiting by the
door. Jack was supposed to have picked him up at
noon for their regularly scheduled weekend visit.

As if by providence, the salon door opened then,
tinging the bell above it. Jenna looked over, hoping
to find Jack, only to see Patsy Lansky arriving for
her two fifteen facial.

Two hours late, and Jack couldn't even call.

Seething inside, Jenna still managed to paste on
a smile and call out a warm greeting to her newest
arrival. She certainly wouldn't allow her anger at
her irresponsible ex-husband to impinge on her
business. IpSnips was Jenna's livelihood, her dream
and her creation, built from the ground up solely
by her.

It hadn't been an easy road to the success she
now enjoyed. After her divorce three years earlier,
Jenna had been desperate. She had suddenly found
herself in need of a job; actually not only a job but

a *career,* one that would allow her to raise her children on a single parent's income but still leave her free to be there to pack their lunches, to soothe their skinned knees, and most importantly, to not make them feel as if they were losing both parents at the same time. She had married young—too young, she now realized—and had never gone to college, instead jumping straight from the carefree world of high school into the adult worlds of marriage and motherhood. At the time, it had felt so right. She'd been utterly, truly, crazy in love, never dreaming she and Jack wouldn't be together until they were old and gray, until death did them part. Blissfully naive, Jenna had been content to let Jack work while she tended to the home. An old-fashioned arrangement, perhaps, but she'd loved it. She'd reveled in being a "Homemaker" while all her school friends had departed their seaside village for colleges or stress-filled careers in Boston, New York, or even L.A.

Unfortunately, Jack hadn't found that same sense of contentment and the incompatibility of two people not sharing the same dreams had eventually been too much to bear, toppling her playdate and PTA world. After she'd picked herself from the wreckage, Jenna had faced the reality that she would have to make it on her own.

With Sam and Cassie.

And without Jack.

She suddenly found herself a single mom. Trying to turn back time by going to college then hadn't been an option. What else could she do? Jenna had taken two years of cosmetology as an elective in high school, and had done pretty well with it, styling her friends' hair and giving them makeovers on slumber party weekends. Everyone had said she had a knack for it.

And *knacks* were something Wren women had relied on for generations.

She and the kids moved in with her mother and after quickly getting her stylist's certification, Jenna threw caution—and a very carefully cast spell—to the wind. IpSnips was born with a single chair Jenna set up in the back room of her mother's small colonial. From there, the business flourished, soon outgrowing the tiny back room, and eventually moving to the antique saltbox next door when Number Eight had come available for sale.

It was the perfect location, just off the village's main shopping street and within walking distance of the central common. Formerly a tailoring shop, photographer's studio, and even a day-care center, the place had been in need of renovation. But the price was reasonable and her mother had cosigned on the mortgage to help Jenna get her start.

In those early days, Jenna cut hair by day, stripping walls, sanding floors, and caulking windows and doors at night with Sam and Cassie down on all fours helping. For the heavier, more complicated work, she called in favors from some of her neighbors who were skilled at carpentry and plumbing, promising them free haircuts for life in exchange. At the time, it was all she had to offer. The work had kept her constantly occupied, a good thing since it didn't allow her much time to dwell on her failed marriage.

Jenna, Sam, and Cassie moved into the house's annex, while the main house comprised the salon and all it had to offer. They uprooted the picket fence that had separated the old saltbox from her mother's house next door, giving them a more spacious lot and allowing Jenna to design and lay out her other dream, an herb garden where she grew many of the ingredients she used in the salon.

And as her garden grew, so did IpSnips. Now she offered not only services for hair, but also manicures and pedicures, massage, all-natural facial and body treatments, even aromatheraphy. The salon's success culminated in a very favorable write-up in a recent edition of *New England Living* magazine, which dubbed IpSnips a "true hidden treasure," a place to visit to be "pampered, coiffed, and preened," and a very special salon filled with an indescribable "enchantment."

That last accolade had given Jenna cause for a wry smile. If they only knew.

Even back when it had been nothing more than a local secret, IpSnips had always done a fair amount of business. But since the article's publication, the phone rang almost constantly, with patrons coming from as far away as Rhode Island and Long Island. Appointments were booked through the end of the year with a waiting list several pages long for cancellations. There were rarely any cancellations, and Jenna certainly wasn't complaining. She'd added two new stylists over the summer months—one she'd kept, the other she'd let go because of sloppy work and, *ahem,* differing philosophies on the treatment of their customers.

It took a certain, special breed of stylist to work at IpSnips and Marcia just hadn't been it. Marcia would be better suited to a place decked out in chrome and glass instead of checked curtains and dried herbs, a place with a sterile and austere environment, where the clients' wants were secondary to the stylist's own "vision" of what their look should be. As a result, Jenna was still trying to smooth things over with Mildred Caldwell, assuring her on an almost daily basis that yes, she was sure it would grow out.

The bell above the salon door tinged again, drawing Jenna out of her reminiscing. While Hannah nattered on about Jim and his latest slip up, Jenna prepared to greet her customer. It was probably Kathleen Spencer-Brown, who was due at three for her monthly waxing.

When she turned, however, Jenna offered no warm smile, no friendly greeting. She simply narrowed her eyes and frowned as her ex-husband ducked into IpSnips.

Jack Gabriele flashed his boyish smile from beneath the brim of a tattered Red Sox cap as he entered the salon. His brown hair, she noticed immediately, had lightened over the summer to a rich burnished toffee. It suited him, she thought, as she remembered a time when she had threaded her fingers through that same hair while lying beneath him one particularly passionate night on the beach at Siren's Cove. But Jenna pushed that thought away just as quickly as it had come. She had to admit that the lighter hair color suited his tanned face even though she could tell his hair hadn't been cut in a while. If she hadn't been so put out with him at being late, she probably would have offered to cut it for him, a gesture of ex-marital harmony.

Purely for the kids, of course.

"Hey, pal," Jack said to Sam, who brightened the moment he laid his eyes, the same glinty hazel as his father's, on Jack.

"Dad! I was beginning to get worried you weren't going to make it."

"You know I wouldn't let you down, Sam."

And as he said those words, Jack's smiling gaze drifted across the salon in the direction of Jenna's booth.

Glinty hazel collided with simmering blue.

Jenna could, and often did, speak volumes with just one stare. She watched Jack straighten and set his shoulders as he headed across the salon toward her, obviously gearing himself up for the confrontation that was brewing.

"I'm busy," she said as she slid her fingers up a section of Hannah's wet hair and neatly clipped the ends.

"Aren't you always," Jack muttered. "Look, I just wanted to say I'm sorry I'm late. I got hung up."

"Aren't you always?" Jenna mimicked. Catching Hannah's interested gaze in the mirror, she motioned Jack toward the back supply room. "Emma," she called to the stylist who was just cleaning up her own booth after finishing Mrs. Chambers' tinting. "Would you comb out the rest of Hannah's tangles while I take a second to hand Sam over to his father for the weekend?"

"Sure thing," Emma said, and stepped right in to Jenna's place. "So, Hannah, did I hear you say something about Jim using your grandmother's handmade quilt for a drop cloth when he painted the backyard shed?"

And in that moment, Hannah's attention turned from Jenna's marital misfortunes back to her own.

"Nice of you to show up," Jenna said as she shut the supply room door behind them. She knew she sounded like a typical petulant ex-wife, hated that she did, but she crossed her arms and stared him down—or rather *up* since he was a good ten inches taller than she—nonetheless. Space in the storeroom was tight. They were so close she could smell his familiar scent, an inexplicable combination of soap, the sea, and *him* that used to have Jenna hugging his pillow every morning when she woke to find him already gone to work.

Jenna took a step away from Jack, backing against the supply shelf in an effort to put some distance between her and him . . . and that scent.

"Look, Jen," Jack said, cracking his cocky smile. "I'm not going to fight with you, no matter how much you want to."

"I don't want to," she said. "I just wish I knew why it is so impossible for you to be a responsible father."

"I am a responsible father, Jen. I send the support checks every month and I'm here to pick up my kid just as I am supposed to. I said I got caught up."

"Couldn't you have at least called him? Do you know he's been practically jumping out of the chair every time that bell rings above the door? You're over two hours late, Jack. That's two hours less that you'll have with your son this weekend. Last time, you were three and a half hours late to pick up Cassie. Part of being a responsible parent is to be there when you say you will. They count on you for that, Jack. And I'm the one who has to be there to comfort them when they're disappointed by you." She looked at him. "It's something I'm becoming quite an expert at."

The look that always crossed his face whenever Jen dug low and gave him a not-so-subtle reminder of their failure to make their marriage work surfaced for but a moment. It was a mixture of hurt, sadness, and raw regret, and it left Jenna hissing in her breath, as if she'd been the one just sucker punched and not he.

Jack, however, did what he usually did, which was to pull the brim of his cap down to shield his eyes and head for the door. Silence and avoidance were his specialties. Dealing with issues was not one of Jack's strong points.

"I'll have Sam back at the usual time tomorrow night."

And then he was gone.

Jen could only stand there, alone in that supply closet, feeling like the world's bitchiest ex-wife for having resorted to the same condemnation she always used, the one she knew stung Jack the deepest.

Damn it.

Later that night, Jenna sat in her kitchen, which was painted a cozy periwinkle blue and decorated with hand painted Delft tiles that she'd found one rather fortuitous afternoon hidden away in an old crate at the 2nd Chance Shop, Ipswich-by-the-Sea's local antique emporium. It was late, past eleven. She had washed the dinner dishes, Cassie was bathed and put to bed, and Jenna could finally unwind from the day while relating the entire episode, Hannah Greer and all, to her younger sister, Hallie, over a bottle of Australian chardonnay.

"Why is it men have to be so . . ."

"Obtuse?" Hallie offered. "Thoughtless? Asinine? Infuriating beyond belief?"

As little sisters went, Hallie was as good as they made them. Even though there were nearly seven years between them, when they were girls, they'd been inseparable. After they lost their father at ages six and thirteen, they'd been each other's comfort. And over the past twenty-three years, Hallie had grown from seedling to gangly adolescent sprig to the brilliant bright sunflower she now was. She was strawberry blond like their father, where Jenna had inherited their mother's pitch-black hair. Hallie had Jenna's same blue eyes, eyes that were always turning toward the light, looking for the best of any situation, and seeing every possibility.

Hallie was also a whiz with computers. At the salon, she had always helped Jenna with keeping track of inventory and searching out the latest trends to make sure Jenna had the best to offer her clientele. Over the summer, Hallie had also taken a second job working up at Thar Muir, the local B-and-B run by Jenna's friend, Flora. Hallie managed the bookkeeping, the reservations, and the technical side of the inn, freeing up Flora to do what she did best, making their guests' stays as unique and unforgettable as possible. Hallie was well suited for the work and she thrived on it. Jenna couldn't be prouder of her sister.

"Men," Hallie repeated, shaking her head. Her eyes sparked in the soft glow of the scented candles Jenna had lit around the room. "Mother Nature certainly left out that sensitivity gene when she tossed in the other ingredients. Too bad she couldn't have left out the penis instead. It's all they're motivated by."

"Amen to that, sister," Jenna replied, topping off Hallie's wineglass and then her own. "You know, I tell myself every time this happens that I'm not going to resort to old arguments, that I'll be the better person and simply learn to accept that he's never going to change. But then he does something, like not show up, not call to say he's going to be late, not care that he's got his kid nearly wetting himself, waiting for him, and all my good intentions vanish like *poof*!"

Jenna snapped her fingers to emphasize her

point. When she did, the cork she'd placed in the wine bottle suddenly popped back out, rolling on the table beside them.

She looked at Hallie. "Oops."

Hallie grinned, shrugging. "Occupational hazard?"

They were both, after all, practicing witches.

Magic, spellcraft, witchery—whatever anyone chose to call it—was a thing of genealogical significance to the Wren women, stretching back to their roots in the ancient Celts. Theirs was a hereditary witchcraft, passed from mother to daughter to granddaughter. They practiced as "hedge" witches, solitary spellcasters, not part of any coven, revering the earth and all its treasures and dispensing their craft within the bounties of nature. Not a New Age craft like that of the Wiccans, but an age-old gift, something to be respected; more than that, something to be *protected* at all costs. It was as much a part of their lives as breathing, yet it was rarely spoken of out loud and when it was, never outside of the private female circle of their family.

"Things like that always happen when you've had too much wine," Hallie said, picking up the popped cork from where it had fallen to the floor. "Remember that time you had everyone over for brunch and had a few too many mimosas? All the eggs exploded out of their shells like little land mines." She made a bursting motion with her hands. "Boom!"

Jenna laughed. "I will never forget the look on Jack's mother's face—Rosa Gabriele, the Italian equivalent to Martha Stewart. I had to tell her that was how I thought scrambled eggs were made."

Hallie's eyes widened. "You didn't!"

"How else was I going to explain it? 'Yes, pardon me, Mama Rosa, but this is what happens when a witch has a little too much to drink?'" Jenna shook her head. "I remember she just looked at me for what must have been an entire minute, and then turned and said something to Jack's aunt in Italian. Good thing I don't know what the word for 'ninny' is in Italian."

"You and Mother," Hallie said. "Give her more than a glass and everything goes haywire. Although she swears she conjured up the perfect recipe for her raspberry 'fertility' chutney once while drinking a bottle of her favorite Madeira."

"Yes, well, Ingrid Bellhorn and her three sets of twins are certainly testament to that," Jenna laughed. "Hmm," she said, twirling the stem of her wineglass before her. "Maybe we should try coming up with the recipe for a perfect man over this bottle of chardonnay. One who doesn't use a grandmother's quilt to paint, and who shows up when he says he will."

Hallie snickered, then snorted. The wine and the moonlight stealing through the kitchen window made her game for just this sort of mindless fun. "So, a recipe for a *perfect* man, huh? It would be a challenge. Sort of like revamping what Mother Nature concocted the first time? Actually, this could be fun. What should we include as the first ingredient?" Hallie thought a moment longer. "Hmm. *Irish*. Definitely Irish."

Jenna grabbed a pen and sheet of paper from the counter by the phone, jotting it down while Hallie thought further.

"And I'm thinking a really big—"

"—heart," Jenna finished, shooting her sister a reproving glance. "So he can love the woman to whom he gives that heart utterly and completely."

Jenna drew a fanciful heart in the very center of the page, then penciled in an arrow à la Cupid for good measure.

"Okay, okay," Hallie agreed. "Add two cups of 'tall.' He has to be six feet at least. We don't want to be staring down at him in our heels."

"Right," Jenna agreed, writing a *6'* beside the heart she'd drawn. "Hair color?"

"Black. No. Blond, and not that dirty beach sand color either, but *gleaming,* with a dash of brilliant gold. Like the gods of Olympus." She sighed as Jenna scribbled on the page. "And his eyes, they just have to be green. Like emeralds. Gold and emeralds . . . perfect."

Hallie sighed again as Jenna finished adding to the list. "Anything else?"

"Yes," Hallie piped in. "Money. A heaping bowlful of it."

"Okay . . . fine, while he doesn't need to have Donald Trump's bankbook," Jenna specified, "he should at least have a stable income. But what about his inner qualities? What about responsibility?" Jenna pictured Jack in his tattered baseball cap that morning, unkempt hair and cocky grin in place. She frowned. "What about reliability?"

"Yeah, yeah," Hallie agreed. "Responsibility. *Blah.* Reliability. *Blah, blah.* But give him good taste, too. No ballgames for dates and he must know the difference between a bottle of good wine and a can of beer." She took a sip from her glass, then added, "Oh! And he must love the woman of his heart to utter distraction. He cannot sleep or even eat without thinking of her. He sees her in his dreams. Everything he does reminds him of her."

Jenna laughed, indulging in the ridiculousness of their game. She wrote Hallie's latest "ingredients" on the page and wondered if she'd ever been that young, that fanciful. She knew she must have been, once long ago, and she wondered where that girl had gone.

"But while all this is certainly good, we cannot forget the most important quality of all," Jenna finished. "Above all else, he must have—"

She was interrupted by the sound of the front door opening down the hall, followed by the staccato clicking of doggie claws on the hardwood floor. Their mother had apparently returned from her nightly walk around the common with her dog, Ogre, a growth-challenged terrier who, despite his fearsome name, ran for his life whenever confronted by the neighbor's cat, Arnold.

The dog scampered into the kitchen a full minute before his matriarch.

"I'm back," yodeled a deep female voice from down the hall. "Did you see that moon? What a glorious night for a walk!"

The two sisters turned just as Eudora "Nanny" Wren came into the kitchen. She cut a formidable figure, cloaked in black with her polished wood walking stick levered before her. Her hair, once as black as Jenna's, was now shot through with gray, rendering it a true salt-and-pepper. When it wasn't wound up in its usual knot and fastened to her head with the sort of long hairpins used a century earlier, it fell nearly to her hips. She always wore lipstick, no matter if she were going only to the front door to meet the package delivery man. And she wore spectacles—and yes, that's just what they were—wire rimmed, round and looking like they had been made around the same time as her hairpins.

Age and two pregnancies and a fondness for dark

chocolate–covered cherries had rounded her once eye-catching figure, but Eudora didn't care. She'd been a widow since the day her Sam, for whom Jenna's son was named, had been taken from her, a fisherman lost to the sea in one of the most terrible storms in New England history. A widow she would stay until the day she joined him.

Eudora's shrewd eyes took in the cloaked expressions of her daughters, the nearly empty bottle of wine, and the candlelight. She immediately asked, "What are you two up to then?"

Jenna quickly turned over the paper she'd been writing on. Mother would never approve of their undertaking, even if it was only for fun. "Oh, just having a glass of wine and complaining about men. You know, typical girl stuff. Care to join us?"

"I would," the matriarch sighed, tossing Ogre a bit of cheese from the cracker platter the girls had been sharing. "But if I have wine this late at night, I'll wake with a headache fierce enough to stir the dead." She nodded to herself then glanced at the clock. "Besides, you two should be abed as well. I trust Cassie's already tucked in for the night?"

Jenna nodded. "Hours ago. You must have worn her out with all that baking today. Didn't even put up a fight."

Eudora grinned. "She's a sweet one, that child. And canny as can be. She'll be a true Wren one day, that's for certain."

"Better later than sooner," Jenna said. She and her mother didn't quite agree on when the best time was for initiating Cassie into her legacy. Jenna wanted to wait until her daughter was at least ten. Eudora, however . . .

"It comes when it chooses to come, dear. There's naught you can do to stop it."

Smiling a mother's knowing smile, Eudora took up her walking stick and headed for the back door. It opened onto a stone pathway that wandered through Jenna's garden to her mother's house on the other side. "Are you coming, Hallie? You've work tomorrow, no?"

"A'yea," Hallie conceded, nodding to her sister. "We've got Betsy Berringer's wedding, with the bridal party staying on till Tuesday. It was a good thing Flora decided to keep Thar Muir open through the winter and stay on with Gavin and the kids a little longer. We're already booked for Thanksgiving and Christmas, and I've almost convinced her to do a good, old-fashioned dress-up New Year's bash. All in all, I'd say the B-and-B had a triumphant first season."

Hallie got up, grabbed her jacket from the back of her chair, and whistled for the dog to follow. Ogre started forward, but skidded to a stop when he heard Arnold's distant meow from the shadows that beckoned beyond the safety of the back door. The dog froze and then began to shiver.

"Come on, you coward."

Jenna scooped him up, tucking him under her arm and rubbing his one folded ear. "You can stay here tonight. We'll protect you."

She walked her mother and sister to the door, and stood watching as they vanished into the shadows that cloaked the garden between the two houses. She glanced up, catching sight of the moon her mother had remarked upon. It was full and fat and ringed in a mist, hovering over the treetops in what was a typical New England autumn night.

What a moon, indeed . . .

Jenna closed the door, slid the latch in place, and put Ogre on his pillowed "throne," an old laundry basket Cassie had done up with cushions and curtains and glued-on ribbons. She took up the wineglasses, washed and rinsed them in the sink, and put them on the dish board to dry. Then, toweling her hands, she circled the room, checking the windows, extinguishing the candles.

She was drained. It had been a full day at the salon, complete with her confrontation with Jack, and tomorrow showed every sign of being just as hectic. Betsy Berringer's bridal party was due in at eight for hair and makeup. And then Marjorie Cummings was coming in at noon, a treat to herself for her fortieth birthday. Jenna made a mental note to include an extra gift of her "Youth Springs Eternal" vervain and rosemary bath sachet to help ward off any birthday gloominess.

As she reached for the last candle, Jenna remembered the impromptu recipe she and Hallie had been crafting. She also remembered that last quality they'd forgotten to write when her mother returned, the one that would complete their "perfect" recipe.

"Honor," she whispered out loud to the dancing flame of her candle, and smiled a wistful smile. "Above all else, the perfect man must have honor."

Jenna turned to retrieve the paper, intending to burn it in the candle's flame. It was never a good idea to leave any spell, howsoever makeshift it might be, left loose. All spells, she had learned from a very early age, must be kept in a proper grimoire.

But when she looked on the table where she'd last seen the paper, turning it facedown she remembered when her mother had come into the room, Jenna saw that it wasn't there.

It wasn't on the chair.

It hadn't fallen to the floor either.

The paper, in fact, was nowhere to be found.

Chapter Two

Seven-year-old Cassie Wren loved her house.

It was old, almost three hundred years old, and there were fireplaces in every room. The glass in some of the windows was wavy and bubbly, not perfectly see-through like at her Uncle Sal's coffee shop where the front window always sparkled onto the harbor. At her house, the steps were creaky and some of the floors were even a little crooked. The banisters that ran up all three staircases were freckled with little nicks and dings. Her mom said they gave the house character, those dings. Cassie didn't know what *character* meant, but she did know that because there were so many, whenever she made another mark with one of her toys, no one ever noticed.

Another thing she loved about her house was that it had lots and lots of hiding places. There was the cellar and the attic, of course, but they were the obvious places. And there was a cupboard under the stairs where her brother Sam told her disobedient little sisters used to be locked away. Cassie didn't really believe him because he always told her things like that that weren't true, just to try to scare her. Brothers were stupid that way.

But sometimes Cassie did imagine the other children who must have grown up in the house before her, one hundred, two hundred years before. Had they ever hidden in the same places she did? Had any of them slept in her room? Had they stared up at the ceiling like she did at night sometimes, imagining shapes in the shadows that moved with the moon across her ceiling? Did any of them have a stupid brother like she did?

Cassie knew that at some time, someone named "Lettie" had once stayed in her room, because her name was written in the darkest corner of the closet wall. She'd found it when Mommy had pulled off the scary flowered wallpaper that someone had put in her room *everywhere*, on the walls, on the ceiling, in the closet, even on the backs of the doors. Now her walls were a pretty pale purple color that Cassie herself had picked out, except for the spot where Lettie's name was written. Cassie had begged her mother not to paint over it, not to hide it like whoever had put up that wallpaper. Instead, they'd bought a tiny picture frame, a white oval painted with green ivy. They'd removed the backing and fixed the frame to the wall around Lettie's name, preserving it for posterity.

Lettie, or rather the idea of Lettie, had become Cassie's secret friend. She even talked to her sometimes, usually late at night when it was really, really dark. She asked Lettie to do something, leave her a sign, make something move, to show Cassie that her spirit still remained in *their* room. But so far, there had been nothing to indicate that Lettie ever heard her. Even so, Cassie felt something sometimes, like she wasn't really all that alone at night. It didn't scare her, that feeling. She liked the idea of having a "sister" spirit with her, and had even written her own name very carefully underneath Lettie's in that corner of the closet as testament to their special connection. She wondered if one hundred years from now some other little girl would be living in her room and would wonder about her, too.

One of Cassie's very favorite spots to sneak into was the dumbwaiter. She didn't know why it was called that, because it certainly wasn't *dumb*. In fact, to Cassie, it was the coolest thing ever. It was just her size and she could go from the hall outside her bedroom down to the back mudroom off the kitchen without anyone even realizing she'd left her room. Usually she went there when she couldn't sleep because her tummy was rumbling for some of Nanny Wren's chocolate chip and cherry cookies. She could get to the kitchen and back with the pocket of her bathrobe stuffed full before anyone—especially Mommy—was the wiser. And of course, she always sneaked a carrot stick for her pet gerbil, Rat.

Tonight she'd started out doing just that, but had ended up crouched inside the dumbwaiter, listening to Mommy and Auntie Hallie, mostly because she hadn't realized they were in the kitchen until she'd already lowered the dumbwaiter to the bottom floor. She stayed on, hoping they'd go to bed before long, pressing her fist into her middle whenever her tummy had rumbled.

Until she'd heard them and realized they were casting.

Cassie loved it when her mommy worked spells. It was all so mysterious the way she spoke softly and closed her eyes, moving her hands in that strange way. She looked like a picture Cassie had once seen of Morgan Le Fey in a book about King

Arthur, beautiful and dark and mysterious. Sometimes, when she was alone in her room, Cassie mimicked her mother, lifting her arms and trying to remember the words, but they were in Gaelic mostly, because the first Wren women had come from Ireland, and Cassie never seemed to get them right. Nothing ever happened when she tried it, except for once when one of her dolls had fallen from her top shelf, landing right on Rat's cage. It had scared him so much, he'd hidden in his little plastic shoe the rest of the day. It scared Cassie a little too, but it had also excited her more than anything ever had before.

Cassie sighed. Of course none of it mattered anyway because Mommy wouldn't let her cast, no matter how much Cassie begged, whined, and even sometimes cried.

"Not until you're old enough to respect your gift," she'd say.

When Cassie asked her how old she had to be, Jenna wouldn't answer her except to say, "When the time is right, I'll tell you."

But Cassie *knew* she was old enough. She knew it in her heart and felt it all the way down to the tips of her toes. And what Mommy didn't know was that Nanny Wren sometimes let Cassie cast, just a little spell. Under Nanny's watchful eye, Cassie could coax a songbird onto her finger simply by calling out a special chant. She could bring a wilted flower back into bloom by cupping her hands around it and blowing once, twice, and then three times while reciting the words her grandmother had taught her. Nanny promised that soon she would even show Cassie how to make a rainbow appear. But Cassie wanted to do more. She wanted to work a really *big* spell. All by herself. Cassie wanted to show her mom that she was ready to be a witch just like her.

It had to be just the right spell. She couldn't do anything to Sam because he'd just tell on her (even though he deserved it). Boys were stupid that way. In all ways, really. Which was why only the girls in her family could be witches. Not the boys. Mommy and Nanny had made Cassie promise she wouldn't ever tease Sam about it, but there were times, especially when he was being a big doofus, like when he refused to let her follow him and his stupid friends when they went looking for salamanders down at Purgatory Creek, that she wanted so much to gloat at him she would almost break that promise.

But she hadn't.

Promises, Cassie had learned, should never ever be broken.

Good thing Mommy hadn't made her promise never to work a spell. She'd only told Cassie she didn't think she was ready yet, but Cassie knew better. She had tried to tell her mother, but it hadn't changed her mind. Maybe if she showed her, proved to her that she could work a spell all on her own, then she'd realize Cassie was plenty old enough.

After all, she was *almost* eight years old.

The spell, Cassie decided then, had to be something that would help someone. That was the first rule of their craft, that it could be used only for good. And as she'd sat crouched in that dumbwaiter, listening to her mother and her aunt, she'd realized just what she should do. She would cast the spell that they had been writing. She would finish up what they'd begun. And she could even add a couple of her own "ingredients" as well.

Such as playing hopscotch for a start. Every good man should be able to play hopscotch.

Oh, and making the perfect egg cream.

Her daddy made the best egg creams, mixing in just the right amount of chocolate and soda to make it the yummiest. And he wasn't afraid to play hopscotch with her either.

So she would take the bits that Mommy and Aunt Hallie had come up with, add her own, and truly make the "Perfect Man" for Aunt Hallie to fall in love with.

The first part, getting the spell so she could work it, had been easy. While her mom stood at the door watching Nanny and Auntie Hallie leave, Cassie had simply crawled along the kitchen floor to the table. It was a good thing Mommy had been holding Ogre because if he'd seen her on the floor, he would have scampered over to lick her face and she would have been caught. Then, without making a sound, she had slid the paper from the table and crawled back to the dumbwaiter to return to her room.

She was there now, under a tent of bedcovers, studying that special first spell she would cast on her own. She would need to figure out all the right things to include to make the spell work, but perhaps Nanny Wren could help her with that. Cassie would ask her questions, like she always did, and if Nanny wanted to know why she was asking, she would just tell her she was trying to learn for when Mommy decided it was time for Cassie to cast.

The light switched on in the hallway and Cassie heard creaking as her mother came upstairs on the way to her bedroom. She quickly switched off her little pocket reading light and tucked it under her pillow along with the spell, which she'd folded very carefully. Curling into a ball beneath her blanket, she heard her mother stop at her door, open it just slightly and take a peek inside. Mommy always did that. Cassie closed her eyes, but her heart was beating so hard, she felt sure her mother would hear it and know she wasn't really asleep.

She waited through a quiet moment, then two, with only the sound of her breathing coming from the lump she'd formed on her bed. Finally her mother stepped back and closed Cassie's door behind her. A minute later, the light in the hall switched off and Cassie heard her mother's bedroom door close softly.

Cassie pushed off the covers and slid from the bed. She went over to the window, parting the curtain slightly to let in the blue light of the moon. She sighed just a little, but enough so that her breath fogged on the glass.

If only she could cast a spell to make Mommy and Daddy love each other again.

She had been only four when they had decided to break up, and she didn't really remember what had happened, except she knew it was right after she'd gotten really sick and had to go to the hospital. She wondered if it had been because she'd gotten sick, because sometimes, when he was really mad at her, Sam almost said that it had been, coming as close as he could to telling her it had been her fault that their parents had gotten divorced. She hated that word—*divorce*—it sounded so dreadful, like *disease,* or *doom.*

Cassie had asked her mother once whether the divorce had been her fault, and her mom had gotten very upset. She'd insisted it wasn't true, but the way she'd insisted so much only made Cassie wonder more if it had been because of her. She knew that she and her mom and Sam had moved in with Nanny Wren right after she'd been sick, and that the next year her parents had gotten divorced.

So how could she not think her being sick had had something to do with it?

Cassie missed her dad. Because he worked and she went to school every day, she got to see him only on weekends and not even every one because sometimes, like this weekend, he took only Sam, to go fishing or camping or some other *boy* thing. Cassie protested about it to her mom once, but Jenna had just told Cassie that Sam needed some extra time with their father alone because the rest of the time, being the only boy in a house full of women, he was overwhelmed by *girl* things.

But maybe, just maybe, Cassie could fix that. When she worked Auntie Hallie's spell to find her the perfect man, maybe she could work another one at the same time, one that would make her mommy and daddy fall in love again.

Because to Cassie, her daddy *was* the Perfect Man.

Cassie stared out the window. The more she thought about it, the better the idea seemed. But she didn't have much time. The moon was full and the fact that it was a *blue* moon had to make it even better. One thing Cassie did know was that spells worked best when they were cast during a full moon.

So that meant she had just one day, maybe two, to figure out how to work the spell.

She would start on it first thing in the morning.

Eudora Wren glanced up from reading her morning horoscope to see her granddaughter cutting across the garden toward her back door.

It wasn't her being there that was so unexpected because Cassie was known to appear at most any time of the day or night, oftentimes curling into bed with her grandmother for their "secret" treat of late night popcorn and peppermint hot chocolate. The odd thing this morning was that Cassie was fully dressed in a pair of overalls and a yellow T-shirt. Her sparrow brown hair was brushed back into two neat pigtails that for once appeared very nearly even. Usually, if Cassie showed up this early in the morning, she was still half-asleep, dragging her favorite blanket as she trudged barefoot through the garden with her nightgown trailing behind her.

"Good morning, sweet one," Eudora greeted, watching over the tops of her spectacles as Cassie set Ogre down on the kitchen floor then slid onto the chair across from her. Cassie put both elbows on the table, and dropped her chin into her hands. Then she sighed loudly.

"Busy day planned then?" Eudora asked.

"No, not really." Cassie took up a chunk of the coffee cake Eudora had already cut and set out for her, crumbling it on her chin as she ate. "What are you going to do, Nan?"

Having had two of her own, Eudora knew little girls well enough to know when they had something on their minds, and when they were reluctant to tell that something for whatever reason. But Cassie would tell. It was all just a matter of getting it out of her.

"Oh, I don't know. Sam's gone with your dad. Your mum's going to be busy all day at the shop, and Hallie's out at Thar Muir to work that wedding, so it looks like it's just going to be you, me, and Ogre. Any ideas?"

"Well . . ." Cassie lifted one brow and in that moment she looked so much like her mother, it left Eudora blinking. "Do you think maybe you could teach me a new spell?"

Indeed. *Just* like her mother.

"Hmm," Eudora considered. "Perhaps we could work a small one. Have you any specific kind of spell in mind?"

Cassie pursed her lips, moving them to one side of her mouth in a way that wrinkled her nose quite endearingly. Granddaughters, Eudora declared to herself, were truly a little piece of heaven.

"I was wondering"—Cassie looked at Eudora, those blue eyes wide and unblinking—"what sort of things go into a love spell?"

So that was it. A love spell, Eudora thought. Well, it would certainly explain her dithering, and if memory served, Jenna had developed quite the crush on little Billy Richards when she'd been around the same age. Apparently some young man had turned Cassie's head, and knowing boys, he was likely oblivious to her. One of her brother's friends, perhaps? Eudora wondered who it could be. Timmy Spencer? Or Flora's eldest, Robbie. Probably him. He was a charmer, that one.

"Love spells can be very complicated, sweetling. It's never a good idea to try to manipulate another's heart."

"Oh, that's not what I meant, Nanny. What if someone just wants to be loved, or they already love someone, but for some reason . . ."

"Ah," Eudora said, "there's an obstacle?"

Such as the boy's friendship with her older brother, perhaps?

Cassie nodded. "Yes, an obstacle. That's it."

"Well, if the love is true and the intentions are

honest and good, then a little spell of encouragement certainly wouldn't be a bad thing. First, though, we'll have to go gathering. A spell of this kind works best with fresh ingredients. So why don't you go and fetch a couple gathering baskets from the closet while I make up a list of everything we'll need?"

Less than a half hour later, grandmother and granddaughter were walking together along the edge of the village common, baskets in hand, with Ogre trotting on his leash alongside them. The weather was brisk even for late September in New England and they each wore the velvet-lined capes that Eudora had sewn. Sure, they could have worn jackets or sweaters like everyone else, and they probably would have drawn fewer stares from passersby. But where was the fun in that?

As they walked, Eudora quizzed Cassie on the various plants they encountered, challenging her to recite their Latin names as well as their more common monikers. The child had an incredible memory and didn't miss a single one. Eudora beamed proudly. They skirted the common and headed away from the harbor, trudging through the cemetery with its ancient slate headstones, some tilting at odd angles, others worn smooth and indecipherable by the salty sea wind. They stopped to lay a posy of rosemary, for remembrance, from Jenna's garden at the foot of one headstone, that of Sam Delaney, Eudora's husband and Cassie's grandfather, before moving on.

At the far side of the graveyard, there was a very old rusted gate, long forgotten, that no one really used any more. It led onto a path that snaked through a small thicket and on into the "Old Settlement" of Little Ipswich. Here the first villagers had settled before eventually moving closer to the harbor where the main town stood today. This was Eudora's favorite gathering ground. Although little more than the outlines of some foundations from those first homes remained, Betty Petwith and the local historical society had succeeded in protecting this section of the town from further development, preserving its place as one of the earliest colonial settlements in Massachusetts.

There were plans to outline a walking trail with placards to describe the history of the various homesites, shedding a bit of light on the village's birth and everyday life in the seventeenth century. But budget constraints had thus far kept those plans on the drawing table, so for now it sat untouched. Thus there were specimens of the herbs and plants that had once filled the physic gardens of the first settlers still thriving among the overgrowth, brought over from England and Ireland and Scotland some three hundred years earlier. What some saw as weeds and wild grasses were really the purest, and sometimes most rare, botanicals, unspoiled by pesticides, modern methods of agriculture, or other pollutants.

Fairy flax, self-heal, heartsease, and meadowsweet grew freely, mixing and twining together among the rocks and field grasses. Eudora was once very pleasantly surprised to find a rare false unicorn root growing down by the creek bed. She didn't take anything unless she needed it, and when she did gather, or *wildcraft* as some called it, she did so in a manner that was both ethical and responsible, preserving the bounty of nature for the generations to come. Hedge witches had a responsibility to honor nature and her gifts. It was a respect Wren women continued generation to generation.

*   *   *

It was well past noon by the time Cassie and Eudora finished gathering. They decided to stop in for a quick lunch at Ipswich-by-the-Sea's only coffeehouse. It was called Common Grounds, and they served not only coffee, but tea and small meals of sandwiches and soup. In the summer, they had the best Italian ices. But the best part was that Cassie could have anything she wanted when she went there because the man who owned it, Sal Capone, was her other grandmother's brother. Which made him her grand-uncle or great-uncle or something like that. She wasn't sure which. One thing she did know was that he was not any relation to the famous Chicago Capone although some of the kids at school still swore he was. Cassie always just called him *Zio* Sal, and his wife was *Zia* Maria.

"Cassandria!" Uncle Sal greeted her in a voice that was both gravelly and accented in Italian. He smothered her against his striped apron, locking his arms around her. His head was balding on top with a dark fringe of hair that he kept slicked back with pomade. It always made him smell a little oily, but Cassie didn't mind. His dark eyes were bright beneath his bushy eyebrows and his nose was a little pointed like her gerbil Rat's. When he was mad, he cursed very loudly and always in Italian.

"Bella, we haven't seen you for so long. Why you have been so long away from here? What? You don't like us no more?"

Cassie grinned, squirmed away from him, and climbed up on one of the tall counter stools. She grabbed a yummy stick of her aunt Maria's fresh biscotti from the jar that always stood waiting for her there. She grinned on the first bite when she realized today's flavor was chocolate. Her favorite.

"No, *Zio* Sal," she answered on a mouthful. "You know that's not true. I love coming here. I've just been busy, you know, since school started again."

Maria Capone came out of the kitchen, reaching across the counter to pinch Cassie's cheek. She had hair like puffy cinnamon cotton that never seemed to move no matter how windy it was outside. And she had the strongest hands Cassie had ever seen. She could open any jar and didn't even need to bang on it with a spoon first, like her mother sometimes did.

"How's my sweet little *nipote* like her classes, eh? Any handsome boys catch your eye?"

"No, *Zia*." Cassie eyed Eudora, who had gone to sit at one of the café tables after exchanging greetings with Sal and Maria. "Well, not really . . ."

Maria chuckled. "Oh, well, he better be good to you, *bella*. Or *Zio* Sal will take good care of him, eh?"

She punched her meaty Italian fist into the palm of her other hand, just like she did when she was kneading her bread dough. Callie found herself wondering if Aunt Maria could crush walnuts, too.

"So where's that big brother of yours, eh?" Sal asked then.

"He's with Daddy this weekend. They went fishing up in New Hampshire yesterday."

"And why you didn't go, too?"

Cassie shook her head. "Fish are slimy," she said. "And they smell."

Sal laughed. "Oh, but they taste good in my Maria's cioppino. Go now. Sit with your *Nonna* Wren and I bring you some, eh? It will put some meat on your bones. Fish meat!"

He laughed out loud and poked her in the ribs,

like he always did. And Cassie squealed in response, like she always did.

After steaming up a couple of *caffè macchiatos* for another table, Sal brought the soup in twin steaming crocks, two chunks of crusty *sfilatino* bread, and a pot of Eudora's favorite mint tea. Behind him, Maria bustled about the café taking orders from two other tables. It was a busy Sunday and they were without their daughter, Julia, who had waitressed at the café throughout the summer.

"How's our Jules liking Harvard?" Eudora asked Maria when she finally found a free moment to stop by their table for a chat.

"Oh, she's beginning to settle in. She's got a very busy schedule. All those classes! *Santo cielo!* She leaves early and comes home late. And always studying now, she is. I feel like we hardly see her anymore."

"Maybe she could find a roommate to share an apartment with closer to campus."

That suggestion earned Eudora a ferret-sharp stare from Sal, and a subsequent gripe. "She's fine coming home every day as she is."

Eudora laughed. "No need to call out the carabiniere, Sal Capone. I just wanted to check if you were listening."

Of course, there was a flashy little red Mini Cooper that had been part of an agreement that Jules would not seek housing nearer to campus—away from the watchful and protective eyes of her father. To Jules, the deal—and the wheels—were worth it.

Cassie and her grandmother had their soup and finished up with creamy chocolate tortoni. As they got up to leave, Sal called out, "*Cassandria,* don't forget to stop by next door now and see your *Nonno* Tino, eh?"

Cassie wanted to get home so Nanny could teach her what she needed to know for the spell. If it got too late, and Mommy came home, she'd never be able to learn it. But Cassie had also been raised to cherish having her grandparents and extended grandparents. She had never known her Grandfather Sam, and the stories she always heard about him made her miss him very much.

"Okay, *Zio*," she said as she and Nanny headed out the door.

D'Agostino Gabriele was the owner and namesake of D'Agostino's, the only pizzeria in Ipswich-by-the-Sea. In many people's opinions, the *Boston Globe* included, it was also the best pizzeria on the North Shore, which made "busy" seem like an understatement. No matter the time of day, the little brick-walled nook always seemed to be humming. And with this being the first Sunday of football season, with the Patriots playing in Foxboro, a good many New Englanders were glued to their televisions, intent on downing as many slices of her grandfather's pepperoni and prosciutto pies as possible.

"Ciao, bella," her grandfather called to her when she ducked inside the crowded parlor. "I must have been crazy to let your padre go off this weekend. I could really use him today. And that phone, it's making me *mezzo matto*! What was I thinking?"

The entire time he spoke, the phone on the wall behind him had been ringing without stop. Tino grabbed his ears and made a funny face that dusted his face with flour and instantly set Cassie to giggling. An older version of her father except for the fact that he was about six inches shorter and his hair was a good deal more gray, *Nonno* Tino always knew how to make Cassie laugh.

"You want a pie to take home with you then, *bella*?"

"No, we just had some cioppino next door at *Zio* Sal's. I'm stuffed." Cassie ballooned out her cheeks to illustrate her condition.

"Ah, your *Zia* Maria, she makes the best cioppino this side of Italy. Good thing you already ate because we've got orders coming in faster than I can make them."

Cassie didn't want to, but she asked anyway, "Can I help, *Nonno*?"

She knew sometimes he let Sam take orders or pound down the dough.

"No, that's okay, *bella*. I've got your *nonna* in the kitchen with the boys, and *Zia* Sofia is on the phone. She knows how to write the codes for all the different orders. But *grazie*."

For once, Cassie wasn't disappointed that he wouldn't let her help.

She and Nanny Wren bid them farewell, but Cassie doubted he even heard her because right as they did, one of the boys from the local high school who worked in the kitchen dropped a big stainless steel bowl of her grandmother's celebrated sauce, splattering crushed tomatoes and secret spices all across the pristine kitchen walls, and eliciting a string of Italian curses that followed them out the door. Cassie didn't know what a *minchione* was, but she could certainly figure out what *stupido* meant.

They arrived back at Nanny's house just before two. From the number of cars parked on the street out front and the humming of blow-dryers coming from the salon next door, Cassie felt confident they would still have time for the spell before her mom finished up for the day.

In Nanny's kitchen, there were little glass jars

filled with all sorts of herbs and colorful powders. Cassie knew the ones that Nanny and Mommy used most frequently, like lavender, garlic, chamomile, and sage. But some of the others were a mystery. They were kept up on the topmost shelf where even Nanny Wren had to use a stool to reach them. Whenever Cassie asked about them, what they were called, what they did, Nanny just shook her head.

"They are very powerful, my lovey. You'll learn about them when the time is right."

"Now," Nanny said, drawing Cassie's attention away from the wall of jars, "you said you wanted to learn about love spells. What kind of love spell did you have in mind?"

"What kind of love spells are there?"

"Well, first, it must be a spell that does not manipulate anyone's heart. True love cannot grow where there is no seed, no soil to nurture it. To force something that wouldn't otherwise be there is artificial and contrived. Always, *always* remember that, okay?"

Cassie nodded. She knew her mother and father loved each other. She'd seen the way her mother would sometimes look at the picture of the four of them, taken when Cassie was a baby, back when they'd all lived together. And whenever she spent the weekend with her father, he always spent a lot of time asking Cassie about her mother, how she was doing, if she seemed happy. She may be only seven years old, but Cassie knew when two people belonged together. They just had to get around whatever it was that had happened to make them forget it. And since Cassie had been the one to break them apart, it only seemed right that she should be the one to fix it.

* * *

Cassie waited until she could hear Nanny snoring from her bedroom across the hall before she slid from underneath the bedcovers.

It had taken a good deal of begging, but she'd managed to convince her mother to let her stay at Nanny's that night. It would be the best place for her to work the spell since Nanny had all the ingredients in her kitchen, and because Nanny slept much more soundly than her mother did. And Sam wouldn't be around to ruin things if he caught her sneaking out of her room.

Whenever she stayed at Nanny Wren's house, Cassie slept in what had been her mother's childhood bedroom. The walls were still decorated in a yellow sprigged wallpaper and there was a picture of her father when he'd been in high school taped to the side of her mother's vanity mirror. Cassie carefully unstuck that picture, intending to use it in the spell, then padded across the room to the door.

Nanny had told her that a witch sometimes used poppets when performing spells. Poppets were some sort of object that was used to direct a spell at a specific person. Sometimes they could be sewn-together little dolls stuffed with herbs, others could be something that belonged to the person the spell was intended for. Or even, Nanny had said, a photograph of the person would work. Cassie hadn't had time to cut out and sew four different poppets for her spell, so she'd had to improvise, making the poppets from the most convenient supplies she had on hand.

Cassie waited at the bedroom door, and when she heard one of Nanny's rather loud snorts, she pushed the door open just enough to allow her to slip through.

The moon lit her way down the narrow hall from the round window above the stairwell. Her feet were bare beneath her nightgown and her hair was still pulled back in the pigtails she'd worn that morning, although they were decidedly more crooked now from the day's activities. There was something to be said for being small, especially in the way it helped to keep the old stairs in her grandmother's house from creaking as she went down to the bottom floor. Once there, she removed the paper with the spell her mother and Aunt Hallie had been writing the night before from the pocket of her bathrobe and set her father's photograph on the table beside it. Then she took out the other poppets she'd gathered.

The first she'd made by twisting some reeds from her mother's garden into a figure and then tying it off with a scrap of yarn from Jenna's favorite sweater. This was meant to represent her mother. The next was one of the gingerbread cookies she and Nanny had baked that afternoon. She'd given it strawberry orange frosting hair and blue candy eyes, making it look as much like Auntie Hallie as she could. The last poppet was a picture of a man she'd seen in an advertisement for toothpaste in one of Nanny's magazines. She'd chosen him because in his picture he had very shiny gold hair and green eyes, just like Auntie Hallie had said he should have. And Cassie liked the name of the toothpaste—PerfectaDent. Cassie wanted to be sure that the man she conjured up for her aunt was as perfect as she'd said he should be.

Setting the poppets aside, Cassie went to the cupboard where she knew Nanny kept her grimoire. The book was old and had been handed down to her by Nanny's great-grandmother. One day it would pass to her mother and then eventually to Cassie. And when she had a daughter, Cassie would pass the grimoire on to her. It was the way of the Wren women, a tradition that had been unbroken for as long as anyone could remember. The grimoire held their spirits, their hearts, and their very souls.

Nanny simply called it her "recipe book" and she used it whenever she made her special cakes and preserves. Nanny had referred to the book earlier that day when Cassie had asked her about casting a love spell, and so Cassie took it out now, turning the pages until she found the one her grandmother had studied.

She read it and then turned toward the shelves where Nanny's glass jars were lined up, searching through them for the ingredients she needed.

Orris Root.

Moonwort.

Rose.

And one other jar, one from the topmost shelf that Cassie had once seen Nanny use when she'd made a secret Valentine spice cake for Mrs. MacPhee. Cassie remembered how Nanny had used only a pinch and had smiled as she'd done so, saying it was her *special love spice*. Cassie also remembered that shortly after Mrs. MacPhee had taken her cake home, she'd met and fallen in love with Mr. MacPhee, and now everyone in town commented on how perfect they were for each other. So Cassie decided, just to make certain it worked, she would add the mysterious ingredient to her own spell as well.

She took down each jar, then fetched a small red candle from the cupboard. She sat at the table and studied the workings of the spell.

First she would need to cast a circle, to gather all the energies around her that would make the spell work. She'd seen her mother do this by marking off a circle using candles or a knotted cord. But in absence of these, Cassie also knew she could "draw" a circle, an invisible boundary, using a wand. Since she didn't have a wand yet, she would have to use something else. She scanned the kitchen and spotted Nanny's walking stick. Picking it up, she gathered the poppets, the candle, and the glass jars. She had everything she needed except for the one last ingredient.

Moonlight.

Cassie was headed for the back door when she heard Ogre come scampering down the stairs on his way to the kitchen.

"Shh," she said to him when he whimpered behind her. "You'll wake up Nanny."

Cassie knew if she left him in the house, he'd whine and bark and scratch at the door, so she had no choice but to bring him with her.

Outside, the moon cast a brilliant blue glow across the whole of the garden, bathing it in a shimmery sort of enchantment. The night air was cold and the grass was damp beneath Cassie's bare feet, but she decided against going back for her slippers. She followed the path to the very center of the garden, where her mother had made a path both forward and back and across. There was a hand-blown glass globe set in a stand that reflected the moonlight in the dark and the brilliance of the sun by day. This was the altar where her mother and her grandmother usually worked their spells.

Cassie set out the poppets first, arranging her mother and father on one side, Aunt Hallie and the man from the toothpaste advertisement on the other. Then Cassie placed the candle between them. As she cast the circle, she would need to call on the elements of nature for protection. Holding out the walking stick, she mimicked the words she'd heard her mother and her grandmother use so many times before, closing an invisible circle around her while calling the energies forth that would work the spell.

Once she finished, she took up the first three jars, one at a time, and mixed a bit from each into her cupped hands. Then she added a pinch from the fourth, the mysterious love spice. She closed her eyes, took a deep breath and concentrated on the images of her mother and father, and then Aunt Hallie and the golden-haired man. She imagined each couple together, happy, in love. Then she spoke softly to the moon,

> *"I call upon thee,*
> *Spirit of the Earth,*
> *Wind, and Fire,*
> *The Endless Sea.*
> *Come to this circle,*
> *This safe haven of the moon's light.*
> *Bring these lovers together.*
> *With your power,*
> *Remove that which stands between them,*
> *Bind their hearts, so that they may*
> *Be as one. Forever."*

Cassie paused, and then added the final words that she knew would seal the spell.

> *"As I will it,*
> *So mote it be."*

Eyes yet closed, she repeated the incantation two more times. Then, opening her hands just slightly, Cassie blew softly, scattering the herbs, mixing them together, letting them fall over the altar and releasing the spell. She stood for a moment, bathed in the moonlight, in the shimmer of the stars above. She waited, thinking she should feel *something* if the magic would work, like a tingle or a tickle in her tummy. But there was none. Only the soft, whispering sounds of the night that surrounded her.

Then Cassie took up the walking stick once more, and turning in the opposite direction this time, opened the circle she'd traced.

The spell was cast.

When she finished, her heart was pounding. She'd done it. She'd worked her first spell, all on her own. All she had to do was collect the poppets and sleep with them beneath her pillow. She would dream of what she'd desired. And then the next day she would find a special place, somewhere in the garden, and she would bury them there.

But when she knelt to retrieve them, Cassie found only three poppets sitting on the ledge beneath the garden globe. There was the reed figure, her father's photo, and the magazine advertisement. The cookie that represented her Aunt Hallie was missing. In its place there was a small scattering of crumbs . . .

. . . and a small dog looking up at her, wagging his tail.

Oh no.

Ogre had eaten Aunt Hallie.

Chapter Three

Jenna loved autumn in New England.

The colors were bold and vivid, bursting to life in brilliant gaiety everywhere you looked. Spices filled the air with the scents of cinnamon and cranberry, pumpkin and clove. Leaves swirled in the roadways whenever cars rushed by and a surreptitious chill crept in day by day, week by week, turning the whispering harbor breeze into a sharp, brisk, surly sort of rebuff, one that had New Englanders pulling their thickest wool sweaters out of storage. It seemed to go from balmy summer one day to bitter fall the next. New England was like that, impetuous, always changing, and never predictable.

This particular Monday was no exception. While the day before had been kissed by sunlight and cool breezes, they'd woken to a morning dew that had stiffened on the lawns in what could almost be called a frost. It was hard to believe that only three weeks earlier, they'd been standing in T-shirts, sipping iced tea and watching the Labor Day parade roll by. Now the sky was cloaked by a sullen swelling of clouds while the wind pulled and teased, slapping at the sails on the boats anchored in the harbor. Rain was certain—you could smell its dampness and feel the weight of it thickening the air. It was just a matter of when. Hours, maybe even days away, but it threatened, keeping all but the most stalwart of seamen ashore. Centuries of experience had taught them never to try to out-guess a New England storm, and to remind them, there was a memorial wall down in Gloucester engraved with the names of those who had tried— and failed.

Among those named was Sam Delaney.

Jenna missed her father. She'd been only a child when they'd lost him, but she could still remember the thud of his rubber fishermen's boots on the step outside. That sound had heralded his return from many a sail. Sam Delaney's hadn't been a nine-to-five job; in fact he had been gone more than he'd been home. But on those occasions when he was at home, Jenna had loved to climb up on his lap with Hallie, burrowing into his arms as he'd regaled them with stories of sea monsters and mermaids.

Her father had been a true Irish teller of tales, weaving imaginary worlds with just the sound of his voice and bringing them to life by the light of the evening fire. How Jenna wished Sam and Cassie could have known him, could have sat with him like she had to hear his tales, too.

After walking the kids to school, Jenna poked through the garden, deadheading, pulling stray weeds, making plans for winter's preparation. She frowned at a spot of freshly turned earth, hoping there wasn't a mole tunneling beneath her bee balm. Afterward, knowing it was overdue, she decided to take on the salon's monthly inventory.

By ten, Jenna was perched on a stepladder in the supply room. She stacked, counted, scribbled notes, counted some more. She had just started sorting through old style magazines, deciding which ones to pitch and which to keep, when she heard the door in the main part of the salon open. Since it was Monday, the one day of the week when the shop was closed, Jenna didn't bother to go out. She knew that it would be Hallie, who actually should have been there earlier to go over the bookkeeping. She'd apparently treated herself to an extra hour in bed after working the wedding up at Flora's B-and-B the day before.

"Good thing for Betsy this ugly weather held off till today, huh?" Jenna called out as she did a quick tally of the boxes of perm rods and endpaper tissues stacked before her. "I'm in desperate need of a caffeine fix. If I promise to be your personal slave for a week, will you go down to the corner and get me a double espresso? There's a ten on the desk. Get one for yourself while you're at it."

A few seconds later, she heard the door open and close. Jenna grinned. Thank heavens for little sisters.

Hallie came back not ten minutes later, the bell above the door tinging her return. Perfect timing, too. Jenna had just finished counting their stock of towels.

"Make a note we're low on Blond Number 7. Must be from all those summer highlights we did," she said as she glanced over the notes she'd scribbled on the back of an empty box of developing cream. "Oh, and we should probably order a couple blow-dryers. Becca's was sounding off yesterday. I have a feeling it's ready to burn out. Probably wouldn't hurt to stock up on combs, too. And towels." She headed for the door. "Sorry, I would have finished with this earlier but Jack didn't bring Sam home till after ten. And on a school night. The kid was a zombie this morning. I had to literally drag him out of bed. I swear, sometimes I could just kill that . . ."

Jenna's words stuck in her throat when she rounded the corner into the main salon. Hallie wasn't standing there at all. There was a man. A very tall man. A very fine-looking man.

"Oh."

The man held up Common Grounds' familiar to-go cup. "Double espresso, as requested." He smiled, revealing a dimple at one corner of his mouth. "And you don't have to be my personal slave."

Jenna felt her face flush with embarrassment as she remembered the conversation from fifteen minutes earlier. "I'm so sorry about that. I thought you were . . ."

"Someone else?"

She nodded. "My sister."

"Ah." He nodded. "Sorry to disappoint you."

Who said anything about being disappointed? Jenna thought, taking full measure of him as she reached for the cup he offered.

Six feet something with the sort of face that one typically found beaming down from a movie screen. Dressed casually in a Ralph Lauren sort of way. Eyes that were . . . green, she decided after a couple covert glances. Nice watch. Good shoes. The sort of guy who just didn't belong standing in the reception area of some small-town salon, especially with her dressed in grubby jeans and the even grubbier hooded sweatshirt she'd snatched from her son's closet that morning.

Jenna went behind the reception desk, hoping it would hide the ragged cuffs on her jeans. She noticed the ten-dollar bill still tucked in the edge of the desk calendar where she'd set it that morning. "Call it a guess, but I'm sure you didn't come here expecting to buy someone you don't even know a cup of coffee."

"You win." He looked at her. "Actually I was hoping I might get in for a trim."

Occupational habit had Jenna glancing at his hair, a brilliant feathering of pure golden blond. A little long, true, but it certainly didn't detract from his appearance. Oh, no. Not at all.

"Um, we're actually closed on Mondays."

"Ah," he nodded. "Just my luck. There wouldn't be anywhere else in town you could recommend?"

Jenna shook her head. "I'm afraid I'm it, unless you feel like driving into Gloucester. A lot of the guys in town go to a barber there. Although the man who owns it is, uh, well, getting on in years, so don't be surprised if you end up with a somewhat crooked buzz cut."

Jenna picked up the coffee cup and removed the plastic lid. As the heavenly scent of Sal's Italian beans hit her, she wondered if it was possible to reach orgasm over a cup of coffee.

For this, she owed him at least a haircut.

"Tell you what. Since you were nice enough to get me this coffee, and not even let me pay for it, I'm sure I can tear myself away from the thrills of my monthly inventory for a half hour or so to give you a trim." She motioned toward her booth. "Come on. Have a seat."

"You're sure?"

She nodded. "In fact, I insist. If you'll just give me a minute . . ."

Jenna slipped into the adjacent bathroom, yanked off the sweatshirt, fluffed up her hair a little, and spritzed on just a touch of herbal body spray. The plain white T-shirt she wore underneath was a little tight, especially across her breasts. Of course, being Sam's, it would be. She fumbled through the drawer for a lipstick, found a nice muted plum, and swept some on.

"I appreciate this, really," he said from the other side of the door.

"It's no problem." She came out, feeling at least somewhat less bedraggled. She held out her hand. "I'm Jenna, by the way. Jenna Wren."

He smiled. "It's a pleasure, Jenna Wren." He wrapped his hand over hers in a way that was a good deal more intimate than any handshake. "Declan Cavanaugh."

Gorgeous *and* Irish. If that wasn't a lethal combination, Jenna didn't know what was.

She sat him down in a salon chair, adjusting the height as she reached to the shelf for a cutting cape. She put aside the one with the bright purple and fuchsia flowers and went for another of plain black. As she draped it over him, fastening it at the back of his neck, she found herself wondering what it would be like to trace her finger along the curve of his ear.

Jenna pulled herself back. *What was she thinking?*

When she looked up again, his gaze met hers in the reflection of the mirror. Was it her, or was he looking at her as if he knew exactly what she'd just been thinking?

"So, what can I do for you, Mr. Cavanaugh?"

"What do you suggest, Jenna Wren?"

That you ask me out for dinner.

The thought came so clear and so stark in her head, Jenna feared for a moment that she'd actually spoken the words out loud. What the heck was wrong with her? She didn't typically drool over her customers. This wasn't like her. Not at all.

"How about we get you shampooed first? Then we'll go from there."

Jenna led him from the chair across the room to the line of gleaming black porcelain sinks. The fixtures sparkled and the bottles of shampoos and conditioners and treatments were lined up neatly on the shelf above the sinks. She leaned him back in the chair, his face tilted upward, and started the tap, adjusting the water's temperature to a comfortable warm. She could feel him watching her as she soaked his hair, slicking it back from his forehead with her fingers.

Why was her heart drumming like that? Why was she so conscious of touching him? And that stare? She was doing something she'd done thousands of times before, with any number of men and women. Why did it suddenly seem so *intimate*?

Jenna lathered his hair, massaging in shampoo from temple to nape, trying to ignore the fact that when she leaned forward to rinse his hair, his face was positioned dangerously close to her breasts. And then he closed his eyes and made a sound, one of apparent pleasure.

"Mmm, that smells nice. What is it?"

"It's an herbal shampoo made with green tea and ginseng and a touch of juniper."

"No. I meant you."

The air around them seemed to double in temperature.

"Oh." Jenna's throat clogged. "Um, it's neroli, I think."

"Smells like summertime." He smiled. "It suits you."

It had been some time since Jenna had been the recipient of such open and obvious male attention, so long that she didn't quite know how to respond.

She worked in a profession that was predominantly peopled by females and opportunities for meeting men were seldom. Most of the men in Ipswich-by-the-Sea knew her, and knew Jack. As such, Jenna had been on a total of two dates since the divorce, and they had both ended in disaster. The first had been with an old high school classmate who'd apparently only been interested in provoking Jack. The other had been a blind date set up by one of her clients whom Jenna just hadn't had the heart to refuse.

Mrs. Evanson's grandson had seemed nice enough when he presented himself at her door, bearing flowers for her and chocolates for her mother. But after a round of miniature golf and a stop at the local walk-up fish and chip shop, at which he ordered for himself and then left her to fend for herself, Jenna quickly realized why the thirty-year-old had to rely on his grandmama to fill his social calendar.

She'd gone on those dates, needed to go on those dates, mostly to assure herself that she wasn't finished, washed up before she'd even turned thirty. But those two dates had served only to keep her turning down any subsequent offers since then. Jenna had virtually sworn off men, at least for the time being, and had devoted herself to her work and her children instead.

She had enough complications dealing with one ex-husband.

The salon had taken off, becoming more of a success than she had ever dreamed. But a salon couldn't listen when a woman needed someone to talk to, and a salon couldn't wrap its arms around her on those nights when she couldn't sleep. Watching as her friend Flora, a widowed single mother of three, had met and fallen in love with her new husband, Gavin, over the summer, Jenna had found herself wondering more and more if she, too, might one day have a second chance.

She was still young, with physical as well as emotional needs. And now that the business was established, and the kids were growing older, she found herself looking to the future, beyond next week, next year. It was a future she didn't want to walk through alone. As she finished rinsing the Irish stranger's hair, Jenna wondered if maybe it was time she started testing the waters.

After drying his hair with a towel, Jenna led Declan back to her booth. As she combed through his damp hair, she tried to come up with small talk, but her tongue was oddly tied.

"So," she managed, "you're new in town." *Obviously, you idiot,* she chided herself. *You know every other person in town.* "Passing through, or staying on?"

"Just visiting," he answered, offering nothing more.

"Well, you've chosen the best time of the year to come for a visit. Some prefer the summer, since we're so near the coast with the beaches and all, but autumn is my favorite time of year."

He looked at her in the mirror. "I have to agree. There is certainly a lot of beauty to behold here."

Jenna's hands stilled when the lights above her mirror seemed to flicker.

Or had she just imagined it?

Jenna blinked, smiled, and started trimming the ends of his hair.

It had been a long time since she'd felt young, free, even sassy. And with a guy who looked like he did? Why shouldn't she treat herself to a little flirtation?

"So tell me about this town," Declan said. "Have you lived here long?"

Jenna nodded. "All my life."

"Well, it's certainly unique. That guy down at the café . . ."

"Sal," Jenna answered. She decided not to tell him that Sal was her uncle, in an ex-in-law sort of way.

"He's the one. Quite a character. I've been to Italy on several occasions, and I had yet to find a place here in the States with the same 'flavor.' And I don't just mean the coffee, which is incredible, by the way."

"Sal takes his espresso very seriously."

"But it's not just that. It's the atmosphere in the place. It reminds me of this little *caffè* I once discovered in Venice, right off Piazza San Marco . . ."

He had to say Venice, didn't he? Jenna thought. It was one of her secret Have-to-See-Before-I-Die destinations; in fact, it topped the list. As he described the glorious architecture, quiet sunsets over the Grand Canal, and the distant lilting song of the gondoliers carried on the breeze, Jenna found herself daydreaming. She imagined sitting sipping *caffè* from tiny white cups at a secluded linen-topped table while Italian musicians played love songs for passersby. She imagined walking down cobbled lanes with her face turned to the warmth of the sun and standing in historic piazzas surrounded by incredible churches with pigeons taking flight at her feet. But she didn't want to imagine doing it alone. Venice was a city for lovers, where couples walked arm in arm, stopping to embrace, to kiss long and slow and passionately while old Italian women smiled down from open-shuttered windows, remembering their own youth.

Jenna sighed, blinking herself back to reality. "Sounds incredible."

"It is. You should go."

"Perhaps I will." She smiled wistfully. "Someday . . ."

Once she'd finished his hair, dusting off his shoulders with a brush, Declan followed her to the reception desk. He started to take out his wallet, but Jenna held up her hand.

"No. No. It's on the house."

He looked at her.

"Please. I made a fool of myself this morning. Let me make up for it by leaving you with the impression I can at least give you a decent cut."

"You definitely did that." He ran a hand through his neatly clipped hair. "But on one condition."

"What's that?"

"That you join me for dinner tonight at that chowder house you recommended."

A date? Jenna stared at him.

"I don't know," she said. "I'm not very good at this."

Declan leaned on the counter. "I'll tell you what. I'll be there around seven. If you haven't had anything to eat, and should happen to be in the neighborhood . . ."

Jenna looked at him. "I live in the neighborhood." She smiled. "Thanks. I'll think about it."

Hallie was just ducking in the door when Declan turned to leave. Not one for suppressing her emotions, she stared—gawked—then watched him go with her mouth hanging half-open.

"Well," she said when he'd closed the door behind him. "Happy Monday to you! Who was that incredibly yummy piece of eye candy?"

"Declan Cavanaugh," Jenna replied. And then she looked at her sister. "Don't get too excited. He's just visiting."

"Ohh," Hallie pouted. "Why is it they are never moving in and looking for that special someone to paint the picket fence with?"

Jenna was staring down at the appointments book. "He asked me out to dinner at the Chowder House tonight."

Hallie gasped. "And you're going."

"I don't know."

"Jenna . . ." Hallie slapped her hand down on top of the book, forcing her sister to look up at her. "You—are—going."

"I've got the kids, Hal, and it's a school night, and—"

"And yadda yadda yadda. Hello? Did you see him? He's perfect."

Perfect.

Jenna looked at her.

"What more do you need? A foghorn blaring? A lightning strike? He's gorgeous, gorgeous in a way that we don't see around here often. He asked you out. Don't you dare let him just walk away. Go. For once have some fun in your life. You of all people have more than earned it."

Jenna chewed it over, trying to find some legitimate reason why she shouldn't meet him. Finally she looked up, giving a small smile. "You know what? You're right. I have earned it, haven't I?"

Cassie turned the hall corner off the stairs with her backpack in hand and spied her mother standing at the bathroom mirror, putting on a pair of earrings.

Jenna was wearing the short black dress she wore only for special occasions. She'd changed her hair, fluffing it up and pulling it back over each ear with jeweled clips that made her eyes sparkle. She had a swath of vintage black draped over her shoulders and high heels strapped over her ankles.

And she was humming.

"Hi, Mommy," Cassie said as she leaned against the jamb. She secretly hoped she could grow up to be as beautiful as her mommy someday.

"Hey there, gingersnap," Jenna answered, smiling at her in the mirror. "What'cha up to?"

Cassie shrugged. "Nothing. Homework. Where are you going?"

Jenna touched up her makeup, dusting her nose. She inspected her reflection once more before answering. "Oh, just out."

"Where ya going?"

"To the Chowder House. Everyone's been raving about the new chef there, so I thought I'd try it out."

"Oh . . ." Cassie tried to sound nonchalant. "Are you going alone?"

"Um, actually I am meeting someone there."

Cassie nodded and grinned. "I know."

"You do?"

"Yeah."

Jenna looked at her. "And you're okay with it?"

"Of course, Mommy. Why wouldn't I be? You look very pretty."

Jenna smiled. "Well, thank you. It's nice to get dressed up every so often." She glanced at her watch. "But I'm going to be late if I don't get out of here. Now you be good for Nanny and Hallie tonight. Don't fight with your brother and make sure you brush your teeth. You'll probably be in bed by the time I come home, so I'll see you in the morning, okay?"

Cassie nodded, lifting her chin so her mother could give her a kiss. "Ogre and me are going to sleep with Nanny in her bed. She said we could have popcorn and watch Nickelodeon."

Jenna smiled, tucking a lipstick into her clutch and then snapping it closed. "Sounds like fun. Just make sure you don't stay up past eight. You have school in the morning."

"I know, Mommy. Lights out after *SpongeBob*."

"That's my girl," Jenna said and headed for the stairs to leave.

Less than a half hour later, the doorbell rang at Nanny Wren's. Nanny glanced at the clock. "Who would be calling here at this hour?"

"I'll go answer it, Nanny," Cassie offered.

She tugged open the front door with Ogre yapping at her heels. "Daddy!"

"Hey there, Cass. I was hoping I'd find you here." He kissed the top of her head then glanced past her, peering inside. "Is your mom here?"

"No. Of course she's not. She left to meet you at the Chowder House."

Jack scratched his head. "Me? Are you sure about that?"

"Yes, Daddy. I'm positive. Did you forget again?"

Jack searched his memory. *Christ, had he?*

"No, no. I didn't forget. I just wasn't sure if I was supposed to meet her here or there. Thanks, Cass. And do me a favor. Don't tell anyone I was here, okay? I don't want your mom knowing I screwed up again. Just tell Nanny there was someone asking directions at the door. It's the truth, after all, right?" He winked.

"Sure thing, Daddy." Cassie watched as he turned and headed down the pathway toward the street. "Oh and, Daddy? Make sure and remember to tell Mommy how pretty she looks, too, okay?"

Jack jogged across the common toward the twinkling lights and muffled murmur of Muzak and conversation coming from the Chowder House.

The rain that had threatened all day hadn't yet managed to break through the clouds, although the wind hissed through the trees, teasing the banner that advertised HALF PRICE HAPPY HOUR hanging above the outside patio.

Jack couldn't recall having agreed to meet Jen that night, but it certainly wouldn't be the first time he'd forgotten something like that, a fact she'd no doubt point out to him the minute he arrived. He'd just tell her he got hung up helping his father at the shop or something. It had become his standard excuse.

He wasn't really dressed for dinner out but he quickly tucked in the tails of his denim shirt and finger combed his hair as he pulled open the door and stepped inside. Food smells, heavy on the seafood, greeted him. The hostess, Angie, looked up from her lighted podium, recognizing him with a smile.

"Hey, Jack. How's it going?"

"Good, Angie. You?" He did a quick scan of the tables, searching for a sign of his ex-wife.

"You lookin' for Jen?" Angie asked.

Was it that obvious? "Uh, yeah."

"Over in the far corner by the fire."

Jack was already on his way. "Thanks, Ang."

He caught sight of her as he came around a line of tables. She was bent over the menu with her head tilted to one side and one hand resting lightly on her chin. The fire behind her cast warm, dancing shadows over her bare shoulders. Just the sight of her had Jack stopping dead in his tracks.

Wow.

He was so used to seeing Jen wearing the smock from the salon or one of her baggy sweatshirts, he'd forgotten how incredible she could look in something that showed her figure. She was stunning, but then Jen had always taken care of herself. Tonight, she wore a sleeveless dress that showed the elegant line of her shoulders and neck, the same shoulders and neck he'd at one time loved to run his hands over. He remembered how she'd get goose pimples when he traced his fingers along the nape of her neck. How she'd sigh and nuzzle closer to him. How he'd never wanted to let her go. It seemed like an eternity ago.

He wondered why she'd gone to such trouble just to meet him even as he wished again that he'd worn something more appropriate.

"Hey," he said, and dropped into the chair across from her. He remembered what Cassie had told him at the house. "You look great, Jen. Really . . . well, incredible."

"Jack." Her expression was less than pleased at the sight of him. "What are you . . . ?"

"Yeah, I know. I'm late. And I'm not exactly dressed for the place, but I got hung up and—"

He saw someone approach just to the side and behind him. Giving the waiter half a glance, he said, "A beer. Whatever you have on draft is fine."

"Jack, please." Jenna looked horrified. "He isn't the waiter."

Jack turned then, giving the man standing beside him a more thorough study. No, she was right. He didn't look like a waiter at all. In fact, he looked more like . . .

A date.

Shit.

Jack shot up so fast, the chair nearly toppled behind him. He turned, offering his hand. "I'm her . . . uh . . ." He thought better of it and said simply, "Jack Gabriele."

The other man gripped his hand, giving it one firm shake. "Declan Cavanaugh."

The two men exchanged a long silent stare.

Jack was the first to break it, turning to Jenna, who was still sitting at the table, obviously mortified. "I'm sorry, Jen." It was all he could think of to say. "I'll . . ." He looked at Jenna once more, feeling like the world's biggest jackass. "I'll see ya."

It wasn't until he reached the parking lot that the weight of what had just happened really hit him.

Jen.

Out.

On a date.

And not just any date.

A *real* date.

A little-black-dress kind of date.

Shit.

And for the second time in his life, Jack felt as if he'd just had the rug pulled out from under his feet. The first had been the day Jenna asked him for the divorce.

They'd been separated about a year, a year during which Jack—rather Jack's pride—had tried to convince himself that he didn't need Jenna. Having her leave him had been a blow to his ego. Yeah, he'd been a jerk and yeah, he'd probably deserved a good swift kick in the pants, but losing Jen and the kids had been more than a kick. It had completely devastated him, but he'd refused to let anyone, most especially Jen, know that.

Jen couldn't leave. They'd always been Jack and Jen, Jen and Jack. Everyone knew that. So he'd convinced himself that she would come back to him, that she would have to. When faced with the sheer burden of finding a place to live, getting a job, paying the bills, raising two children, Jenna would realize that while he'd been an ass and her anger at him was justified, they were better together than apart. Jack had convinced himself that Jen needed him.

Only he'd been wrong.

Instead, Jen did the unthinkable. She started a business, and built it into an incredible success. And she'd managed to do it all without depriving the kids in any way. She hadn't bad-mouthed him to them even though they both knew she easily could have. She'd done everything she could to give them the stability and the security they deserved.

The stability and security he should have given them.

She had much more strength than he'd ever given her credit for. And Jack had learned something else because of it.

He'd discovered that it had been he who had needed Jenna more.

Inside the restaurant, Jen was mortified.

She sat in her chair, hitting the replay button in her mind over and over again, watching Jack order a beer from her first real date in more than a year. It was like one of those news clips showing some horrific event.

Like an earthquake.

Or a twenty-car pileup.

Only this particular disaster was her date.

"I'm so sorry," she said again as Declan took his seat across from her. She was thankful they had lowered the lights in the dining room so he couldn't see how hideously red her face had gone.

"Is he . . . ?"

She frowned. "My ex-husband. I don't have any idea what he was doing here."

Declan shrugged. "Forget it. I'm sure if I'd had you and then made the mistake of losing you, I'd probably be on the defensive if I saw you with another guy, too."

Jenna shook her head. "It's been over for a long time. Jack knows that."

Or at least Jenna had thought he did.

Declan topped off their glasses from the bottle of Shiraz he'd ordered. The ruby wine glimmered in the light from the restaurant's stone-fronted hearth. "You're certain of that?"

Jenna decided she didn't care to answer the question, and took up her glass, sipping slowly. The wine was smooth, warm, and it soothed her agitation. Thankfully, the waiter was blessed with perfect timing, and came up a moment later to take their order.

"So," Jenna said when the waiter left again, hoping to change the topic from Jack's peculiar appearance to anything—anything else at all. "What is it you do?"

Declan set down his wine. "I guess you could say I'm in acquisitions."

"Acquisitions . . . you mean as in art?"

"Sometimes," he answered. "Sometimes, other things."

She wondered why his response sounded cloaked in more than one meaning. "You have a collection?"

"No, nothing like that. I acquire strictly for others. Out of the ordinary things. A client tells me what it is they want, and I do what is necessary to provide it. For a price."

Jenna swallowed, feeling peculiar of a sudden. "And have you ever not been able to provide what they want?"

Declan just looked at her, letting his silence be his response.

"Oh." Jenna fidgeted beneath his stare, pulling her wrap more closely around her shoulders. The way he looked at her was so bold. It left her feeling *exposed*.

"So is that what brings you to Ipswich-by-the-Sea?" she tried again.

"Perhaps."

"What sort of treasure are you looking for? Maybe I can help you find it."

Declan raised his glass. "Oh, but I think you already have."

He stared at her again in that odd way and Jenna felt her face flush anew. She toyed modestly with the stem of her wineglass, telling herself to relax, to enjoy the attention of this handsome and interesting man . . .

. . . until she spotted Hannah Greer making a beeline for them across the room.

First Jack. Now Hannah. Who next? Her mother?

"I thought that was you!" Hannah said in a voice that carried clearly over the soft music purring through the sound system. "Don't you just look amazing!"

"Thank you, Ha—"

Hannah spun to face Declan, holding out a manicured hand. "Hannah Greer. I'm one of Jenna's very satisfied customers, Mr. . . . ?"

He took her hand, eliciting a smile from her. "Cavanaugh. Declan Cavanaugh."

"Pleasure to meet you, Mr. Cavanaugh." She turned back to Jenna. And winked. "Isn't he just a hottie?" she whispered, only *whispering* wasn't something Hannah really had a knack for. Declan must have easily heard her. "I just wanted to thank you for whatever it was you did with my makeover the other day. Got me those shoes," she held out a shapely braceleted ankle to show off her pretty purchase. "*And* the dishwasher, *and* a second honeymoon to Hawaii." Hannah clapped her hands with glee. "Can you believe it? Hawaii!"

Jenna smiled. "I'm glad to know you're pleased."

"Sugar, I am tickled pink. You work some sort of magic in that salon of yours, Jenna Wren. Some sort of magic indeed."

Jenna glanced at Declan, then back to Hannah. "No, really. You're too effusive. I was just doing my job."

"Well, you do it very well." Hannah glanced across the dining room to where her husband, Jim, decked out in a sports coat and tie, sat waiting. She blew him a kiss and he waved, smiling at her. "Well, I better get back to my honey. It's not a good idea to keep a hungry man waiting." She attempted another whisper—*"You'd do well to remember that, sugar"*—and failed. "You two have a wonderful dinner. Save room for dessert. The chocolate soufflé is to die for!"

Hannah swept off, heading back to her table and the waiting Jim.

Jenna waited a moment before glancing back at Declan, only to find he was staring at her. Again.

"I find myself curious to know what else you offer at your salon to leave someone gushing like that. Maybe I should come back again tomorrow for the full treatment."

"Not unless you want your toenails painted red and a bikini wax," Jenna quipped.

That made him blink. In fact, Declan's face shifted from his assured grin, reflecting instead his reaction to the idea of any sort of waxing. "Maybe I'd be better off sticking with the haircut."

Jenna chuckled. Men were such babies.

Chapter Four

"So? Tell me! Was it fabulous?"

Breathless from apparently having run the breadth of the garden to get there, Hallie gasped out the question even before she got through the kitchen doorway.

Her abrupt arrival, however, was nothing compared to the outrageous sight she presented.

She wore her thick yellow chenille bathrobe over a T-shirt and a pair of candy-striped pajama bottoms. On her feet she wore the pink bunny slippers Jenna had given her for her last birthday. Her hair was twisted up in a towel from her morning shower. Ogre was tucked under one arm. And to complete the ensemble, a mask of dark, algae-looking green that Jenna recognized as her own "A New Day" almond and sea kelp facial was slathered all over her face.

The privileged beholders of this "vision," Jenna, Sam, and Cassie, were sitting at the table, one sipping coffee over the morning newspaper, the other two finishing up their respective bowls of oatmeal. Not one of them batted an eye at the green-faced harridan who'd just shattered the peace of their breakfast.

Jenna simply looked at her kids, then glanced at

the clock, ignoring her sister's impatient and exasperated "Well?"

"You two better head off for school," Jenna said. "Dishes in the sink and brush your teeth."

Sam and Cassie pushed back their chairs in unison. They filed to the sink, and then headed off for the stairs. Jenna waited until they were gone before turning to her sister.

"Oh, it must have been good," Hallie said. "You're glowing."

"I am *not* glowing."

"Yes, you are. Look at yourself."

"All right," Jenna said, smiling as she poured Hallie a cup of coffee from the countertop pot. "Maybe I am." She slid the pitcher of half-and-half and a spoon across the table to her. "All things considered, it was a very pleasant evening. He was"—she searched for the right word—"different. Attentive. Gallant, even. And he made me feel so *interesting*. Like I wasn't, you know, just a single mom who works in a small-town hair salon. We talked all through dinner, and it was intelligent talk—*adult* talk. World issues, current events, and not one single mention of Nickelodeon or Nintendo, which is a definite switch from what I'm used to. And then afterward, we took a walk along the harbor. The moon was out. It was a little chilly and"—she glanced at Hallie and smiled again—"he put his jacket over my shoulders. It sounds stupid, I know, to care about something so ridiculously old-fashioned. But it definitely scored points with this gal."

Hallie nodded, waving her hands impatiently. "Yeah, yeah, yeah. Enough about that. Get to the good stuff. Did he kiss you?"

"Shh." Jenna looked toward the stairs, lowering her voice. "The kids will hear you." She waited a

moment, listening for bathroom sounds coming from upstairs. "You know, I thought he would, but he didn't. Afterward, he just walked me to the door and kissed my hand."

Hallie squealed.

Ogre barked.

Jenna *shh*'d them both.

Around the corner, Cassie leaned against the wall with her backpack clutched before her. She grinned with glee and whispered softly to herself, "Good job, Daddy."

When she heard Sam coming down the stairs, Cassie raced to the door, grabbing her jacket off its hook on the wall. She shoved her feet into her sneakers and tied them by making bunny ears, just like Nanny had shown her.

"I'm going to stay here with Aunt Hallie so you two better hurry," Jenna called. "You've got exactly seven minutes before the first bell."

Jenna bid the kids good-bye, waiting for the sound of the front door before turning back to Hallie, who was now picking bite-sized morsels off a cranberry muffin.

"The night was almost a disaster though," she went on. "All thanks to Jack, of course."

Hallie groaned. "What did he do now?"

"Oh, well, do I start with when he showed up and plopped himself down at the table while Declan was in the restroom? Or how about when Declan came back, and Jack assumed he was the waiter? Even proceeded to order himself a beer!"

"Please tell me you're making this up."

"Believe me, I wish I were. I could have *killed* Jack. I mean what are the chances of his being at the Chowder House the same night I go out on my first date since . . . since . . ."

"Since Mrs. Evanson's Dutch-treating-miniature-golf-playing grandson, Stuart?" Hallie finished, cracking a smile. "Sorry. Couldn't resist. But you're right. That *is* a little freaky, isn't it? It's not like the Chowder House is one of Jack's usual hangouts. Was he maybe there with someone?"

"No. That's the weird part. He seemed like he was there to see me. It was almost like he thought he was supposed to be meeting me or something."

"That *is* weird." Hallie shook her head. "What did he do, I mean, after he ordered the beer?"

Jenna tore off a chunk of her sister's muffin, unable to resist. If there was one thing their mother was best at baking, it was muffins.

"What could Jack do? He left as soon as he realized Declan wasn't the waiter. But you should have seen the look on his face when it hit him that I was out with someone. Someone other than him. And someone who looked like Declan. If I didn't know better, I'd have sworn he was jealous."

"Poor Jack . . ." Hallie looked at her. "Well, it had to have been hard on him, seeing you out with a successful handsome stranger."

Jenna sipped her coffee, trying to ignore the knot that had settled in her stomach as she remembered the way Jack had looked. His eyes, the way he'd stared at her. He hadn't seemed jealous at all. He'd seemed almost . . . crestfallen.

"You know, why am I letting this bother me so much? It's been three years, four if you count the separation. And it's not like he hasn't been out there, seeing other people. I don't think the ink was dry on the divorce papers before he was sniffing around Diana DeNunzio's"—she coughed—"*tree.*"

"Along with half the other mongrels in town. Good old 'Double D' *De*Nunzio," Hallie muttered, grimacing as if the cream in her coffee had gone sour. "I mean, I just don't get the attraction. Bottle blonde and not even a good bottle blonde, but something she obviously did in her kitchen sink because we both know she isn't coming in to the salon. And on top of that, a complete vacancy between the ears. A walking cliché if ever I saw one. What are they thinking?"

"It's not *what* they are thinking, rather what they are thinking *with*. And it sure isn't a brain. I can just hear them now down at the pub." Jenna lowered her voice, thickening it with a South Boston accent. *"Hey, who needs brains when you've got a set of double D's like those?"* She shook her head, as ever unable to comprehend the vagaries of the male species. "It's certainly something we Wren women would know nothing about."

Hallie nodded, polishing off the muffin. "Ugh, would you want to? It's like carrying a set of twins, only around your neck! I swear sometimes that girl looks as if she'd topple over from a good wind. Don't they realize by fifty, she'll be stooped over like Quasimodo? No, thanks," she added, squaring her shoulders and straightening her posture. She struck quite a pose with her towel-wrapped head and green face. "I'll stick with the 'almost C's' that Mother Nature gave me."

"Likewise," Jenna added, and the two sisters shared a kindred chuckle as they finished their morning coffee.

Cassie just couldn't contain herself.

Outside on the leaf-littered sidewalk, she was skipping, actually skipping, as she walked with her brother to school. It was a glorious day. The sun was out, her birthday was coming, and now her parents were falling back in love. Even Mrs. Murphy's nasty beagle, Bagel, barking at them from the other side of the picket fence couldn't dampen her spirits.

"What's with you?" Sam asked. "You look like an idiot, grinning like it's Christmas or something."

"Oh, it's better than Christmas, and I'm grinning, Sam Gabriele, because I know something you don't," she said, lifting her chin just a little. Brothers, she decided, were just so clueless.

"Oh, really?" Sam said. "What is it?"

"I can't tell you. It's a secret."

"So?"

"So, it's a secret that I know and you don't."

She started humming, singing the words of that familiar song to herself in her head:

> *Mommy and Daddy sitting in a tree,*
> *K-I-S-S-I-N-G . . .*

Her refusal to share the secret with him sparked Sam's temper. "Who cares? It's probably some stupid little girl thing anyway."

"No, it's not. It's something really, really good."

"Shut up, Cass."

"Better than Disney World even . . ."

"I said *shut up!*"

"And it's about Mom . . . and Dad."

Sam stopped on the sidewalk, grabbed his sister by the arm and held her, yanking her back midskip. "What about Mom and Dad?"

"Ow! Quit it, Sam. That hurts."

He stared at her without a hint of anything but seriousness in his expression. "I mean it. Tell me, Cassie. Tell me right now, or I'll . . ."

She glared at him, wrenching her arm away. "Fine. I'll tell you." She rubbed her arm, even though it really didn't hurt that much. She just wanted to make him think that it had. Finally, she said, "Mom and Dad went out on a date last night."

Sam looked at her as if she'd just said she had walked on the moon in her nightgown. "You're full of it."

"No, I'm not. You saw Mommy all dressed up last night in her black dress, didn't you? Well, they met at the Chowder House for dinner, and afterward they walked down by the harbor together. And Mommy told Aunt Hallie it was fabulous. That he was different. A true gentleman. Daddy even kissed her hand."

Cassie wanted to add that it was all her doing, by way of the spell she'd cast, but knew she couldn't. Because if she told Sam what she'd done, then he'd tell their mother. And if he told their mother, then everything would be ruined.

Boys were such blabbermouths that way.

Sam chewed over his sister's news. "Do you think they're getting back together?"

Cassie just grinned, then turned and ran when she heard the school bell start ringing down the street.

Chasing after her, Sam couldn't help but smile as well.

Jack shifted his truck into reverse, spitting up gravel as he backed out of the drive.

The small two-bedroom cottage he rented looked down from the heights onto the harbor and the line of houses and shops that ringed the common above it.

After the split, he'd needed to put some distance between himself and Jen. His parents had offered him the studio above the pizza shop, which would have been fine, except the location—down the street and around the corner from Eudora's house, and then later Jen's salon—had been just too close for his comfort. If he didn't have to face it, he could almost convince himself sometimes that it hadn't really happened, that Jen and the kids were just away visiting family or something. He'd been stung deeply by her rejection, and had been less than comfortable at having to play a part in the public disintegration of their marriage.

Theirs had been Ipswich-by-the-Sea's hometown match made in heaven, the one that was supposed to last where others had failed. Most of the town had been at their wedding, a two-day celebration that had taken place on the common with food, dancing, and high spirits drowning out an Italian wedding band.

His parents had been together more than forty years, through thick and thin, across an ocean and halfway around the world, and with two children and a successful business to show for it. It must not always have been easy, but they'd managed to weather the storms that had come their way. And Jack had believed he and Jen could do the same.

Until that weekend.

He would never forget the day he'd come home after Cassie had recovered to find Jenna gone. At first, Jack had been incensed. How could she? How could Jen have just left? Even though he knew now that he—and his behavior—had brought it on, back then his male pride had been far more important. He'd simply refused to acknowledge what life had decided to throw at him.

The worst part was that it seemed as if *everyone* had known before he had. And overnight love turned to resentment. The truth was, the resentment was just easier to contend with. Seeing Jen whenever he went to pick up the kids, having to ring the doorbell like some sort of delivery person, had been salt rubbed into a very new and raw wound. He'd needed to distance himself far enough away that he didn't have to see the looks on everyone's faces, the disappointment, the blame.

So he'd hidden himself away, to wait until he felt he could breathe again, until he could stand back and look at what had become of his life, and figure out what he was going to do with the pieces of it lying all around him like a shattered mirror.

The house where he'd holed himself up was really more of a cottage that a friend of a friend of his father's had picked up with a thought to renting out during the summers. The bargain he'd gotten it for had shown in the outdated fittings and worse-for-wear trim. The place had been in sorry need of repair, updating, an "out with the old, in with the new" renovation. But it was livable and it had suited Jack well enough. There was an extra bedroom for the kids when he had them, and a loft where he could set up the office for the business no one except his father and a few closemouthed others knew he intended to start. Jack had offered to work off part of his rent in doing the renovations himself.

It turned out to be the perfect place for him to renovate himself as well.

Up here he could sit on the small covered porch, legs stretched out from a weather-beaten Adirondack chair, sipping a beer while watching the moonlight ripple on the sea. A man could do a lot of thinking in such a place, and Jack had done just that. Even while blaming Jen during most of that first year of their separation, in more lucid moments, Jack had managed to take a long look at his life. He'd looked at the choices he'd made, and the place those choices had brought him to. He and Jen had married out of high school and he'd gone to work on a construction crew, putting in time at his father's pizza shop on weekends to help make ends meet while Jen stayed home with Sammie first, then later Sam and Cassie. Rent payments, truck payments, bills, responsibility—it had been a daily load to bear. There was no time or allowance for the freedoms his friends had enjoyed like going off to college, backpacking through Europe, taking the time to decide exactly what they wanted to do with their lives.

Jack had had the decision made for him.

He didn't blame anyone. It couldn't have been easy on Jen either. Nineteen, pregnant, rushed to the altar. Life just worked that way sometimes, and they'd both stepped up to accept the responsibility at the cost of unrealized dreams and forgotten aspirations. But stress had a way of burning in the belly, clouding the vision, weakening the brain. Instead of pulling together and working out a plan, they'd drifted. Jen wanted more than the small two-bedroom apartment they'd rented on the outskirts of town, and she'd deserved more.

But when she pushed, he pulled away, and the stress of it turned to resentment. Feeding that resentment became a daily requirement, one that took him further and further away from Jen. He started going to the pub each night with the boys to sit around complaining about their wives, the boss, the loss of freedom. He hadn't even realized how deep into it he'd fallen.

Then came that weekend, when he'd made a decision that would change the rest of his life. Not only his life, but also Jen's—and the lives of his two children.

At the time, he'd seen it as making a statement, drawing a line in the sand and standing his ground. The truth of it was Jen had needed him, needed him more than she'd ever needed him before, and he hadn't been there for her. In fact he had abandoned her. Utterly and completely.

It had taken Jen doing the same to him, moving out and then moving on with her life—without him—for Jack to realize just what that must have been like for her. And Jack had learned it was the worse possible feeling imaginable. Everything that had really mattered to him was gone, and he was left alone. Truly alone.

The nights were the worst of it. During the day, he could throw himself into his work, working himself to exhaustion in hopes that it would leave him no option but to fall into bed, insensible to the rest of the world. But more often than not, no matter how exhausted he was, he would still lie there numb and awake, staring at the ceiling and remembering the way Jen used to curl up against him, or the smell of her skin.

God, he missed her.

Once he'd picked himself up from the blow, Jack had conceived a plan. He was determined to do what he did best—he would fix that which needed fixing—make it stronger, better, safer. He would show Jen that he was not the screwup, the selfish jerk, she believed him to be. That was something he had shown her for too long. He would give her what she'd deserved to have that first time around. He would give her the man, the husband and father, she'd always believed he could be. He'd just needed the time to do it right.

Jack's dream in high school was to study architecture in college, maybe even travel to his parent's native Italy to see firsthand the great palazzos and villas. Instead, after getting married, he'd ended up working on a crew for one of the many home builders in northern New England who slapped as many modern colonial boxes on an acre of land as they could get away with. Jack had spent his days putting up cookie-cutter houses with windows sashed in plastic and walls sided in vinyl in subdivisions where one house could barely be distinguished from another. Houses without souls. It wasn't what he'd planned on, but it paid the bills and that had taken priority over any dreams he'd once had.

After Jen left, Jack decided he could no longer take it. Without her, without the kids, none of it mattered. So he quit the construction crew and hooked up with an old school friend of his, Brian O'Connell. Brian's father, Jimmy, ran a business out of his home doing renovation, particularly for the older properties in and around Ipswich-by-the-Sea. O'Connell & Sons was known for being a small operation, just a man and his three sons, but they paid careful attention to detail and craftsmanship.

Brian, the eldest O'Connell son, who had gotten his architecture degree while working with his father and brothers, had often talked with Jack of bigger things, of preserving heritage, building houses with souls. So he and Jack had sat down and come up with a plan that would include a partnership with the elder O'Connell. The partnership would take the core business into true architectural restoration, renovation, salvage, and design.

Without telling anyone, except for his father who

had given him the encouragement and support he'd needed, Jack went back to school, studying at night while working during the day. It had taken three long years, but now Jack had a newly framed degree in architectural design hanging on his wall to show for it. At the same time, Jack and Brian O'Connell had laid the foundation for their business with Jack apprenticing under both Jimmy and Brian on various O'Connell projects. It had eaten into his time with the kids especially, but Jack learned the things that books and classrooms couldn't teach.

Recently, they had renovated what had once been the boathouse up at the old Hutchinson place, Thar Muir. One of the oldest properties in town, it had been converted from a family home into a B-and-B earlier that year. Jack had done some of the work in it, finishing with the boathouse renovation, which had been carefully restored for use as a long-term studio rental.

That boathouse had been O'Connell & Sons' last project. Just the week before, the newly named O'Connell & Gabriele had landed their first official job, a Revolutionary era home restoration in Newburyport. It was to be the start of the last phase in a new path for Jack, a path that was to take him back to Jen and the kids. He was older and wiser now, and he knew the cost of forgotten dreams. Just as Jen had realized her dream with the success of the salon, Jack had promised himself he would have the success of a career he could be proud of behind him before he would try to win her back.

That time had finally come.

Only after seeing her the night before, looking so beautiful—so beautiful for another guy, and a guy who obviously already came with all the things Jack had been busting his tail for—Jack could only hope he wasn't too late.

"Good afternoon, IpSnips," Jenna answered when the salon phone rang on the reception desk beside her.

"I have *news*," burst Hallie's voice from the other end of the line.

Jenna counted out Mrs. Mahoney's change, whispering a "Thank you" and giving her a smile before answering her sister. "Aren't you supposed to be working today?"

"I am. Flora had an appointment at her obstetrician's this morning for a sonogram so I came in early. Which is how I found out this absolutely juicy bit of news, something I think you're going to be very interested in . . ."

Hallie paused.

"So, are you going to tell me or are you just going to sit there breathing into the phone like some perverted teenager?"

Hallie huffed. "You're no fun! Fine, I'll tell you. You know the boathouse cottage here at the B-and-B that was just renovated?"

Jenna scanned the appointment book for her upcoming clients. Of course she knew about the cottage. She and Flora and Hallie had spent more than one late night earlier that summer deciding on its design so Jimmy O'Connell and his sons could bring their vision of what it should be into reality. Jenna had yet to see the finished work, but Flora had been very pleased with it when she spoke to Jenna the week before. "Yes, Hallie, of course I do . . ."

"Well, we just took its first booking. Someone

took it for an extended stay. An *open-ended*, extended stay."

"Oh really? Well, that should please Flora to no end considering she's decided to keep the B-and-B open through the winter while their place in Scotland is being fixed up."

"Yes, Flora will be quite happy about it, I'm sure. But aren't you going to ask me *who* took it?"

Jenna sat back in her chair, fiddling with her pencil. "Okay, I will. Hallie, who took out the cottage for an extended, open-ended stay?"

She could almost see Hallie's grin through the phone. "A certain Declan Cavanaugh."

Jenna sat up, dropped the pencil. "He did?"

"Yes. We'd only had him booked here for a room through Friday, but he's decided he wants to stay on, and wants to move into the boathouse. Wants more space. Some privacy. Seems something in town has caught his eye. Something, or rather *someone* . . ."

Jenna thought back to the night before and the way it had felt to be with a man who openly admired her, who treated her with respect, who'd cared to hear her opinions. So different from—

The salon bell rang. The door swung open. Jenna glanced up, expecting Mrs. Jaffrey for her afternoon wash and set.

Jack stepped through the door a moment later.

"Hallie, I have to go."

She didn't even wait for her sister to respond before hanging up.

He hadn't shaved that morning and his hair was still too long and still stuffed beneath that tattered ball cap. As she shoved the receiver back in its cradle, Jenna wondered why she was feeling like she had been caught doing something she shouldn't have been. It wasn't like she and Jack were still married. So she'd gone on a date. She had nothing to hide. Nothing at all.

"Jack," she said.

"Jen."

"You need your hair cut."

"Huh?" He pulled off the cap, raked a hand over his head. "Yeah, I guess I do. I've been busy."

"You can come by the house tonight if you want and I'll cut it for you."

He nodded. "Thanks. Listen, I wanted to talk to you. About last night."

She looked at him, frowning as she remembered how he'd almost ruined the evening for her. "Is there really anything to talk about, Jack?"

"Look, Cassie told me you were there. I had no idea you were"—he paused, "*out* with someone."

Their gazes locked.

"Who is he?" Jack finally asked.

"I don't see how that is any of your business."

Her refusal spoke straight to his Italian temper. "It is if he's going to be anywhere around my kids," Jack bit back. "Who is he, Jen? A client?"

"He stopped in for a cut, and we started talking. He's new in town. He asked me out. We had dinner. That's all it was."

"Fine." Jack nodded. "Jen, I went there last night because I wanted to talk to you about—"

The door behind Jack opened and in walked the biggest bouquet of flowers Jenna had ever seen. Deep wine-colored roses set off by brilliant white orchids, it eclipsed the delivery driver who was carrying it.

"Ms. Jenna Wren?" asked the voice coming from behind the blooming profusion.

"Yes, that's me," Jenna answered. She circled the desk and took the crystal vase, setting it on a plinth where she'd intended to arrange a display of decorative scented candles. The flowers would be a definite improvement.

Breathing in the heady scent, she plucked the card from inside, reading it quickly.

Dinner was a pleasure. How about an encore? Tonight? I'll pick you up at seven thirty.

He'd signed it simply *D.C.*

Jenna felt herself smile as she slid the card back into its envelope.

Another date.

He was staying on for an extended time.

Things were definitely looking up.

When she turned back, she found Jack staring at her.

"Must have been some date."

Saying nothing, Jenna just stared at him.

"Be careful, Jen," he said. "You don't even know who this guy is. You don't need to be jumping for the first one that comes along."

With that, her own temper, rooted in her father's Irishness, flared.

"You needn't worry, Jack," she snapped. "In case you've forgotten, I've been taking quite good care of myself, and our children, for the past three years. And long before that, for that matter."

Jack shoved his ball cap back on, shaking his head. "You know, I came over here to apologize. To try to talk to you. Not to have my nose rubbed in it . . . again."

And then he turned, shoving the door as he headed out and nearly running down Mrs. Jaffrey who had arrived for her appointment.

Chapter Five

When the doorbell rang at Number Eight Elm Street, Cassie rocketed from the kitchen table with a *whoosh* that left her math homework fluttering to the floor.

She knew who was there. It would be her daddy. She knew this because she'd just seen her mother upstairs, putting on her makeup and fixing her hair.

They were going out on another date.

"I've got it!" she shouted and raced to be the first one to the door. She didn't want anyone, most especially Sam, getting there first. She smiled when she grabbed the door handle, giving it a good hard yank.

"Hi, Da—"

But her words got stuck in her throat like a big glob of peanut butter when she saw who stood on the other side of the door.

It wasn't her father, not at all. It was a stranger. Only he wasn't *really* a stranger. In fact, he looked just like . . .

His blond hair was a little lighter than it had looked in the magazine, and his face was more tanned, but there was no mistaking that Perfecta-Dent smile.

Cassie's mouth fell open as she faced him.

"Hi there," the man said, flashing that smile. "You must be Cassie. I'm—"

"I know who you are," Cassie answered him, somewhat stunned that he was there, actually *there,* standing before her.

She wanted to tell him she knew he was the Toothpaste Man, but decided that would probably be rude. Nobody would really like to be called Toothpaste Man, would they? So instead she said, "You're at the wrong house, you know."

"I am?" He raised one eyebrow then looked around. "Are you sure?"

Cassie nodded. "Auntie Hallie isn't here. She's next door at Nanny's house."

"Oh. Well, that's nice to know, Cassie. But I was actually looking for—"

"Declan."

Cassie turned and found her mother standing on the stairs behind her. Jenna had put her hair up with tendrils curling down around her neck, and Cassie could smell the faint scent of her perfume, the one that reminded Cassie of the sweet peas that grew in the garden. She was wearing a long, narrow, filmy skirt and her pretty blue sweater with the shiny pearl buttons—it was Cassie's favorite because it was made of something called *cashmere* and was the softest sweater Cassie had ever felt. It always made her mommy look really elegant, like a princess.

"You look stunning," the Toothpaste Man said, stepping into the doorway. What had Mommy called him? Cassie tried to remember and thought it began with a *D.*

David? No.

Dennis? Not that either.

Jenna smiled softly and came down the last few steps to meet him. She gave him her hand and leaned forward to kiss his cheek. "You're looking rather well yourself," she said. "Thank you for the flowers. They are beautiful."

Flowers? That big bouquet of flowers Mommy had been giddy about all night were from *him*?

Not Daddy?

And suddenly Cassie realized why the Toothpaste Man was there.

No!

This couldn't be. Why would he be coming to take Mommy on a date when he was supposed to be madly in love with Aunt Hallie?

Aunt Hallie. That was it. Maybe the Toothpaste Man just needed to see her. Then he would realize he had made a mistake.

"I'll be right back!" Cassie said and she slipped around them both, dashing through the door and running straight for Nanny's house next door.

"Cassandra Wren," Jenna called. "Wait! Where are you going?"

But Cassie didn't stop. She raced down the walkway, jumping over Nanny's hedgerow, and shoved the door open without knocking.

Nanny was sitting on her sofa, an afghan over her legs with Ogre sleeping beside her, curled on a pillow. Until Cassie came tearing in. At her thunderous arrival, the dog sprang up and started yapping like mad.

"Child, what on earth is the matter?" Nanny asked, closing the book she had been reading as she tried to *shh* Ogre calm.

"Auntie Hallie," Cassie gasped out. "Where is she?"

"Upstairs in her room, I think. She was taking a shower. Why? Has something happened?"

Cassie didn't pause to explain. She didn't have the time. Instead she tore up the stairs and found her aunt plucking her eyebrows in the bathroom mirror. Cassie didn't say a word. She just grabbed Hallie's free hand and pulled her out the door.

"Cass! What the . . . ? What are you doing?"

"You have to come with me. Right now. It's urgent!"

"What is it? Is something wrong?"

"Yes . . . No . . . Just come!"

They scrambled down the stairs, past a startled Nanny, a still yapping Ogre, and on out the front door. They raced down the walkway and back to Cassie's house where Cassie tore through the front door to find Jenna and the man with the funny name standing in the living room with Sam. The moment he saw her, Sam gave Cassie a sour look.

"Cassie, what is going on?" Jenna asked, clearly perturbed. "Why did you go tearing out of here like that?"

"I had to go and get Aunt Hallie. So she could meet the Too—, I mean De—, De—"

"Declan," Hallie answered for her. "His name is Declan Cavanaugh. And we've already met, silly."

Cassie stared at her aunt in disbelief. "No, you couldn't have."

Because if you'd met then he'd be coming to take you out on a date, not Mommy.

"Yes, sweetie, I have. Declan is staying at Thar Muir. In fact, we spent the afternoon getting him settled into the boathouse apartment." She looked at him, and smiled. "Declan's going to be visiting Ipswich-by-the-Sea for a little while and your mom's offered to show him around so he knows where to buy groceries, how to find the post office—you know, that sort of thing . . ."

As the adults chatted, Cassie could only stand by helpless and perplexed. If Aunt Hallie had already met the Toothpaste Man, and he hadn't fallen instantly in love with her—and she with him—then that had to mean that Ogre had eaten Aunt Hallie—her poppet cookie, that is—before Cassie had been able to finish casting the spell. So that must mean that without the poppet cookie, the spell had somehow been redirected, and instead of Aunt Hallie, the Toothpaste Man had fallen in love with . . .

Mommy.

Cassie gasped, covering her mouth.

"Now come on, you crazy pixie," Hallie said, tugging one of Cassie's pigtails. "I promised your mom I'd sit with you and your brother tonight. We've DVDs to watch and popcorn to pop."

"Only until eight," Jenna reminded her. "They have school tomorrow."

"But wait! Mommy, I need you to help me with my math homework and—"

"Aunt Hallie will help you, Cassie. We've got to get going. It's getting late." Jenna kissed the top of Cassie's fretful head. "Go with Aunt Hallie now and I'll talk to you later, okay?"

She and the Toothpaste Man said good-bye to Hallie and Sam.

"It was a pleasure to meet you, too, Cassie," the man—Declan—said, flashing her that same sparkling smile before he turned and led her mother out the door.

Unable to tell them what had gone wrong, she could only stand and watch them go.

Sam hissed in her ear after they'd left. "You're a big fat *liar*."

Aunt Hallie had headed off to get the DVDs and it was just the two of them standing in the living room. Next to the huge vase of flowers the man had given their mother. "Mom and Dad are not getting back together." He pointed to the door. "I think *he*'s going to be her new boyfriend."

"No, Sam, you're wrong," Cassie insisted desperately. "And I didn't lie. It's a mistake. You don't understand."

But Sam just shook his head and went back up the stairs to his room. She heard his door close, more loudly than usual, a minute later.

How? How could this have happened?

Cassie couldn't concentrate on the Harry Potter DVD that Aunt Hallie put on. Even at her favorite part, when Hermione punches Draco Malfoy and makes the bully wizard cry, Cassie didn't even crack a smile. She was staring at the popcorn kernels in her bowl, troubling over what she was going to do, how she was going to fix whatever had gone wrong with the spell.

What if she dug up the poppets from where she had buried them in the garden, and tried casting the spell again? Would that cancel out the first spell, or would the two spells cross somehow, and make even more of a tangle? The result could be disastrous. But what if instead she dug up only the Toothpaste Man's poppet and then burned it in the hearth? Would that take him away just as suddenly as he'd appeared?

There was a knocking on the door but Cassie barely heard it. She didn't even notice when Aunt Hallie got up to answer, coming back a few minutes later, this time with Cassie's father.

"I'm sorry, Jack. I don't know why Jen didn't leave any message. She didn't mention you'd be coming by."

"Apparently her mind was occupied elsewhere." Jack was frowning. "Look, it's no big deal. I only came by because she offered to give me a cut. I'm glad to see the kids anytime." He looked at his daughter and his frown vanished. "Hey there, Cass. How's my girl?"

"Hi, Daddy . . ."

Cassie slid off the couch with all the enthusiasm of a snail. She felt so bad. He should be the one out with Mommy. She wanted to tell him what she had done, how she had messed everything up, but knew she couldn't. So she crossed the room and gave her father a tight hug, squeezing him extra hard and extra long. She wanted to tell him how sorry she was for bringing the Toothpaste Man to meet Mommy. She wanted to tell him it was all her fault that now they weren't going to get back together again. Just like when she'd gotten sick. Now she'd done it again. She'd only wanted so badly to make it better.

Cassie closed her eyes, swallowing hard as she struggled to squeeze back her tears.

"Hey there," Jack said when he noticed his daughter crying. "What's the matter?"

But Cassie couldn't answer him. She just hung her head and stared through watery eyes at her toes.

Jack looked to Hallie, who only shook her head. "She's been quiet all night. Ever since Jen left."

Jack put his finger under Cassie's chin, lifting her face so she had to look at him. He brushed away the tears still swelling in her eyes. "Cassie, are you upset that your mom went out tonight?"

"I don't . . ." She shook her head, then nodded, then shook her head again. "I can't . . ."

"It's okay, Cass. You don't have to talk about it if you don't want to." Jack took Cassie's hands, enfolding them in his own. "Hey, do you know why daddies are made with such big hands?"

Cassie sniffed, blinked at him. "No. Why?"

"Because it's their job to take all the things that upset their little girls, all the problems they might have, and make them disappear."

Jack opened his hands, cupping them before her. "Now, I want you to take whatever is troubling you and put it in here. You don't even have to tell me what it is. Just imagine it locked up tight in your fist, then open your hand and drop it right here."

Cassie looked at him, screwing up her mouth in disbelief. "Daddy . . ."

"I mean it, Cass. It works. Trust me in this. I promise. It's like magic."

Magic.

When she heard that word, Cassie looked into her father's eyes. Did he know? Had he somehow found out what she'd done and knew a way to make it better? For a moment, as she stood there so close to him, feeling the warmth of his hands on hers, it felt as if she truly could give him her troubles and have him spirit them away.

"Just try it," Jack said.

Cassie clenched her hand into a ball, picturing the poppets, the spell, and the mess she'd made all stuck together inside. She placed her fist into the hollow of her father's large hands and then slowly opened her fingers, letting it all ooze away as she lifted her hand. Jack closed his hands around one another as if he were holding a very dangerous and precarious thing. He looked at Cassie, smiled, and then walked to the kitchen. He motioned her to follow, and then stepped on the trash can to lift its lid so he could toss the invisible glop away.

If only it were that easy.

Her father was the strongest, bravest man ever. But Cassie knew even he couldn't fix this problem. Still she loved him all the more for trying. She kissed his cheek. "Thank you, Daddy."

"You bet. I'll always be here for you, sweetie. You don't ever have to feel like you're alone when something is bothering you. Remember that, okay?"

Cassie hugged her father, suddenly knowing what she would have to do to fix her mixed-up spell.

She would have to go to Nanny.

Cassie waited until after school the following day when she was sure she would have the best chance of being alone with her grandmother. Sam was going to Timmy's house to play some dopey video game. Mommy would be working at the salon, of course, and Aunt Hallie would be at Thar Muir.

As always, she found Nanny in the kitchen. She was brewing, covered bosom to knee in her well-worn apron, and sprinkling herbs, spices, and various other bits into her big cast-iron pot. Nanny had a new stove, one of those stainless silver ones like in her grandfather Tino's pizza shop, bigger than most other stoves because Nanny was always cooking and she'd burned through the two before. As she worked, Nanny would pause to scribble little notes in her grimoire, which she kept open on the kitchen table. Cassie knew when she did that she was creating a new spell. Behind her, there were dozens of little glass jars lined up neatly on the countertop, waiting to be filled.

Waiting for those who would come for them.

Nanny's specialty was fertility spells. The women of Ipswich-by-the-Sea and nearby towns, and even farther away than that, had been coming to Eudora Wren for as long as Cassie could remember, looking for hope where medical science had offered them none. Many of them had spent years and thousands of dollars on doctors and special procedures in hopes of having a baby, only to be disappointed in the end. Only to be told there was no hope. But those doctors didn't know Nanny Wren, and they didn't know her recipes.

Hers were "recipes" that had been handed down in their family for hundreds of years. The women would come to Nanny's kitchen, take home one of her special "chutneys," and their dream of having a baby would come true. Inexplicably. *Magically.* When confronted, those doctors who had failed simply said it had been that one in a million chance, and not due to anything else. Certainly not due to a jar of homemade preserves. But Nanny had scrapbooks filled with photographs of tiny babies and happy families. And she even knew the names of every single one.

So, Cassie thought, if Nanny could make that many people happy where they had been hopeless before, then surely she would be able to help fix something as simple as her mixed-up spell.

Eudora Wren was standing at the stove, stirring a pot of her newest potion while her favorite Enya CD murmured from the countertop stereo. She liked listening to the songstress' Gaelic selections when she was brewing, and especially when she was casting something new and untried. Something about the earthy Celtic voice helped to get her in the "conjuring" mood.

This afternoon, she'd been concocting a special new "salsa" made with basil and fennel, some kidney bean and just a touch of cayenne pepper. It was meant for those men whose "confidence" was in need of a little "elevating." Her inspiration for this particular recipe was a local fisherman named George Templeton. George's wife, Rose, had come to Eudora in obvious desperation. It seemed she had done everything she could to inspire the conception of their long-awaited first child, but she had two things working against her.

First, with George being a fisherman, he was away through most of the summer. But then once the cold weather arrived, Rose couldn't manage to get her partner off the living room sofa long enough to bring things to fruition. George was a football fan—a football *fan*atic. His fortunes rose and fell on the success of his hometown team. Now that the season was upon them, Rose was frantic. She had lost the months of September to February to the Patriots and their prolific Super Bowl runs every year of their six-year marriage. Even those years when they didn't bring home the trophy, George would only end up blubbering into his beer about interceptions and fumbles and missed opportunities.

Meanwhile, Rose was bemoaning her own missed opportunities. This season, she was determined that things were going to be different.

Rose had come to Eudora with a heartfelt plea, a rapidly ticking biological clock, and a desperate gleam in her eyes. This coming weekend, the Patriots were on the West Coast, playing in Seattle, which meant George would once again be couchbound. And according to Rose's pharmacy-bought ovulation predictor kit, her fertility was coming to its peak. But Eudora could have told her that just looking at her. Rose had a definite "greenness" to her natural light. Indeed, time was of the essence.

Eudora had readily accepted the challenge.

Just wait, George Templeton, till you dip your chips into this. . . .

With a pinch of cinnamon for the finishing touch, Eudora said a quick incantation before putting a cover on the slowly bubbling cauldron . . . eh, pot. She was just about to change Enya for Van Morrison's "Moondance," a song she always did a celebratory little dance to whenever she brewed up something new, when she caught sight of Cassie standing in the middle of the kitchen behind her, watching her. Goodness but she hadn't even heard her come in. Sometimes, she swore the child moved on cat feet.

"Hey there, kitten," Eudora said, forgoing the "Moondance" ritual for the moment. "How long have you been home? How was school today?"

"Not long . . . and okay." Cassie went to the fridge to pour herself a glass of milk. That and one of Eudora's brownies was her usual after-school snack.

"Homework?" Nanny asked, sliding the brownie before her.

"A little. Spelling test on Friday, but I already know all the words."

"That's my girl," Eudora smiled. Cassie was a voracious reader, poring through chapter books hundreds of pages in length, and as such had developed a vocabulary years beyond her age. "And . . . what about math?"

Cassie pulled a face. Math, however, was *not* one of her favorite subjects.

"Okay, let me put that pot on simmer and we'll go over your problems together."

Cassie quietly ate her brownie until Eudora came to the table to join her. "Okay, let's see what you have."

"Nanny, I need help."

"Yes, dear. I know you do. Double-digit subtraction can be tricky. But don't worry. We'll figure it out together."

"No. That's not what I mean." Cassie's voice dropped. "I need help with something other than math."

Eudora recognized the sound of a child's distress. Cassie was troubled by something. Something deep. Which meant the math was going to wait. She settled back in her chair. "Okay . . . why don't you tell Nanny what it is, then?"

She waited, sipping her tea until Cassie found the words to tell her.

"I did something, Nanny."

Tears were already welling in the little girl's eyes. Whatever it was, it must be something big. Eudora took her hand and squeezed it. "It's okay, Cassie. You know you can tell me."

Cassie chewed her lip a little bit longer, then slowly raised her eyes. Her voice was little more than a whisper. "I did a spell."

Was that all?

But before Eudora could say anything in response, Cassie went on. "I know I shouldn't have, Nanny, not without telling you first. But I was only trying to fix things. It was for good, not for bad, just like you said it should be. I just wanted to show Mommy that I was ready to learn how to cast for real."

"Well, you know how your mommy feels about that. But if it was for good, like you said, then I'm sure a little spell won't do any harm."

"But it's not okay, Nanny. Something went wrong with the spell."

Eudora felt something then, a chill that most other people would shrug off as a draft coming through an open door or some inexplicable "cold spot." But Eudora knew better. She knew very well what those chills could mean. And it was certainly nothing auspicious.

"What do you mean 'something went wrong,' Cassie? How do you know?"

Cassie looked at Eudora and her mouth started to tremble as she struggled to let go of what she had been keeping bottled up inside of her. Eudora just waited, not wanting to pressure her, knowing eventually it would come out. And when it did come, it burst like a swollen, contemptible balloon.

"I don't know how it happened! I was so very careful, Nanny. I heard Mommy and Aunt Hallie talking and they were both unhappy because they didn't have a perfect man. They were writing a recipe, just like you do, to make one. So I thought I would help them. I made sure to follow everything you ever taught me. Every rule. The moon was right. I lit the candle. I cast the circle. But then Ogre ate Aunt Hallie and now everything is a mess because the Toothpaste Man came, only he is with Mommy, not Aunt Hallie, and now Daddy is . . . Daddy is . . ."

Eudora just let her blather it out, not understanding more than a fraction of what the child said. She waited until Cassie, now sobbing, finished by saying, ". . . and now I don't know what to do!"

Calmly and as reassuringly as possible, Eudora responded. "Okay. Now, let's take this one step at a time, all right? First, tell me exactly what you did."

It took almost a half hour before Eudora had a clear idea of what had taken place. And it was quite a muddle. The fact that it involved Jenna would make it a challenge to put right. When spells went awry on non-witches, it was fairly simple to fix them because most people didn't ever consider those odd little coincidences and peculiar happenings as anything more than that. They certainly never suspected for a moment that it might just be magic.

But on a witch . . .

. . . that was another story.

First, though, Eudora had to make Cassie believe the world wasn't going to come to an end just because of her little magic misstep.

"Okay, the good news is that you tried a spell, a spell with truly good intentions, and it worked, at least in theory anyway. So you should be proud of yourself for that."

Cassie, however, wasn't seeing the bright side of this pickle.

"But Mommy is going to be *so* mad at me when she finds out. She'll never let me learn to cast after this. And I've ruined everything! She's not getting back with Daddy and now instead she's going to fall in love with the Toothpaste Man and—"

"Sweetheart, wait! Now listen to Nanny. Even with the most powerful of spells, you could not make your mother fall in love with someone she wouldn't otherwise love. You might create an attraction for a time, and I suspect that is what your mother is feeling. It's nice to get the attention of a dashing, sophisticated man, such as this Toothpaste Man seems to be. But in the end, you cannot create love where there is none."

"But she needs to love Daddy again! She's so

unhappy and so is Daddy. And it's all because of me. I know it. Because I got sick."

Eudora looked at her. "Who told you that, child?"

Cassie stared at her grandmother. She didn't want to get Sam in trouble. He was already mad enough at her for making him think Mommy and Daddy were getting back together. And he'd never really said it, out loud. He'd just made her think it had been her fault, once, when he'd been really really mad at her.

"No one. I just know, and that's why I tried to fix it. But look what I've done! I have to turn off the spell, Nanny. I just have to! I have to make the Toothpaste Man go away."

"All right." Eudora took a deep breath, thinking as she tapped a finger to her chin. "There are some things we can do to try to redirect the spell. We can also cast a bit of a barrier spell to keep this Toothpaste fellow at a distance." *At least until I've had a chance to check him out,* Eudora thought to herself. "Now, I'll need to know exactly which ingredients you used and the words you recited when you cast the spell. Just trust Nanny in this, Cassie. We'll find a way to make it right."

Cassie looked at her grandmother and found the comfort and reassurance she needed in Eudora's warm smile and wise dark eyes. Her face brightened and that dimpled smile Eudora loved so dearly broke through the worry that had etched her tiny child's face.

"Thank you, Nanny," she sniffed. "I knew you could fix it."

But as Cassie slid off the chair to put her brownie dish in the sink, even Eudora could only hope.

*   *   *

Jenna was just closing up the salon for the day when Jack came to the door, drumming softly on the window with his fingers to draw her attention. The minute she saw him wearing his backward ball cap, she remembered she'd told him to stop by the night before for a cut.

She turned the latch to let him in. "Jack, I'm sorry I forgot about last night."

"It's fine. Don't worry about it."

She glanced at the clock. "I have time now if you do."

"Sure. That's good." He nodded. "I wanted to talk to you anyway."

He crossed the salon to Jenna's chair and dropped into it.

"What did you want to talk about?" she asked as she fixed a cutting cape around his neck. She adjusted the chair to his height, locked it in place.

"It's about Cassie. She was pretty upset last night."

Jenna looked at him in the mirror. "She was? Hallie didn't say anything to me when I got home."

"No? I figured she would have. Cassie was fighting tears when I got there. I'm not sure but I think she was upset that you went out."

"But I've left her with Hallie before."

"No, I mean out *with someone*."

Jenna thought back to the night before and the odd way Cassie had gone tearing out of the house when Declan had arrived. She had seemed wound up about something, but Jenna had just figured she was excited to spend the night with her aunt watching movies. Now she wished she'd taken the time to listen to the little girl's concerns.

"I'll talk to her tonight."

Jack nodded, and Jenna sprayed some water on his hair to dampen it for cutting.

She started combing through it, checking its length with her fingers when Jack said, "Look, I know it's none of my business, but I'm going to ask anyway. Are things getting serious with this guy? I mean, two dates in two nights and a flower delivery that must have put quite a smile on old Mr. Valentino's face down at the flower shop. I mean neither of us have really hooked up with anyone else since . . . well, since we split."

"Oh, really?" Jenna raised an incredulous brow.

Jack frowned. "I know you have never believed it, but there was—is—nothing between me and Diana. In fact, if you knew . . ." He shook his head, abandoning the old and recurring argument. "Never mind. I'm only asking about this guy because I just would like to know how to approach it with the kids if they happen to bring it up again."

Jenna nodded. Jack was right. They both knew no matter how either of them felt about the other, and about the past, the kids mattered first.

"His name is Declan Cavanaugh. He lives in California—Monterey, I think he said—but has rented out the boathouse up at Thar Muir for an extended stay. He's in the business of some sort of acquisitions. I don't know his blood type, or where he went to kindergarten yet. We've been out all of twice. Do I like him? Yes. I have enjoyed what little time I've spent with him. That's it. I have no idea if it's going to go any further than that."

As she snipped away, Jenna found herself remembering the first time she had cut Jack's hair, back when she'd been just a student, learning her trade in the school's vocational program. They'd been dating only a short time and she'd complained about the fact that she didn't have any opportunity to practice on "real" hair. Without a moment's hesitation, Jack had volunteered. She'd wanted so badly to give him a good cut, but she'd ended up botching it by trying too hard. The result was uneven and sloppy; the more she'd cut, the worse it had gotten. And at the time, Jack Gabriele had been known around the girl's locker room for his Brad Pitt (the younger Brad) locks.

But Jack hadn't cared. He'd simply slapped on his ball cap, assuring her it would grow out so she could try again, and then proceeded to kiss her frustrated tears away.

And it was in that moment she had first realized she loved Jack Gabriele.

God, but that seemed a lifetime ago. What had ever happened to those two kids who had been determined to conquer the world together? Where had they gone wrong?

Jenna didn't realize it but as she'd harkened back, reminiscing over happier times, her fingers had stopped snipping, combing, and were now lightly stroking the side of Jack's neck.

But Jack certainly noticed.

He had been watching Jenna in the mirror and noticed the moment her face softened, shedding the defensiveness she usually wore whenever he was around. He knew he had put that there, that buffer, that armor. He hadn't been there for her when he should have. He'd left her vulnerable. He'd *hurt* her. He hated that he'd done that to her, that he'd taken away the once trustful faith, that optimism, that had made him fall in love with her in the first place.

Where would they be if only he'd done things differently?

He'd beaten himself up about it so many times over the past four years. He couldn't turn back the clock, no matter how much he wished he could. But he sure as hell didn't intend to give Jenna up that easily either.

"Okay . . ." Jenna's voice summoned Jack out of his thoughts. "You're all set."

Jack combed his fingers through his freshly shorn hair. "Thanks, Jen. That looks much better."

"Yes, it does." She smiled, stepping back as Jack rose from the chair. She reached up, brushing away some hair clippings from his shoulder and neck. "Keep the ball cap off every now and then, okay? It looks much better that way."

Jack looked Jenna deeply in her blue eyes. For a moment, the years seemed to flutter away, like pages flipping back on a calendar. Suddenly they were nineteen again, with nothing but the future ahead of them. A future *together*. Something pulled at him inside, refusing to let go. Jenna seemed to feel it too because when Jack reached for her, tipping her face up to meet his mouth, she simply slanted into him as she had all those years ago.

Time stopped for the length of that one kiss. Jack heard nothing except the sound of his own pulse, he felt nothing but the warmth of her body against his.

God, it felt good to hold her again, to smell her skin, to taste her. Heat and years of pent-up emotion jolted through him, making him tighten his arms around her. He wanted to tell her how sorry he was for everything that had happened between them. He wanted to tell her he loved her, always had loved her, and always would. He wanted to tell her he would be there for her the way she wanted him to be, the way he should have been. But he'd told her those words countless times before and had failed her. This time words weren't going to cut it. He was going to have to prove himself to her. But for now, for this moment, this kiss was all he needed, and he sure as hell wasn't going to be the one to break it.

"Jenna, you're still here. I wanted to check if I could get in for a—oh, *geez*!"

Hannah Greer stood frozen in the salon doorway, one hand on the door handle, the other flattened over her open mouth. It was probably the only time in the woman's life she'd ever been left speechless.

"Hannah," Jenna said, jerking away from Jack.

"No! Never mind. . . . I'll come back later. Just forget I was ever even here. . . ."

She was gone before either Jenna or Jack could say another word.

Too late, however.

The spell that had wound around them that moment before had broken down.

Chapter Six

Jenna had just finished treating her eleven thirty's sadly overworked ash blond hair to a hot rosemary oil treatment, one of her favorite salon services because it soothed her overworked hands and left them smelling simply heavenly. She'd tucked the thirty-something from Providence into a cushy armchair by the fire in the client's lounge with a fresh cup of tea and a stack of style magazines for a twenty minute warm towel wrap. She was just coming back to her booth when she happened to catch a snippet of the conversation coming from the adjacent chair.

"Nothing but an overgrown, overblown grizzly! Insufferable, I tell you. The man is completely insufferable."

A quick glance confirmed that Ipswich-by-the-Sea's historian and head of the preservation commission, Betty Petwith, had come in for her regularly scheduled six-week trim.

Jenna was fond of Betty, who despite a deceptively small frame and an air of gentility as strong as any drugstore perfume, was not what anyone would call a shrinking violet. True, she kept a tidy appearance, donned sensible dresses and neat matching cardigans, and she had stuck to wearing her horn-rimmed glasses even after they'd gone out of style. Although now that those glasses were considered "vintage" and "trendy" again, Betty saw it as yet further proof that newer was not always better.

In fact, to Betty P., newer was *never* better, and eventually the less enlightened souls realized this, only by then it was too late since they had already traded in their _____ (fill in the blank with *car*, *house*, *clothes*, *wife/husband*, *children*, or any combination thereof) for newer versions.

In her mid-fifties, Betty was as classic as the Mini 850 she drove, an *original* 1959 Mini and not one of the souped-up twenty-first century models like the one Sal Capone had bought for his college-bound daughter. Betty's car had been her late husband Archibald Petwith's pride and joy, and she cared for it as lovingly as she'd cared for him before she lost him to cancer some eight years before. The car was known about town simply as "The Duck" because it was as yellow as a daffodil with bright orange trim and whenever she drove through town, everyone saw her coming.

Indeed, Betty Petwith was a force to be reckoned with. And as preservation commissioner, she was adamant about safeguarding the past, so adamant that she often came across as a bit of an eccentric. Old-fashioned some called her, even outdated. But there was nothing *outdated* about her. She was simply passionate, a true and dedicated advocate in that fervent sort of way that only served to endear her to most of the town.

With the exception of a notable two.

If the conversation Jenna had just overheard was any indication, Betty P. had been doing recent battle with one of them. Judging from the adjectives she'd been tossing about, Jenna would bet her day's tip money it had been Betty's foremost adversary, Lou Prichett.

It was sort of a local ongoing soap opera between the preservation commissioner and town planner, who were like opposing poles of two very stubborn and opinionated magnets. Where Betty was conventional, Lou Pritchett was an activist for change, prone to using words like "improvement" and "progress," always on the lookout for a way to do things "better" even if the *old way* was perfectly good enough.

It had once even come to the point that the two had refused to walk on the same side of the street.

Added to the tangle was Lou's brother, Blair Pritchett, a local home builder—in fact *the* local home builder. Unlike Betty, who had married Archibald and had come to make his town her home, the Pritchett boys had been born and raised in Ipswich-by-the-Sea. And to them, that meant they had the right to determine what was best, more so than some incomer.

Blair Pritchett had started out at the age of sixteen as an apprentice carpenter, and had gone on to found a solid business in home building to the point that he was now the single largest employer in town. In fact, Jack had been one of the many locals who worked for Blair. It was said by some that Blair Pritchett had built so many boxlike, single-family colonials in and around Ipswich-by-the-Sea, he could probably do it in his sleep. Some even suggested he should erect a sign, similar to the golden arches, with an ever-escalating figure of houses built instead of hamburgers served.

That number would be far, far greater if Betty

Petwith didn't do everything she could to keep him in check.

Self-made and thus filled with his own importance, Blair Pritchett would stand up at the town meetings and crow about wanting their tiny hamlet to be so much more, the "Envy of Massachusetts," even all of New England. But to do so, he declared, they would need to make the town accessible to anyone who might want to live there, no matter how many that might be.

After all, what right did they, the good people who already knew and gleaned the many benefits of their town, have to keep others who wanted to join their ranks at bay? It went against the very principles of the democracy that had been born in their Commonwealth nearly four hundred years before.

"This was the Land of the Free," he would preach, and if that meant filling every empty plot of land with one of his houses so newcomers would have a place to live, then so be it.

Campaigning to have his younger brother installed as town planner had been a stroke of genius. Blair Pritchett's proposals for multihome, modern and efficient subdivisions slid through town approval as if they'd been greased in butter, making him not only the largest employer in town, but the single most wealthy citizen, as well. He lived in a big stone house right on the shore with tennis courts, a swimming pool, and an ice rink in the winter. And he drove about town in a fully loaded Hummer H2 that was oil-slick black and trimmed in gleaming chrome. He liked to call Ipswich-by-the-Sea "His Town" in that blunt, irascible New England way, but it was a way that was beginning to make people narrow their eyes at him in suspicion.

Most especially Betty Petwith.

Together, Blair and Lou Pritchett would openly mock Betty's efforts to preserve the town's precious open spaces, alternately painting her as a zealot or a bothersome little widow with too much time on her hands. Two summers earlier, she'd single-handedly mapped out a walking trail of the town; she even printed up a small booklet that gave information on the more prominent houses and landmarks, their founding families, their histories and the role they had played in putting the village of Ipswich-by-the-Sea on the map. The book sold moderately well at the local pharmacy, mostly to tourists and interested residents, but the Pritchett brothers were often overheard referring to it as "Little Betty's Comic Book."

Meanwhile, the brothers did everything they could to urge the good citizens of Ipswich-by-the-Sea to embrace the twenty-first century instead of clinging to the seventeenth. They had lobbied the telephone and cable companies to install updated cabling to the village first so that even the most remote homes in town could receive high-speed Internet and more television channels than they would ever possibly need. They proposed and succeeded in getting voter approval for a skate park that was built adjacent to the school, and were looking for investors who would be interested in converting the old textile mill off the main road leading out of town into luxury condominiums.

Yes, their town had seen quite a lot of history, dating back to the arrival of the Pilgrims in 1620 down the coast in Plymouth, and even before that.

Natives had called the area that comprised this and the surrounding towns "Agawam," but history didn't pave roads and history didn't build little league baseball fields. Tax dollars did that and with a larger population, it only made sense that the town could offer more while taxing those who lived there less. They could build better schools, attract more industry. They could and would save their tiny coastal village from extinction beneath the weight of the ever-restrictive government fishing regulations that were threatening to do away with the very livelihoods of many of its citizens.

Situated as it was at the mouth of a river and protected by its own natural harbor, Ipswich-by-the-Sea had been an ideal site for settlement. Colonial farmers and fishermen had come and generations afterward had thrived on the rich soil and even richer sea waters for nearly four hundred years. But now the farms were nearly gone, swallowed up by those who'd moved out of Boston for the very thing they were devouring. And the government had placed limits on the number of days the third, fourth, and even fifth generation seamen could spend netting the famous cod and haddock of the North Atlantic to the point that a man could no longer make his living or feed his family working on the sea.

No, to the Pritchett brothers, the security and very future of the town lay in building and bringing in more tax-paying bodies to ease the financial burden. They were masters at instilling fear, in making people believe their salvation lay in developing the prime real estate Ipswich-by-the-Sea had been blessed with, usually at the expense of the town's very unique historic character. And when it came time for a town vote on a particular development issue, Blair Pritchett was not above impressing his opinions upon those who worked for him, slathering on the underlying threat to their future employment should it be found anyone had voted against him.

His biggest success had come in the defeat of a growth management bylaw that would have strictly limited the number of houses he could build in any given year within the confines of the town boundaries. He was certainly still free to go to the neighboring towns or even nearby New Hampshire, reasoned the committee that had brought the bylaw forward, one headed by Betty P. herself. But Mr. Pritchett preferred building closer to home because the further he went outside in search of buildable land, the more he had to pay his workers to get there each day. So he'd strong-armed his employees into voting against the bylaw by convincing them that if it should pass, he'd only be forced into a layoff. And while most agreed in theory that growth should probably be monitored and controlled, they also needed to keep food on their tables.

So the growth bylaw had been defeated, much to Betty Petwith's chagrin, and Blair Pritchett Homes just went on building.

First one historic home then another had been sacrificed to the Pritchett brothers' "greater good." But when he turned his attention to the old Essex House, seeking to demolish one of the earliest properties in the village in order to make way for a new twenty-home subdivision, Betty Petwith's tolerance had reached its end. She stood up against the Pritchett brothers, and much to their surprise, she won the battle, succeeding in getting the proposed "Essex Acres" quashed. And she had been standing up against them on every issue ever since.

Jenna did a quick tidy up on her booth then glanced at her watch. She had at least another fifteen minutes before she needed to rinse and finish with her client. Certainly time enough to lend Betty P. a sympathetic ear.

"So what's he done this time, Mrs. P.?" she asked, bringing the older woman a fresh cup of lavender and lime blossom tea to soothe her obviously upset nerves. She tucked one of her mother's clove cookies on the saucer.

"Oh, thank you, dear."

Betty took the cup, pushing back her horn-rimmed glasses before taking a sip. Her stylist, Becca, winked at Jenna as she stood behind her chair, tidying Betty's sideswept, naturally auburn helmet of hair.

"This time he's gone too far, I tell you," Betty said, shaking her head. "Too far indeed!" She took another sip, setting the flowered teacup in its saucer. "You remember when he had his brilliant idea to develop the old settlement into some sort of adult entertainment facility with a miniature golf course right through the middle of seventeenth century house foundations?"

Of course Jenna remembered. That had been Ipswich-by-the-Sea Showdown Number Three, if memory served, and fortunately Betty had come out of it the victor. There had been a handful of subsequent skirmishes since and apparently now, Mrs. Petwith was gearing up for yet another.

"So what brilliant idea have they come up with this time?" Jenna asked. "A twenty-screen movie cinema? A water park?"

"They think they are going to sell Hathaway Island, that's what! And I tell you, Jenna, I'll be deviled if—"

Jenna blinked. "What did you say?"

"Yes, dear. Exactly. *Sell Hathaway Island.* Apparently a private party has expressed an interest in buying it outright. Has offered quite a lot of money for it, too. Four million, in fact."

"Four million *dollars*?"

Betty gave her a grim nod. "Imagine how many baseball fields they could build and name after themselves with that much in the town coffers."

She was referring to Pritchett Park, with its miniature rendering of Boston's Fenway Park, complete with its own Green Monster and Yawkey Way. The kids all loved it, of course, as well as all the middle-aged jocks who sought to reclaim their lost youths, but to Betty Petwith it was one step shy of being a theme park.

Meanwhile, Jenna was still trying to get her mind around the idea that someone actually thought to buy Hathaway Island.

Ringed in mist and timelessness, the fifty-five acre enclave lay some four and a half miles as the crow flies from the main harbor. Three smaller islets known as the Stepping Stones reached from its western shore toward Siren's Cove on the town's northernmost point of the mainland. Uninhabited, the smaller islands were havens for seabirds, cormorants and piping plovers, and a protected population of harbor seals. Hathaway Island, however, stood apart, both in size and in legend.

It was a legend that was very close to Jenna's heart.

"What does this 'private party' want to do with an entire island?"

"Seems whoever it is wants to build a private residence on it, make it into some sort of exclusive personal sanctuary."

Jenna couldn't believe what she was hearing. "But the island has always been open to everyone in town. People picnic out there in the summer. They spend weekends camping there. And we just opened up the new boat jetty this past summer, with the walking trails mapped out for visitors."

Not to mention that my first child was conceived on that island one long ago summer night . . .

"I know, dear. I know. Believe me, I am going to do everything I can to fight it. I've already started contacting preservation offices on a state level, and I've alerted James Dugan to look into any legal hindrances we can use to oppose them. The problem is the island isn't registered as a site of historic value. A serious oversight, to be sure. In fact, with the exception of the lighthouse addition back in the late 1700s, the island has just sort of sat there for the past three hundred years. They are calling a special town meeting to address the proposal on Thursday at the Town Hall. Eight o'clock. I have until then to research and come up with everything I can find. We also need to get the word out so we can convince as many people as possible to attend and voice their opposition to the sale. I hope I can count on you, dear."

Jenna nodded. "Of course you can, Mrs. P," she said. "You know that Mother, Hallie, and I will certainly be there for you."

The historian returned a comforted smile. "Thank you. I know sometimes people say I'm old-fashioned and I just don't want to accept change but . . ."

"Now, Mrs. Petwith, that's not true."

"Jenna, I may be old but I'm certainly not deaf. I hear what they say about me, but the truth is, I only try to look out for the best interests of this town. I love our place and her people—even those idiot Pritchett brothers. I just want to protect the very thing that makes us so unique. Without our past, who are we, really?"

Who, indeed? Jenna agreed.

Betty's eyes had grown misty and Jenna patted the woman's hand. "We know that, Mrs. P. And the majority of us appreciate all that you do for the town. We'll be there to support you. Don't you worry."

The timer bell dinged, signaling to Jenna that her client was due for her rinse and blow out. "You can count on my support, Mrs. P. You know if there is anything I can do to help save that island, I will. I'll certainly do my part to spread the word and we'll post a flyer here at the salon for the meeting. I'm sure Sal and Maria will put one up at the café as well. Don't worry. We'll get everyone there next Thursday. And those Pritchett boys . . . well, they won't know what hit them."

Betty P. was smiling when Jenna turned from the booth.

After finishing with her client, Jenna decided to take a short break, and sneaked off to the corner for a cup of Sal's espresso. Her next appointment wasn't due until one thirty.

"Jenn*ina*!" Sal greeted her when she slipped through the café door. "How's my favorite niece and neighbor?"

Jenna smiled. *"Ciao, Zio."*

She called him uncle even though technically, after the divorce, it no longer applied. Sal and Maria Capone had always been kind to Jenna, had always treated her as family no matter the marital accord—or disaccord—between her and Jack.

"Espresso, *si*?"

"As always, *Zio*."

"I've got some beans fresh from *Italia*, bella. The best I could find."

Jenna slid onto one of the counter stools to wait while Sal got to work behind the puffing and steaming copper hammered machine. Like Betty Petwith, Sal held fast to the traditional, refusing to exchange his vintage golden-domed monstrosity for one of the sleek stainless automated models found in every Starbucks. When he was standing behind it, working its knobs and dials, Jenna often thought he resembled the "wizard" in *The Wizard of Oz*, the one Dorothy had uncovered when she'd gone seeking a way home. All he needed was a red velvet curtain.

Maria came out of the kitchen, and blew Jenna a kiss with one meaty hand. "*Ciao*, bella," she called in her singsong Italian voice. "Biscotti?"

She was filling the huge glass jar at the end of the counter.

But before Jenna could answer, someone jumped onto the stool beside her and leaned over her shoulder.

"Jenna Wren, you sly thing."

It was Hannah Greer and she was beaming ear to sparkling diamond-studded ear.

Jenna had dreaded this moment, even as she knew there was no way to avoid it. "Hullo, Hannah. How are you?"

"Oh, I'm doing just fine, but certainly not as fine as you. I mean, I about fell over on your doorstep when I walked into the salon to find you lip-locked with none other than Jack Gabriele. I always wondered how you could have let that fine piece of man go, but then, after seeing you two together in a kiss that would most assuredly have led to the bedroom had I not made the mistake of coming in, maybe you haven't let him go after all, eh? It would be so completely fabulous to see you two get back together."

"Hannah . . ." Jenna tried to interrupt, even held up her hand and shook her head, doing everything short of slapping a piece of duct tape over Hannah's mouth to stop the woman from blathering on. But it was futile. Once Hannah glommed on to a subject, she didn't let it go willingly. Jenna could do nothing but sit there and wait till she paused to draw breath. Surely she would have to sometime, wouldn't she? She caught a glimpse of Maria, who was glued to the conversation, biscotti jar all but forgotten.

Maria met Jenna's gaze and smiled, and that smile spoke volumes. The Capones doted on Jack, their only nephew, as if he were their own son. By the time Sal finished steaming the espresso, word would have reached Jack's parents at the pizza shop next door about what Hannah had walked in on.

"Hannah, what you saw, between Jack and me . . . it's not what you think. It was not something I ever planned to do. It just *happened,* completely out of the blue."

The more Jenna tried to explain, the worse it sounded. Even she realized that.

And there was Hannah grinning like the Cheshire cat.

She cocked her blond head and lifted a brow. "Are you going to sit there and try to tell me you didn't enjoy it? That it didn't curl your toes and make you go weak in the knees?"

Truth was, it had done all that, and more. In fact, Jenna had done little else since that afternoon but replay it in her mind over and over again. Even after all the time since their separation and then divorce, Jack could still manage to take her breath away. All it had taken was one little kiss.

Knowing that scared the living hell out of Jenna.

"It doesn't matter, Hannah. We've both moved on," Jenna insisted. "He's been out. I've been out. It was just . . ."

Jenna searched for a sensible explanation for that kiss, that incredible, mind-numbing kiss, but came up with nothing plausible.

"It's okay, honey. You don't have to try to sugar-coat it for me. Some men are just impossible to get over. My Jim is one, which is why I put up with all the crap he does, like ruining my grandma's quilt." She leaned across the counter and snatched a fresh biscotti from the jar Maria had started to fill, pointing it straight at Jenna's nose. "And Jack Gabriele is certainly another. Face it, darling. You miss him. You need him. And no stupid divorce paper is ever going to change that."

Jenna could only stare, speechless, as Hannah handed the still eavesdropping Maria a dollar for the biscotti and headed out the door. She practically swayed as she went, singing an off-key rendition of "I Saw Mommy Kissing Santa Claus" only she found it necessary to substitute "Jenna" for "Mommy" and "Jack Gabriele" for "Santa Claus."

When Jenna turned back, Maria was still standing, still smiling, only now she'd been joined by Sal, who had Jenna's espresso ready and waiting in a paper cup.

And he was smiling, too.

Dear God, by later that morning, the entire town would be talking about it.

"Thanks, *Zio*," Jenna said, taking the coffee and

spinning off the stool. She made a beeline straight for the door.

As she hurried down the leaf-littered sidewalk back to the salon, Jenna cringed as she replayed Hannah's less than demure insinuations. Yes, Jack had kissed her, and yes, she had kissed Jack back. But that didn't mean they were suddenly going to get back together. Not with everything that had happened between them.

Face it, darling. You miss him. You need him. . . .
Need.
Him.

If there was one thing Jenna had vowed the day she'd walked out of her marriage, it was that she would never *need* Jack Gabriele again. Needing him had hurt too much, had left her far too vulnerable. And anyone who thought differently, especially Hannah Greer, had oatmeal for brains. Jenna had managed just fine without Jack these past few years, taking care of the kids and building a successful business all on her own. Just because she'd let her defenses down long enough to get lost in one stupid little kiss, didn't mean anything.

To prove it, as soon as she got back to the salon, Jenna picked up the phone and called Thar Muir.

Hallie answered the phone at the B-and-B on the third ring.

"Hal, it's me. Don't ask any questions, just connect me to Declan's line."

Hallie must have heard the seriousness in her sister's voice, because she didn't even ask why. Just said, "Hang on," and clicked whatever button she needed to in order to transfer the call.

He'd been out of town the past several days on business, Jenna knew, and truthfully, she'd been glad for the space. It had given her the time to come to terms with Jack's kiss, at least that was what she told herself. She wasn't really sure where things were going with Declan, but at the moment, he was the only thing she could turn to in order to make the statement she needed to, both to the world and to herself.

So she'd just leave him a quick message, a "Hello" and "How are you?" simply because she could. She was a single woman and he was a single, sophisticated man. She enjoyed being in his company. There was certainly no crime in that.

Jenna sucked in her breath when Declan answered the phone on the second ring.

"Declan Cavanaugh . . ."

She nearly hung up without speaking. But before she knew what she was doing, she had blurted out an invitation to dinner next week.

"I would love to" was his reply. "I'm glad you called. I've been thinking about you . . ."

And so began Date Number Three.

Chapter Seven

Eudora Wren bumped her ample hip against Jenna's kitchen door, closing it with a sharp *thwack*.

"Hello, dear!" she crooned to her daughter, who stood at the stove, sprinkling a green herb into a steaming pot.

Eudora had come prepared, bringing a fresh loaf of marjoram bread wrapped in linen, a basket with bunches of dried herbs tied off with ribbon, and a small potted plant, among other things. With the fragrant and spellstruck pomanders she had tucked inside her cape pocket, she considered herself to be both *charmed* and *sorcerous*.

Eudora chuckled to herself at the private pun, setting her bundle on the kitchen counter just as Jenna turned to face her.

"Well, don't you look lovely?"

Although Jenna always kept herself looking smart, she had obviously taken extra care with her appearance that evening. Her dark hair shone, falling in its sleek under-the-chin bob that she kept tucked behind one ear in a way that her mother had always thought particularly dear. She wore an ankle-length skirt in shades of dark violet and burgundy with a deep boysenberry colored scoop-necked sweater. The sweater must be new, Eudora thought, and decided that the color suited her. It was made of a soft-looking knit and the sleeves hugged her arms to just below her elbows, flattering her delicate shape. Even her eyes were especially bright, sparkling along with the silver and garnet earrings that dripped from her ears.

When Jenna turned, Eudora caught a minty-rose whiff of the rose geranium that Jenna had dabbed on her pulse points, wearing it, her mother knew, for the boost it would give her confidence. Even while her daughter was trying to appear calm and poised for the evening ahead, Eudora could sense that Jenna was on edge. The air around her was thrumming with anticipation.

Jenna peered at the feathery leaves and white flowers growing in Eudora's small clay pot. "Is that . . . motherwort?"

"Yes, dear. Mine was simply overrunning its planter, so I decided to make a cutting. It'll look lovely here in the window. One can never have too much motherwort after all."

Or the protection it offers, she thought to herself.

Eudora set the plant on the kitchen sill, at precisely the spot where it would guard her daughter best. She sniffed at the pot simmering on the stove. "So what's this you have cooking?"

"Rosemary pot roast," Jenna answered. "With fettucine." Then she asked because Eudora had given her no choice but to do so, "I don't suppose you would . . . want to stay for dinner?"

Eudora crinkled a smile. "Oh, how sweet of my girl to invite her mother to dinner. Of course I would love to. You know how much I adore your cooking."

Eudora did love her daughter's pot roast, but what she didn't tell Jenna was that Hallie had let it slip over the weekend that her sister had invited the handsome newcomer, Declan Cavanaugh, to dinner that evening. Ever since Cassie had confessed to her about the misdirected spell she'd cast—*potentially* misdirected spell—Eudora had been troubled with a mother's natural concern at the stranger's sudden appearance. So when Hallie told her about Jenna's date, Eudora had decided it was time to have a look at this Declan Cavanaugh for herself.

Since she couldn't know whether he had come into Jenna's life because of the spell or simply out of the blue, Eudora had decided to take steps both to counter the magic and to protect her daughter against any adverse attentions. She'd spent the past few days gathering the best guardian herbs, preparing spells, and had even driven to nearby Salem for those ingredients that were a little more difficult to come by.

Like powdered Dragon's Blood.

Eudora Wren was taking no chances.

While Jenna went to add another place setting to the dining table, Eudora began hanging the bundles of dried herbs she'd brought with her from the kitchen beams—mullein for protection, centaury to ward against unwanted attention, squill for hex breaking, rue for countermagic, and Saint-John's-wort to make malevolent energies flee. As she secured them, she murmured words in Gaelic to charm the herbs and charge their natural properties with the energies they offered. She finished, peering quickly around the corner to where Jenna was still otherwise engaged in the dining room.

"I hope you don't mind but I've put some cuttings on the ceiling to dry, dear. I've no space left in my kitchen."

Jenna nodded. "Of course."

The tavern-style dining table, made of eighteenth-century cherry, had once offered travelers on the post road between Boston and New York a place to take their ale and lobster pies. It could seat eight, although Jenna typically set it for no more than six. She'd found the piece at their local antiques dealer, the 2nd Chance Shop and had spent nearly two years afterward searching across New England for a collection of comb-back Windsor chairs close enough to match.

Tonight, Jenna had set the table with the creamy Belleek china Eudora's grandfather had brought his wife from his native Ireland. Eudora had given the dish set to Jenna as a wedding present, just as her mother had her. One day, saints willing, Cassie would use it in her own home, perhaps even on that very table.

Tradition was deeply seated in the Wren women.

"The table looks lovely, dear."

And it did. The wood shone from a fresh lemon-oil rubdown, and the tableware sparkled. She noticed Jenna moving to the sideboard for fresh candles. "Here. I'll get those. Why don't you put the bread I brought into the oven to warm and fetch us a nice bottle of that red wine you keep?"

While Jenna disappeared back into the kitchen, Eudora slipped the two candles she had tucked into her cape pocket, the ones she'd anointed earlier with the Dragon's Blood and frankincense, into the waiting holders.

She stood back, drawing her breath deeply.

"Protect this table, and the family who partakes here," she murmured as she lit one, then repeated it for the next, then again a third time to seal the spell. She blew out the matchstick, then finished. "As I will it, so mote it be."

The candles sparked and then the flames danced, burning brightly as the energies within them alighted.

Eudora smiled. Now, just one last thing.

"I'll be right back, dear."

Outside, dusk had already fallen as it did quite early during autumn in New England. Night rode in on the whispering breeze and the moon above the harbor was a lopsided sliver, appearing at ready to scoop up the stars. Cloaked in shadows and wading through the mist that was rolling in off the coast, Eudora walked the perimeter of Jenna's home, sprinkling a mixture that included dried angelica while reciting a final incantation to form a closing barrier.

"What were you just doing?" Jenna asked when Eudora returned to the kitchen.

"Oh, nothing. I thought I'd dropped something outside," she fibbed. "I was looking for it."

Jenna looked skeptical. "What was it?"

"Oh, nothing to trouble yourself over. Never you mind. I probably just left it at home." She rubbed her hands together. "Now, what can I do to help with dinner?"

Jenna hesitated. "Mother, before we go any further, there is something you should know. I have a guest coming to dinner tonight."

"Indeed?" Eudora did her best to appear genuinely surprised. "Who is it? Flora and Gavin?"

"No. I've invited Declan Cavanaugh. It's nothing

formal. Just dinner with me and the kids. And now you. In fact, I'm glad you came. I'd like for you to meet him, too."

"So you're getting serious with this Cavanaugh fellow then?"

Jenna sighed. "Mother, I know you've always felt that Jack and I were somehow"—she shook her head—"I don't know, *fated,* or whatever. But after all that happened, and all the time that has passed since, I just don't know how we could be. There are some things that can't be gotten over. Some words just cannot be unsaid."

Eudora looked at her daughter. "And people change, Jenna Wren. I would hope that you wouldn't forsake a chance for happiness—for you and for the children—simply because you've told yourself you mustn't ever forget."

Jenna looked at her, unblinking. This was not the conversation she wanted to be having, especially with Declan due to arrive at any moment.

"As for Declan," she said, skirting the issue of Jack, "I don't honestly know what will come of it. If anything will come of it at all. He's the first guy I've really gone out with and . . . I mean, I don't know. I like him. I like being with him. He makes me feel . . ."

She searched for the right word.

"You don't have to say it, darling," Eudora said, smiling at her flustered daughter. "It's been a long time since you've had the attention of a man, and from what Hallie tells me, this one is quite the charmer."

Jenna smiled "He sure seems to know the right things to say."

"You know, I'm not so old that I can't remember what it is like to be appreciated by someone of the opposite sex. And no, I don't just mean your father. You never knew this, but about a year after your father's accident, James Dugan started coming around quite often."

"I remember seeing him, but I thought since he's an attorney, it was something to do with a legal issue, with Dad's estate or the insurance."

"Well, it was. In the beginning," Eudora said. "James helped me quite a lot with things like that. But eventually I began to realize that his reasons for coming by were more and more contrived. Then one day, he just came out and kissed me."

Jenna tried not to laugh. "You're joking! James Dugan? Tweed-wearing, doughnut-crumb-covered James Dugan?"

"Oh, yes, dear. And right in the middle of a sentence, too. One moment, he was spouting off some legal gibberish and the next he's got me cornered against the kitchen sink. He's hiding quite a passionate heart beneath all that lawyerly tweed. Said he wanted to take care of me, and you girls."

"What on earth did you do?"

"I thanked him for the offer, and told him I would think about it. I was so very lonely then, more lonely than I ever thought possible. And I did consider it, but mostly because of how it made me feel to know that I was still attractive, still desirable. But at the same time, I knew I would always love your father more, and was that fair to James Dugan? Was it fair to me, either? In the end, I decided I wanted, no, I *needed* to be able to take care of myself and my daughters first. I needed to know that I could."

Jenna knew exactly what her mother meant. She just had never known her mother had gone through the same feelings. "I had no idea."

"At the time, you were going through your own struggle from losing your father. It was a difficult period for us all."

Jenna nodded, remembering. "The thing about Declan is I don't really know how he feels about dating a woman who is also a mother. We've had all of two dinners out. He briefly met Sam and Cassie, but that's been it. And the kids are as much a part of this . . . whatever it is . . . as I am. So I decided to throw him to the wolves, so to speak. Let him spend an evening with all of us. I guess after tonight's dinner we'll know whether he will stick around for anything more substantial."

Eudora hooked her arm around her daughter's narrow waist. "Don't worry over it, dear. It he's worth his salt, he'll survive the evening well enough."

The doorbell rang at precisely six thirty. Eudora lingered in the kitchen, stirring the gravy over a low flame so that she could get an open observation while Jenna went to greet her guest.

"Hi." Jenna smiled at him when she opened the door. "I'm glad you could make it."

Goodness, but he was a handsome one, Eudora thought. Just like Cassie had said. Right out of a magazine. Brilliant blond hair, very easy smile, and the sort of eyes that could make a woman forget herself. Jenna had mentioned he was from California and he looked every bit the part. He was tall, tanned, and just his arrival seemed to charge the air around them.

He handed Jenna a bouquet of flowers—roses, of course, although not the typical red. These were a pale, pale apricot, very delicate. Eudora watched as he kissed Jenna on the cheek. She couldn't hear what he said in response to Jenna's greeting, but it made her daughter laugh and even blush a little. Thinking back, Eudora couldn't remember the last time she'd really seen Jenna smile like that, let alone blush. Jenna was usually so grounded, so serious, and so damned cynical.

Be careful, baby girl, Eudora thought. *Don't let him too close just yet.*

Setting the gravy spoon in its rest, Eudora murmured a quick mini-spell, armed herself, and went out to meet the man Cassie was convinced she had conjured up.

"Hello there," Eudora said as she crossed the living room to join them. "You must be Declan Cavanaugh."

She didn't go straight to him. She'd brought a small spray bottle with her, and on the pretense of freshening the row of potted plants Jenna kept in the window, managed to mist an infusion of agrimony and sneezewort about the room to secure her last spell. Jenna was looking at her strangely as she spritzed away, but Eudora paid her no mind. She just smiled, and spritzed.

Smiled.

And spritzed.

Finally she set the bottle aside and extended her hand. "I'm Eudora Wren, Jenna's mother."

The man smiled easily as he took her hand. "A pleasure to meet you, Mrs. Wren."

The moment her hand touched his, Eudora felt a frisson. It came to her in a mixture of dark greens and browns and yellow-oranges, a clash of colors underscored with a conspicuous darkness. It was a powerful combination, that impression, and one she'd never sensed before.

"Oh, please," she managed, slipping her hand away from him. "To most of the people around here, I'm just Nanny Wren." She looked at him. "Although a refined young man like yourself might feel more comfortable with just 'Eudora.' "

"Eudora it is," he replied.

"Supper is nearly ready," Jenna cut in. "Mother, would you show Declan to the dining room while I go and call the kids?"

Eudora knew Jenna would be wanting a few moments with Sam and Cassie, to talk to them about the evening ahead, remind them to be on their best behavior. She smiled sweetly. "Certainly, dear."

She led Declan into Jenna's dining room.

"Great house," Declan said, taking in the architectural features that were original to the house, the post-and-beam construction, the low ceilings, huge brick fireplaces. "First period?"

"Very good, Mr. Cavanaugh. You know your architecture. This dining room was the first room Jenna renovated after buying the place. It's my own favorite, as well." She shook her head. "We discovered these beautiful wide pumpkin-pine floors hidden beneath a covering of ugly green shag carpeting. Why anyone would deliberately do something like that is beyond me. But it proved to be a boon. All it needed was to be stripped and refinished and it looked as good as it must have three centuries ago."

Declan nodded, looking around the room. "The decor is all very faithful to the time period."

"My Jenna's got an incredible sense for tradition and history. Wouldn't even paint the walls until she'd researched the proper colors and techniques. She settled on this soft cream with the muted moss green trim. I quite like it. Even followed an old recipe for milk paint and mixed it herself. You should have seen this place when we first moved in. They'd blocked up the original fireplaces and covered over the ceiling beams with plasterboard. I think we scraped off eleven different layers of wallpaper in this room alone, and even discovered a curious "speaking tube" that runs to the topmost floor of the house . . ." Eudora showed him the very thing, a trumpet-shaped "horn" sticking out of the wall. "Undoubtedly it was used to summon the servants from their beds. Now we just use it to yell for the kids."

Eudora smiled, satisfied that she'd managed to remind him of Jenna's children.

"You mentioned when you moved in," he said. "So you live here as well?"

"Oh, no. Well, not *officially* . . ." She parted the curtain slightly, to show him her own house next door. "That's mine, where Jenna and her sister were born and raised. But truthfully, the garden there between us is really more like the heart that connects us together. I'm here just as much as I'm next door. They are there, too. There is no dividing line."

She stared at him, wondering if he had gotten her not-so-subtle message. She decided to push her point home.

"Buying this house and restoring it has been an adventure, but more importantly, it brought me and my daughter so much closer than we'd ever been before."

Declan nodded, and the slight smile on his face told Eudora he had gotten the message.

No doubt he thinks I'm some meddling, overprotective mother. But the truth was, this man could never understand Eudora's reasons for wanting to safeguard her daughter so fiercely.

From the time Jenna was, oh, about eighteen

months old, Eudora realized her daughter was the kind of child who just wasn't going to be told what to do. Telling her "no" was met as more of a challenge than a refusal. In some ways that was a good thing, because it allowed Jenna to think for herself, and taught her never to give up, never to accept defeat. But in other ways . . .

Somehow, no matter how much Eudora would try to teach her, Jenna would just naturally rebel. It was as if doing the opposite of what she should was her only option. Being the older of her two daughters meant that the loss of their father, Sam, had been especially hard on her, coming at a time when Jenna was just entering her teens. And Sam's passing had been so unexpected. None of them had seen it coming. It had quite simply devastated them.

For a time afterward, Eudora had been lost in her own grief, and instead of coming together, mother and daughter had drifted. It was at that time that Jenna abandoned her gift, as if somehow blaming the magic for not being able to save her father. Eudora had never been able to understand it, but Jenna decided she would seek what she thought would be a *normal* life, and refused to take any further instruction from Eudora in their custom. Even more so, she'd scorned Eudora for practicing what she had deemed was both a useless, eccentric art. Even a curse.

As such, Jenna's high school years were almost unbearable. The older she grew, the more she distrusted both the craft and Eudora. Her senior year in high school came and went in a blur of heated clashes and tense silences. She couldn't have run out the door fast enough, getting pregnant with Sam, marrying Jack, and staying determined to keep her dreams small. Because to Jenna, keeping them small meant keeping them safe.

But she didn't realize there were no such guarantees.

For as long as she lived, Eudora knew she would never forget the day that horrible phone call had come. She'd known even before she answered it, that something had been wrong, just as she had when she lost her Sam. Even the ringer on the phone had sounded mournful and when Eudora picked it up, a traumatized Jenna had only been able to whisper three words to her mother . . .

I need you.

Eudora had gone to her without even pausing to hang up the phone.

By the time she'd arrived at the hospital, they'd already moved Cassie to the Intensive Care Unit. When she saw that tiny three-year-old face lying so still, eyelashes unmoving, her breathing coming by way of a machine, Eudora's heart had splintered in her chest.

Comatose, they'd said. *Possible brain damage.* Her granddaughter was hooked to machines through tubes and wires and the doctors hadn't been optimistic. There was no way to know how long Cassie had been under the frozen surface of the water, no way to know if she would even wake again. And if she did, would she ever have normal brain function?

Jenna had been shell-shocked. It was the only way to describe her vacant, silent stare. She wouldn't eat. She wouldn't sleep. She just sat and watched Cassie breathe, watched the machine breathe for her. Finally she allowed herself to be taken outside by Eudora, walking with her in silence until the wail of the arriving ambulances at the E.R. could barely be heard in the distance. Eudora found them a bench in a park beneath a huge oak tree. Jenna sat with the mother she had forsaken, and when finally she spoke, she begged her to use her knowledge to save her baby's life.

"Please, Mother. I know you can do something to help her. I'm begging you. . . ." Jenna's eyes had been so desperate, and so very frightened. "I know I turned my back on you, on our gift. And I'm so sorry for that. Somehow, I cannot help but fear that doing so is what caused this to happen. But I had it wrong. I disrespected something I should have held dear. Please, please don't make my baby pay for my mistakes."

Eudora knew it was never wise to question Nature's will. But she could no more refuse her daughter's pleas than she could hold back the ocean's tide.

Seeing her sweet Cassie now, with her seven-year-old exuberance beaming from her face as she came tearing down the stairs to dinner, Eudora knew she had made the right decision.

"Nanny! Mommy didn't tell us you were coming to dinner, too!"

"Well, I hope you won't mind," Eudora said, squeezing Cassie tightly against her bosom. "Especially since I brought your favorite blueberry crumble for dessert."

"Yum!" Cassie squealed, and flopped into her usual seat at the table. She drank half her glass of milk even before the meal began.

Her brother, Sam, came into the room moments later and with a great deal less enthusiasm, dragging his overlong pants cuffs behind him. "Hey, Nan."

"Hey there, Sam. How's my boy doing?"

He wasn't looking at her when he answered, but instead, he stared at Declan who was chatting with Cassie. His mouth barely moved from its stiff frown. "Fine."

Eudora noticed that Sam took the seat farthest away from Declan, even though he usually sat in the chair beside. As close as he was to his father, it was evident how Sam was feeling about his mother's dinner guest.

"Come on, now," she tugged on the ragged collar of his sweatshirt and whispered in his ear. "It won't be all that bad."

Sam's frown deepened all the more.

Eudora went to the kitchen to help Jenna while Declan opened and poured the wine.

"T-Q-T time," Cassie exclaimed as soon as they were all seated and the roast had been sliced.

Declan looked at Jenna. "What is a T-Q-T?"

Jenna smiled. "Oh, you're about to find out."

"I'm afraid it's a tradition in the Wren household, Mr. Cavanaugh," Eudora explained. "Any newcomers to our table must submit to a round of T-Q-T, or Twenty Questions Tag."

"Consider it like one of those annoying chain e-mails that are always circulating around the Internet," Jenna added. "Those ones that ask you to answer questions like 'What's your favorite color?' or 'Who do you expect to respond to your e-mail first?' and then send it on to fifty or so of your closest friends. You know the sort."

"Yes, I'm afraid I do."

"Only we all get to make up the questions," Cassie finished. "And you have to answer, no matter what we ask." She whispered, "Even if it's embarrassing."

Declan glanced around the table with obvious unease. "Okay . . ."

"And, since I am the eldest one here, I get to choose who asks first." Eudora scanned the table. "Sam Gabriele, looks like you're It first."

Sam frowned, seeming less than eager to play the game. He was slumped in his chair, twirling his fork in his fettuccine. "I don't feel like playing."

"Come on, Sam," Cassie said. "You *have* to."

He rolled his eyes at his sister. "Whatever. Fine." He gave Declan the barest of glances. "So what's your favorite color?"

Declan took a sip of his wine. "That would be gold."

"Ah," Eudora said. "Interesting. Not your typical 'blue' or 'red.' Okay, now you get to 'tag' who you want to ask the next question."

"Hmm . . ." He rubbed his chin, smiled and glanced to where Cassie was nearly spouting from her chair. "Cassie, you're It."

The little girl clapped. "Okay . . ." She glanced at Eudora then asked him, "What kind of toothpaste do you use?"

Declan had clearly not been expecting that question, but then he couldn't know that Cassie was convinced she'd conjured him up from a magazine advertisement. "Uh, let me think. I believe it's PerfectaDent."

"I knew it," Cassie whispered out loud, looking again at her grandmother. "I told you, Nanny."

"Told her what?" Jenna asked.

But Eudora just smiled and quickly moved on. "Who is It now, Mr. Cavanaugh?"

Declan looked right back at the elder Wren. "Well, I suppose you are, Eudora."

She nodded. "Okay. Are you now or have you ever been married?"

"Mother!"

Jenna looked mortified, shaking her head and closing her eyes, but Declan simply grinned.

"No. It's all right. A perfectly legitimate question for a mother to ask." He glanced at Eudora. "No, ma'am. I am not nor have I ever been. Guess I just haven't found the right girl. Yet." He looked at Jenna then, who immediately reddened. "Jenna?"

"What? Oh. My turn." She thought for a moment. "Okay. If you could go anywhere in the world, or even in the universe, where would your idea of 'paradise' be?"

"Hmm," Declan said, clearly thinking. "That's difficult to say. I'm not certain I've really found true 'paradise' yet." He looked at Jenna, his voice warming. "But I'm definitely getting closer."

Sam didn't appreciate the way the newcomer was looking at his mom nor did he much care for his obvious insinuations. He scowled. "My turn again. Yankees or Red Sox?"

Eudora smiled. A loaded question. And she couldn't wait for the answer.

"Sorry, pal, but I'm a Cubs fan to the core."

Sam screwed up his mouth. "Figures."

"Sam . . ." Jenna warned.

"My turn," Cassie jumped in, immediately diffusing the tension. "What's your favorite ice cream flavor?"

On it went, a ping-pong salvo back and forth around the table, revealing Declan's taste in music (jazz), his most embarrassing moment (falling asleep during his college graduation ceremony, at which he was giving the valediction and while seated on the stage), and his middle name (Patrick, for his father). Eudora managed to pry a little further, too, cornering him on where he was born (a small Virginia coast town called Cape Charles) and his age (thirty-seven). All in all, she had to admit, Declan was a good sport about it.

Over dessert and coffee, Jenna turned the conversation to Hathaway Island and its proposed sale.

"Why is this island such an issue?" Declan asked over his espresso. "Why not just sell it if it will benefit the town so well financially?"

"Because it has significance in this town," Jenna said. "And no amount of money can replace that. To sell Hathaway Island would be like selling a piece of history. *Our* history. It's always been the town's island, open to anyone who wanted to go there. If someone buys it, there will be no more picnics. No more camping sleepovers. Horace Fenwick proposed to his wife Myrtle there more than sixty-five years ago. And once, that island saved the lives of some young boys who'd gotten into trouble while out on a midnight sail. That's history."

Declan nodded. "Is it true there's supposed to be buried treasure there, too?"

When Jenna and Eudora both looked at him, Declan explained, "I read something about it in a newspaper."

"No one knows for certain. There was always this sort of 'belief' that pirates once used the island as their haunt because of certain things that were discovered there, but that was some time ago. More than two hundred years."

"But didn't someone discover something just recently?"

"It was a piece of eight," Cassie piped in. "And it was stolen from the King of Spain. My friend Annie found it!"

Jenna explained. "Our town historian did authenticate it as early eighteenth century, but there have been countless shipwrecks out in the harbor going back hundreds of years. Any one of them could have been stirred up by a storm, or an errant anchor . . ."

"It's possible," Declan agreed.

"And for the rest of the summer half the town was out there with metal detectors scouring every inch of shore. Other than the usual bottle caps and fishhooks, they didn't come up with anything of any significance."

"But wasn't there something else 'notorious' about the island? Something about a witch?"

Until then, Eudora had been quiet, simply enjoying her blueberry crumble while listening and observing as the conversation went on around her. But Declan's question got her attention. "You've heard of the Salem Trials, haven't you, Mr. Cavanaugh?"

"Sure. Tituba. Cotton Mather. Hasn't everyone?"

"And what's your opinion of them?"

Declan hesitated. "My opinion . . . you mean of the trials themselves?"

"Yes. Your opinion. For instance, do you think the twenty-four people who were executed were actually witches?"

As Declan regarded Eudora, his eyes, which were so green, suddenly went dark. "They were tried, weren't they? By a court. A judge. Their peers."

"But what exactly were they tried for? For being witches, whatever being a witch might have been three hundred years ago . . . or were they accused simply for being different? For not conforming to what was considered to be the Puritan standard?"

Eudora stared at Declan, awaiting his answer.

But Jenna, obviously knowing her mother's sensitivities about the subject, decided to step in.

"Goodness, it's late. And the kids have school tomorrow. Sam, Cassie, time to get ready for bed."

Cassie moaned, but after a stern look from her mother, she followed her brother to the stairs.

Declan and Eudora were still sitting at the table. Eudora waited, leaving Declan to break away first. He did so, turning that PerfectaDent smile on Jenna, but not without a last glance at her mother.

After Jenna shooed the kids up the stairs, she walked with Declan to the door. He draped an arm around her shoulders.

"Dinner was really a pleasure, Jenna."

She smiled at him as she turned to face him. "I'm glad you could come."

"Sam and Cassie are great kids, too. You've obviously done a terrific job with them."

They were standing in the living room, suddenly alone, with only the moonlight filtering in through the windows. Upstairs, Jenna could hear the sounds of Sam and Cassie getting ready for bed, performing their usual rituals—washing hands, faces, brushing teeth. Her mother was in the kitchen. Jenna could hear the dishes in the sink, the water running. For the moment, it was just the two of them. Alone.

She jumped slightly when she felt Declan reach for her, then let herself be drawn toward him. His breath brushed her forehead and he tipped her face up. He was going to kiss her. She could feel it, and her pulse quickened in anticipation. Jenna closed her eyes, waiting for the touch of his mouth on hers . . .

Until he sneezed.

Once.

Twice.

Three times.

"Bless you," she said.

Declan blinked, shook his head a little, then reached for her again. "Now where was I . . . ?"

His mouth hovered inches from hers. Jenna held her breath, waiting . . . waiting . . .

He turned his head, pulled away from her and sneezed again.

Four more times.

"I don't—"

Ah-choo!

"Know—"

Ah-choo!

"What the hell—"

Ah-choo!

"Is wrong with m—"

Ah-choo!

But Jenna knew. She glanced toward the kitchen, which had suddenly grown very quiet.

She remembered her mother earlier, spraying the plants as if they hadn't been watered in weeks.

She picked up the bottle Eudora had left on the window sill, twisted open the top, and gave it a quick sniff.

Her nose tickled immediately.

Sneezewort.

As Declan sneezed his way out the door, and all the way down the walkway, Jenna turned and headed for the kitchen.

"Mother, I'd like a word with you. . . ."

But when she got there, Eudora had gone.

Chapter Eight

Jack was sitting at the bar in the local watering hole nursing his fourth Heineken while Aerosmith sang from the corner jukebox about that same old song and dance.

The lyrics were fitting, considering his mood. He'd had a real mother of a week. And since it was only Wednesday, that was saying something.

On Tuesday his beloved primer-and-rust-colored F-150 decided that nine years and two hundred twenty-seven thousand miles were more than its fair share of the automobile/owner bargain. It died, flat out refusing any attempts at resuscitation, and left him stranded a hundred seventy-eight miles from home in the middle of Notown, Vermont.

And yes, that was the actual name of the place, population just short of a handful.

He'd had to call his sister, Sofia, to come for him, a favor she made clear she was none too thrilled to perform. But she did because she was his sister and because Gabrieles could always count on each other.

Jack, however, had had no choice but to bide the three hours and eighteen minutes it took her with an eighty-three-year-old woman who lived with enough cats to cast an entire Cat Chow revue.

In fact, he suspected the cats might just outnumber the population of Notown two to one.

"I've lost track of how many there are," Granny Feline had admitted to him as one was figure-eighting its way around his legs. Another dipped its whiskers into his coffee. He'd even found one curled up on the top of the toilet tank when he'd excused himself to go to the bathroom.

Jack hated cats. Always had, ever since he'd been a kid and one had eaten his pet hamster. He hated their alien-looking eyes. He hated their claws, which they felt they had the God-given right to hook into *everything*. And he most especially hated the way they acted as if their very existence didn't depend on that person, that human—in other words, their *owner*—whose presence they made it so obvious they were forced to endure.

So there he'd spent the afternoon, sitting in Granny Feline's parlor with at least a dozen of them rubbing up against him, watching the ancient clock tick on its ancient mantel, and cursing his sister for being such a sensible driver.

But he'd gotten it.

He'd been looking for an original claw-foot tub for some time. And not just any claw-foot, but *this* claw-foot. While claw-foots weren't exactly an architectural rarity, a six-foot claw-foot tub was more difficult to come by. But he wasn't about to settle for anything less.

Back when he and Jen had first been married, lying in their cramped little double bed in their cramped little single apartment, they would whisper to each other during the earliest hours of the morning after they'd made love and were wrapped in each others arms. It was then they'd made all their plans for their dream home, and the one thing Jen had always wanted was a real claw-foot tub, cast-iron, preferably at least a hundred years old and certainly not one of the acrylic facsimiles found in special order catalogs or at every Home Depot in the country.

When Jack had started designing the House—a project he'd been working on in his spare time over the course of the past two years—he'd envisioned a master bathroom created around *that* tub. He'd looked at probably a hundred of them in the past eighteen months alone, stopping at antique shops and salvage yards whenever he'd gotten the chance. His only requirement was that the tub be big enough to fit two comfortably and not with knees bent at odd angles just to squeeze in. And the two people, surrounded by mounds of bubbles and candlelight, he'd always envisioned had been him and Jen.

So he'd gone all the way to Vermont to get it.

Granny Feline, whose real name was Aggie Middleton, had lived in the Victorian farmhouse in Notown since December 6, 1941. That was the day she arrived as a young bride of seventeen to live at the family home of her new husband, Humphrey Middleton. The very next day, Japan bombed Pearl Harbor and Humphrey ran off to war.

Never to return.

But he did leave Aggie with a small wedding night part of himself, a part that nine months and two days later would be christened Humphrey Middleton Jr.

Even after the terrible news had come, Aggie stayed on at the house, raising little Humphrey and living with Humphrey Sr.'s parents and four sisters until one by one they either left to get married (the sisters) or passed on (the parents). The house eventually became hers and Humphrey Jr. studied to become a doctor, opening a successful practice in nearby Rutland. He'd wanted to move Aggie to the city with him, but she'd staunchly refused to leave her home.

It was as if she was still waiting for Humphrey to return from war.

But Aggie's eighty-three-year-old bones had come to ache more and more during the harsh Vermont winters and so she'd decided to pull out the old tub and put in a Jacuzzi model, complete with a bath seat and safety handrail, one that would bubble her aching back and limbs in effervescent bliss. Jack could have the old tub, she'd told him on the phone when he'd called about her newspaper ad, if he would remove it and haul it away himself. Luckily Aggie's grandson, Humphrey III, had been on hand to help.

Jack had sat at Aggie's table, surrounded by an orchestra of strident mewing and purring. He could see the tub stretched across the bed of his dead F-150 and wondered how the hell he was going to get it home. Yet, even with this situation, he still thought it had been worth it.

He spent the whole of the following day renting a U-Haul and driving all the way back to Aggie's to retrieve the tub while his truck was towed back to Massachusetts for a proper burial. He'd arrived in Ipswich-by-the-Sea just in time to hear from his mother, who'd heard it from his aunt, who'd heard it from his son, Sam, that while he'd been sitting up in Vermont with Mrs. Middleton and her forty cats, Jenna had been cooking dinner for Declan Cavanaugh.

And even that wasn't the whole of Jack's misery.

The final blow had come just that morning when Jack had gotten an early call from his partner, Brian O'Connell.

"We lost Newburyport, Jack," he'd said, and Jack, still half asleep since it was barely going on six, thought he'd surely heard him wrong. They'd just landed the job. And now it was gone?

"What? How?" he'd managed as his eyes squinted against the glare of the lamp to look at the blurry *5:54* blinking red on his clock.

"I don't know. I went up yesterday to finalize the contracts and they suddenly decided they wanted to go with another firm. Something about reputation and proven track record. Said we were too new, and while they liked our proposal, they just couldn't gamble on something untried. I'm sorry, man. I tried everything I could think of to convince them otherwise, but they wouldn't budge."

So here he sat with no truck, no job, and a bathtub big enough to grow corn in, which was a good thing, Jack supposed, since if they didn't land some work soon, he might just end up sleeping in it.

And things had been looking so bright just a few days before.

After their kiss that day in the salon, Jack had convinced himself that things were finally on the right track with Jen. He had felt the way she had responded to him, recognized the way holding her again, touching her, tasting her again had rocked him to his core. It had just felt so *right,* as if the past four years somehow hadn't happened. He knew Jen had to have felt it, too, had to know things between them had never truly died.

He'd followed it up by driving to Vermont to get her dream bathtub.

And what did she do?

She invited another guy to dinner.

Women.

Shaking his head, Jack downed the rest of his beer, and slammed the empty glass down on the bar.

"Hit me again, Carl," he said to the barkeep and pub owner.

Carl O'Keefe was a carrot-topped giant of an Irishman who'd inherited the bar from his father, whose father had come over from mother Eire back in 1921. But America was a "dry" country then, which to an Irishman like Sean O'Keefe was akin to keeping oxygen from a suffocating man. What is a man, he used to say, without his pub? He and some fellow countrymen put their heads and finances together and spent the next eleven years sailing the coast to Canada by day, only to bring back cargoes of Canadian whiskeys by night. But Sean O'Keefe was a churchgoing man who lived in fear of the hereafter. As soon as Prohibition had been lifted, he abandoned the sea and opened the Pub for *legitimate* business.

His words, painted in gold, hung on the bar above his framed picture to the present day:

What is a man without his pub?

"You got a ride home, Jack?" Carl said when Jack asked again for another beer.

The question only served to piss Jack off further, since it reminded him of his dead F-150, which reminded him of the bathtub, which reminded him of Jen. Again. "Don't worry about me. I can take care of myself."

Carl wiped the polished wood bar beneath the empty beer glass with the towel he kept habitually slung over one shoulder. "I know you can, Jack.

But I make it a policy not to serve a man more than he can take when he's got a set of keys in his pocket. You've got your sister's van parked out there. You haven't eaten anything since you arrived. You're obviously working your way to shit-faced, but I sure as hell ain't going to be party to your driving yourself off a cliff or slamming into a tree when you decide to leave. So unless you've got another ride, you can forget the beer."

"Dammit, Carl," Jack snarled.

"It's okay, Carl," a soft voice suddenly said behind him. "I've got Jack covered."

Jack turned to find Diana DeNunzio standing just behind him.

She was wearing her usual painted-on sweater and painted-on jeans with her too-blond hair teased into a tousle around her too-made-up face. Presenting herself thus and with her very generous bust-line, Diana drew a very obvious sort of male attention. She was aware of this. There was a reason for her doing it, but one only Diana and a select few knew.

Jack was one of the few.

"Hey, 'D,' " he said, and took up the beer Carl set before him. "Buy you one?"

She slid onto the barstool beside him. "Sure. Make mine a white wine, Carl. With a splash of soda."

Diana had been one of Sofia's best friends all through their school years, a friendship that had endured even into adulthood. Growing up, Diana had practically lived at their house, more so during high school. Her home life wasn't the greatest and her parents ended up splitting in a divorce that had her father running off with a twenty-two-year-old and her mother falling into a depression that left her prone on the sofa watching *Oprah* and *The View* while she popped antidepressants. She managed to rouse herself only on Friday nights when she ventured to the local church for Bingo Night.

Diana, who had issues of her own, including a very early puberty, which resulted in an over-developed bustline and an under-developed self-esteem, had found solace and acceptance in the noisy Gabriele home. Jack and Sofia's parents had taken her in all but in name, designating one of the twin beds in Sofia's room for her, even giving her her first job working at the pizza parlor. They treated Diana like their third child, and in turn, she trusted them, and Sofia and Jack, with the secret she had always carried deep in the darkest part of her heart. And unless she said otherwise, it was a secret the Gabrieles would take to the grave.

A Gabriele never went back on his word.

"How's she doing?" Jack asked. He didn't have to specify who. Diana knew he meant her mother.

"She's actually pretty okay so long as she's popping her Prozac. It's when she forgets that life gets unbearable."

Jack knew that Nita DeNunzio could go from being a couch ornament one moment to a fire-breathing, abuse-hurling harpy the next. He'd been witness to it on more than one unfortunate occasion. And when she did hurl insults, she usually turned her abuse on her daughter, the only one she had left to blame for her miserable life.

At times, Jack could remember her as she'd been when they'd been much younger, before the divorce, back when Nita DeNunzio had been the hip Italian mom who gave all the kids candy. It was criminal how betrayal and abandonment could shred a person's very soul.

"Last night was . . . pretty bad," Diana said.
"Apparently Dad and his wife came by." Diana
never called her stepmother anything but *his wife*.
"They said they were there to see me, but truthfully, I think he just wanted to rub Mom's nose in
the fact that his wife is eight months pregnant
again. The other two, the twins, just started first
grade. It's got to be so hard on her, seeing how
he's gotten himself a whole new life, and how he
completely forgot the one he had with her."

Jack shook his head. "We both know that it's no
excuse for her to be ragging on you, 'D.' You
should have moved out a long time ago, gotten a
place of your own."

"What can I do?" she shrugged. "I'm all she has
left. If I walk out, that'll be it. I am not ready to
face that kind of guilt, if she were to do something
to herself, you know?"

He knew, but that didn't keep him from feeling
sorry as hell for her. "Look, you give me a ride
home, and you are welcome to crash at my place
tonight. I have to get up early anyway and find a
new set of wheels now that my truck has bought
it. I'll be gone all day, so feel free to linger as long
as you want."

Diana smiled. It was something she did so rarely
anymore. "Thanks, Jack. You know, if you really
don't mind, I think I will. It's so nice out there, by
the sea. Peaceful. Quiet."

Jack certainly understood.

The next morning, Jenna saw the kids off to
school and then got into her car for a quick errand.

It had been a while since she'd been behind the
wheel. With the salon situated as it was in the center of town, most everything she ever needed—the

market, the pharmacy, the café—was all within walking distance. While she loved that convenience, she had to admit that driving along the New England coast with the wind slashing through the windows and whipping through her hair while Aretha Franklin belted out "Respect" on the stereo did serve to get her blood to pumping.

It even made her feel a little bit young again.

When she came around the first bend in the coast road, Jenna caught sight of Hathaway Island in the distance. It was shadowed by the mist of the early morning, seeming almost to float in the dawn's pearly haze. She slowed the car and pulled over onto the shoulder so she could take a moment to drink the sight in.

From the mainland, the isle looked so lonely, so far away, so *forgotten*. It was precisely what the people of the town had wanted when they'd banished Rachael Hathaway there three hundred years earlier.

All because they'd believed she was a witch.

It was for that reason Jenna, Hallie, and Eudora and generations of Wren women before them remained so steadfast in keeping their silence about that part of their lives. Because no matter how the times might change, however tolerant society might claim to be, they always had that forsaken isle to look to . . .

. . . and to remember.

Jenna eased back onto the road and headed farther away from town. As she turned from the coast, the road started to climb, winding its way through straggling trees that were permanently slanted from the sea winds. She'd heard about the demise of Jack's truck from Sal and had decided to drive out with the intention of offering him the use of her car, should he need it. She could have called, she knew, but the offer of the car was really just an excuse for her to see him. They hadn't spoken since that day in the salon when Hannah had walked in on them, and Jenna sensed the weight of that kiss was becoming a "thing" between them.

She could see it in the faces of Jack's parents and his aunt and uncle. Even Sofia had that unspoken sense of anticipation about her when she'd run into Jenna at the market the day before.

"Maybe you, me and Jack could sneak off to Boston some time," she'd said. "You can leave the kids with Ma and Pop. They'd love it. Just like old times . . ."

Old times.

Jenna didn't want anyone, most especially Jack, to be under the wrong impression. She certainly didn't want it to become an issue that would affect the casual rhythm they'd managed to settle into in their lives, particularly when it came to the kids.

The cottage where Jack had been living since the divorce was set off from the road, cloaked in trees and perched, it seemed, on the very edge of the rocky headlands. It was small and the last time she'd been there, Jenna had thought that it had certainly seen better days. But as she rolled to a stop on the dirt drive, she felt her mouth drop open when the cottage finally came into view.

She hadn't been out that way since the previous winter and the work Jack had done over the spring and summer had truly transformed the place. The patchy roof had been reshingled and he had fixed the broken porch banister, repainting it a bright and sunny yellow. It stood out nicely against the weathered gray shingle siding and peekaboo windows, to which he'd added planter boxes that were

teeming with bright orange and red chrysanthe-
mums. There was a fresh stock of logs already piled
by the door for the hearth that coming winter.
Newly whitewashed wicker chairs were set at angles
on either side of the porch. And the screen door
that had once hung from one hinge had been put
right and given a coat of the same lemony yellow
paint. Seeing the improvements on the outside
made Jenna wonder all the more what he must
have done on the inside.

She was so intent on the changes to the cottage
that she didn't notice the car parked around the
back along the far side of the tool shed. Instead,
she got out, went to the front door, and softly
knocked.

After a moment, she heard movement coming
from inside, and took a deep breath, readying her
words as she waited for him to come to the door.

"Jack, I—"

It wasn't Jack who answered the door.

"Diana," Jenna said, so startled to see the busty
blonde standing there—and wearing nothing but
one of Jack's old T-shirts—that she couldn't keep
the acrimony from sharpening her voice. It lodged
in her throat like an unswallowed pill, dissolving
with a slow, unpleasant burn.

"Jenna . . ." Diana said, clearly feeling awkward.
"Um, Jack's not here."

"Oh, well, that's fine. I just . . . I heard about
the trouble with his truck and—" It was then Jenna
noticed Diana's car. "Apparently he found another
offer"—unwittingly, she glanced straight at Diana's
overstated breasts—"of transportation, I mean. So,
I'll just be going. You know what? Don't even
bother to tell him I stopped by."

Jenna spun about so fast, she nearly fell down

the porch steps. She stumbled down the walkway,
wishing she could run.

God, I am such an idiot!

"Jenna! Wait!"

But Jenna just kept going, pretending she hadn't
heard her. At that moment, the very last thing she
wanted was to stand before Diana "Double D"
DeNunzio—even worse a scantily clad Diana
DeNunzio—looking inadequately endowed, inadequately everything once again.

"Jack, I should have stopped her."

Jack had just returned to the cottage after spending his day haggling over a new truck that at the
moment he had no income to pay for. It was
parked out on the dirt drive, sticker still in the
window. Another F-150, this one black and sleek,
not primer gray and rusted.

"I knew exactly what Jenna was thinking when
she saw me," Diana went on. She was still upset
about Jenna's odd visit that morning. "I should
have stopped her," she said again.

"And told her what?"

Diana shook her head. "I don't know. The truth.
'Jenna, I crashed here last night because my mother
is borderline manic-depressive and Jack was kind
enough to lend me his shirt to sleep in.' Something.
Anything. Even 'Jenna, I'm not sleeping with Jack'
would have been a start."

"And what would that have accomplished? I
know Jen. She wouldn't have believed you. She
would have thought you were covering and it would
only make things worse."

"But I feel bad! I've never intended it but ever
since we were in school, Jenna has felt threatened
by me, by our friendship, for whatever reason. I

can't help but think that it's part of what split you two up."

Jack shook his head. "No. Jenna should have trusted me."

"Jack, she might have trusted you if you hadn't let it be known, or rather believed, that you and I had been together *while* you were dating Jenna. And there she was, pregnant with Sam, too. I'll always feel horrible about that."

"None of us knew about Sam at the time. But even so, I wouldn't have done anything different. I still would have said what I said to shut that asshole's mouth."

Twelfth grade. Senior prom. And a silver spoon-fed Blair Pritchett II was spreading a very ugly rumor about Diana in retaliation for her well-placed knee to his overly horny groin. If not for Jack stepping in when he had, Diana would very well have been banished to high school Siberia, and not crowned, as she'd been and deserved to be, prom queen.

Diana's eyes swelled with tears. "You know, I couldn't have asked for a better brother if my parents had ever had one."

"They didn't need to, 'D.' I'm here. Don't worry about it. I'll talk to Jen."

The town meeting later that night was well attended. So well attended, in fact, it had to be moved from the meeting room in the Town Hall to the high school auditorium across the street. And even then the auditorium was packed to standing room only with a fair amount of spillover into the outer foyer.

Members of the football team were enlisted to fetch chairs from the classrooms. A microphone, usually not needed since no more than a coffee klatch typically attended, was hastily arranged. A group of high school girls turned the gymnasium into a makeshift day-care center so parents could sit in on the proceedings without being interrupted for bathroom runs and water fountain breaks.

Ipswich-by-the-Sea had not seen the likes of a town meeting this well attended since . . . well, perhaps since the redcoats had been coming back in 1775, when Massachusetts had still been a fledgling colony and not an independent Commonwealth.

And they owed it all to Betty Petwith.

Over the past few days, Betty had worked tirelessly, making calls, knocking on doors, writing letters, posting flyers, and stopping anyone and everyone in the street to make them aware of the proposed sale of Hathaway Island. She had scoured through mounds of old documents—property surveys, town histories, and photographs—and had prepared a PowerPoint presentation that she would use to illustrate her cause. Even the media had picked up on the story; there were local reporters and news teams from Boston camped outside, anxious to tie in to the eleven o'clock report.

It was Modern Expansion versus Historic Conservation and preservationists had come bearing signboards, ready to picket and march. Many of the locals had brought their own personal camcorders to record the event.

Jenna took Sam and Cassie's coats and then left the kids in the gym to play with their friends. She stopped to chat with George Feswick, her neighbor across the street, and then joined Eudora and Hallie where they had managed to save her a place in one of the middle rows of the farthest section of seats from the stage.

She spotted Jack sitting with his parents and his aunt and uncle near the back. He gave a wave as she moved past, and looked like he wanted to say something, but then got lost behind the others who were milling about in search of empty seats.

Jenna noticed Declan standing against the far wall and wondered at his being there. No doubt the sophisticated Californian would be amused by their antiquated manner of town government, complete with "ayes" and "nays" when the time for a vote came.

She smiled at him and waved as she folded down the seat next to her mother.

"Quite a turnout," Eudora said.

"Betty's certainly outdone herself," Jenna agreed.

It had all the makings of a true showdown.

On the stage there was a long table with folding chairs lined up behind it. Seated were the town selectmen, an ancient trio who won reelection more out of sentimentality than anything else. Next sat Town Planner Lou Pritchett, Finance Committee chairman Blair Pritchett, and of course, Betty Petwith, who had brought the local attorney, James Dugan, for advice.

The town moderator was standing at the podium testing the microphone and making some final notes while the town clerk sat to the side at a small desk, waiting to record the proceedings into her stenograph for posterity. The local cable TV channel had set up a camera behind her, planning to broadcast the meeting on public access later that week for any who hadn't attended. And Chief of Police Barrett stood at the door, checking in the voters to keep everything legal.

Betty looked every bit the part of the crusading historian, dressed in a proper skirt and blouse with her cardigan draped over her squared shoulders and buttoned at the very center of her breastbone. Her hair was tidy, her glasses in place, and she had the expression of someone gearing up to do battle.

All she needed was a sword and charger.

She kept her composure while the meeting was opened, making a few last minute notes. Several other issues were discussed—dog license renewals, easements, and the upcoming Christmas festivities— before they arrived at the place on the typewritten agenda designated as the "Proposed Hathaway Island Sale."

Since the sale had been brought before the board by Lou Pritchett, he would speak first, outlining his reasons for recommending the sale. His brother would follow with the Finance Committee's points and recommendation. Then finally, Betty would offer her rebuttal.

After an introduction that had the reporters in the room keying Lou's name into their Black-Berries, the town planner rose with all the austerity of a Boston Brahmin and took the podium.

Betty Petwith wasn't far off the mark when she said that Lou Pritchett was certainly full of himself. Even at sixty-three, he had a head of silver hair with most of his face covered by an equally silver beard. He wore Hawaiian shirts year round and spent most of his day parked at table number three in Common Grounds, debating the rivalry of the Red Sox and Yankees, or reminiscing about the great blizzard of '78 over bottomless cups of Sal's coffee. A number of the men who shared that table with him each day sat beside him on the dais in the true "good old boy" fashion that was their small town government.

His older brother, Blair, a near carbon copy

minus the beard, was wearing his Blair Pritchett Homes golf shirt and matching jacket. He sat with his mouth glued to his two-way, conducting some sort of last minute business.

Betty Petwith was the only female seated, and it was obvious the scale was tipped out of her favor by sheer virtue of testosterone.

She had her work cut out for her.

"Evenin' all," Lou drawled into the microphone. He stuffed one hand into his trouser pocket as he leaned casually on the podium, gripping the microphone in his other hand. "Now, you all know me. You know me and my brother here are hometown boys born and bred." He glanced at Betty, as if to remind any who had forgotten that she had married into the town instead of spewing forth from it. "I have served this town through most of the past thirty years, volunteering at the town-wide yard sale, coaching ball . . ." He pointed to someone in the first row, one of Jenna's schoolmates. "Tommy Tipton, you were my catcher when we brought the state trophy home." He nodded his head reverently, scratching his beard. "That was a great day for the town of Ipswich-by-the-Sea."

Jenna frowned, shifted in her seat. Lou Pritchett had missed his calling, she thought, beginning to grate under his patronizing litany. He should have been a preacher. Coffers over at the congregational would be filled each Sunday with him up there pontificating.

"Now, you all know the issue before you. A private party has contacted the Board of Selectmen with a proposal to purchase Hathaway Island. The offer stands at four million, a very healthy offer for a piece of unused, mostly inaccessible land, the bulk of which would go into the town's very over-extended general fund. As most of you are aware, especially you who have children, our town is in a pattern of tremendous growth. Our classrooms are nearly at capacity. In fact, the art teacher, dear Mrs. Price, had to give up her classroom and now travels room to room with a supply cart. That four million would certainly go a long way toward funding us a second school . . ."

Murmurs of agreement rippled through the crowd.

Someone—Jenna recognized him as Mel Johnson, the green grocer—called out from his seat in the second row, "We don't even know who the person is who wants to buy it."

An echo of agreement followed.

Lou frowned. "The party wishes to remain anonymous."

Someone else blurted out, "Who is it, Pritchett? Madonna?"

Another laughed, then added, "No, it's Elvis!"

Soon everyone in the audience started to chuckle.

"The point of the matter," Lou scolded into the microphone, "is not *who* wants to buy the island, but whether the town agrees the island should be sold in order to help fund—"

"No, the point of the matter," Betty Petwith broke in, standing at her place across the stage, "is that the town cannot legally sell Hathaway Island at all."

For the first time in as long as anyone could remember, Lou Pritchett actually fell speechless.

But it only afforded his brother the opportunity to tag in. Blair Pritchett stood up, then faced down Betty Petwith like Boss Tweed on election day.

"What the he—" He caught himself, remember-

ing that middle America was watching. "What are
you talking about?"

"What I'm talking about, Mr. Pritchett, is this
document that I discovered among a collection of
early town papers. I have verified its language with
Mr. Dugan. In it, the whole of Hathaway Island is
deeded to one Rachael Hathaway, in exchange for
her farm."

"Hathaway?" Blair narrowed his eyes. "You
mean the witch woman?"

Betty stared at him. "I mean the Rachael Hathaway who was incarcerated on the island by the governing members of this town at that time. On
simply a suspicion of witchcraft, they seized her
farm and put her out on that isle, where they left
her to die. Meanwhile, they then split up her land—
one of the best farming parcels in the county—
amongst themselves. Only after they realized that
since Rachael was never formally charged or con-
victed what they had done was patently illegal, did
they draw up this document in order to protect
themselves for posterity." She slipped on her reading glasses and recited, " 'The island, hereafter to
be known as Hathaway Island, is given to the
widow Rachael Hathaway in fair exchange for the
former Hathaway Farm.' " She looked up again.
"The handwriting of the signatories can, I'm certain, be authenticated."

Blair just looked at her, and then suddenly he
smiled. A moment later, he started to laugh, the
microphone making the sound echo throughout
the theater.

Finally, he said, "You're not saying you actually
think that Hathaway woman is still alive three hundred years later, are you, ma'am? I mean I know
some have claimed to have seen her ghost every

now and then, mostly at Halloween or when they've had one too many down at the pub, but I'm thinking you're going to have a tough time convincing most of the sensible people here that she'll be walking through those doors to object to this proposal."

Lou was chuckling along with his brother, but curiously, most everyone else was silent.

"Perhaps, Mr. Pritchett," Betty said quietly. "Although the deed clearly states that in the absence of Rachael Hathaway herself, the island then becomes the property of any heirs."

Blair Pritchett threw up his hands. "You've got to be kidding me, woman! This is just another one of your ploys, your delaying tactics to try to sway the vote on this issue. You know you can't win on this one, Mrs. Petwith, so you're grasping at straws in order to try to put it off long enough to get some fat lawyer in here"—he glanced at James Dugan, but went on—"who will smooth talk some liberal idiot judge into your archaic way of thinking."

And there he was, for everyone to see in all his native New England brashness. No doubt that clip would air numerous times on the eleven o'clock news.

Betty held her ground. "We are required by law, Mr. Pritchett, to seek out anyone who is entitled to ownership of the property. And according to Mr. Dugan, we are also duty bound to cover the costs of conducting that search."

"Cover the—!" Lou Pritchett suddenly found his voice again and blew loudly out his nose and into the microphone. "You expect the people of this town to *pay* to conduct a search for someone who doesn't even exist? It's a colossal waste of the taxpayers' money, and I for one, won't do it."

"It is the law, Mr. Pritchett."

Voices erupted, murmuring at first, then growing louder.

Lou turned, leaning on the table, and started conferring with the trio of selectmen.

Betty whispered something to Dugan, who nodded in agreement.

Blair Pritchett just stood back and let the discord swell, all the while staring at Betty with vengeance in his eyes.

Finally, Lou turned back to the microphone and said, "You've gone too far this time, Mrs. Petwith. As town planner and a voting member of this community, I move that the town's preservation commissioner be removed under the charge that she is abusing her position. Do I hear a second?"

"There will be no need for a second," called a voice from the audience, preventing him from taking his initiative further.

Every voice in the auditorium fell silent, as those seated searched through the countless faces around them for whoever had spoken.

Blair Pritchett shaded his eyes against the stage lights overhead. "Who said that? Can we get some damn lights turned on in the auditorium?"

Someone offstage tripped the main switch, washing the whole of the chamber in light.

"Nor will there be a need for any search," the voice spoke again. "Rachael Hathaway has an heir."

A moment later, Jenna stood from her seat, rising in the midst of the crowded room.

Everyone stared at her in uncertain silence.

Lou Pritchett barked into the microphone. "You, Jenna Wren? Are you saying that you are the witch woman's supposed heir?"

"Not *supposed,* Mr. Pritchett." Jenna lifted her chin. "I am descended from Rachael Hathaway."

A moment later, Eudora rose to stand beside her. "As am I, Mr. Pritchett."

"And me, too." Hallie came to Jenna's other side.

And on that moon-kissed Thursday night in October, the Wren women finally came out of the closet.

Chapter Nine

It was astounding.

The secret of the Wren women, left unspoken for centuries, had been revealed—

And still the sun managed to rise the next morning.

Jenna lay in her four-poster bed, curled among a nest of pillows and wrapped in her favorite blanket, a fisherman's wool Aran-style afghan her grandmother, Eulalie Wren, had knitted a half century before.

It was early yet, barely past six, and day was just breaking over the blue-gray waters of the North Atlantic. She lay there and gazed at the soft light filtering through the sheer cotton curtains.

Outside she could hear the morning sounds of her hometown. Songbirds were chirping in the garden feeder. Gulls circled high above the rustling treetops, crying out their familiar *kee-rah* as they scrounged for scraps on the ground below them. The newspaper delivery boy, Timmy Spencer, was riding his bike along the cobbled street; rubber wheels humming as he tossed papers with astounding accuracy on each front door step.

Thunk.

Hearing him at the corner, George Feswick's little demon of a Jack Russell started barking—*yip, yap*—chasing Timmy the length of his yard from the other side of the picket fence. The dog fell silent, as he did each morning, as soon as Timmy's bicycle reached Mitch and Abbey Darlington's crab apple tree.

But not without giving one final *yip*.

Thunk.

Out in the harbor, a lone fishing boat sounded its somber horn, bidding farewell to the home port until it would return, laden with silvery herring. A gate hinge squeaked, needing oil. Someone dragged their trash can to the curb while the soft canzone of Sal Capone singing to the accompaniment of his espresso machine drifted from the corner café.

And there went Timmy Spencer again, tossing his paper on the last doorstep before turning the corner onto Main Street.

Thunk.

It was a daily concerto that played itself out in various ways on any given day. The instruments might be different and the lyrics would change. Sometimes it played to the *rat-ta-tattoo* of the rain, other days to the murmuring rush of the winter wind. But to Jenna, the symphony playing outside her window would always bear the same title:

Home.

She loved her home. She loved the comfort that it gave her, the security of knowing *this* was her little place in the world. Where she lived. Where she belonged. The only thing missing was someone to lie among the pillows with her, someone to wrap his arms around her, to warm her, to listen to the song of the morning with her.

There were times, especially like now, when

Jenna would find herself thinking back to the earlier days of her marriage. They had been so young, she and Jack, so determined to conquer the world.

And so incredibly in love.

When had things gone wrong between them? Just how had they lost each other so completely?

She remembered how she'd woken in the early hours of a morning like this, back when they'd lived in their tiny apartment on the outskirts of town. Her morning song then had been the roaring of the interstate, the creaking footsteps of their upstairs neighbors, and the gentle rush of Jack's warm breath playing against her neck.

And she'd cherished it.

Jenna knew now they'd been too young. It hadn't been easy, those first years of struggle, but she hadn't expected it to be. They'd taken on too much and then did what they could, what they had to, in order to see it through. She'd been eighteen and pregnant, and she had never fully been able to trust that nothing had happened with Diana as Jack had sworn. But she knew what it was not to have her father and she'd wanted so badly for her baby to have Jack fully in his life. And on the day they'd married, when Jack had promised his life, his fidelity to her, she'd clung to his words, believing them, believing in him. She knew Jack had hated his work, but she'd just thought, perhaps naively, that they'd manage to find a way, that things would get easier in time.

But time passed, and the distance between them only grew.

Jenna had come to believe their problem was they hadn't really had a plan. At least with a plan, they could have felt they were working toward something, not just sitting in the same place, stuck

in a muddy rut, watching their wheels spin hope-
lessly.

But for so much of their time together, none of
it had really mattered. The leaky faucet that never
seemed to get fixed, the noisy neighbors, the attempts to stretch out their last dollar until Jack's
next paycheck. Somehow, when they'd been in each
other's arms, when Jack had been loving her, filling
her, touching her more deeply than anyone else
ever could, it was as if the rest of the world hadn't
existed. They could be in that apartment, or on a
sun-kissed island beach, or halfway to the moon.
All that had mattered was that they were one.

Jack and Jenna.

Man and woman.

Soul to soul.

It just hadn't been enough. Somewhere along the
way, after Sam and then Cassie had come, after
rent increases and jumbo-sized packages of diapers
and the other obligations that had Jack working
morning till night, somewhere along that road, he
had begun to drift. Jenna hadn't noticed it at first
because she'd been so busy caring for an infant and
a toddler she got lost in the day-to-dayness. Jenna
remembered how even their lovemaking had become tinged with it, an ever-present tension, that
shadow of apprehension of what they'd do if they
suddenly found themselves facing baby number
three.

And then baby number three had been there,
that white stick turning bright blue one freezing
winter morning. It came on the very day Jack
learned he'd be facing a temporary layoff because
of the winter and its seasonal slowing of the home-
building business.

Jenna remembered she had been waiting to tell

Jack the news when he came home from work that night. She'd seen the dullness in his eyes as soon as he'd come through the door, and he'd told her about the layoff. They'd just had to sign a new lease on the apartment, with an increase in rent, the week before. So Jenna had decided to wait, tucking the news of the baby away for a better time.

And then Jack told her about the plans some friends had made for a snowmobiling weekend in the White Mountains of New Hampshire. Without telling him why, Jenna had suggested perhaps he shouldn't go, that they should save the money instead. But Jack had seen it as just another freedom denied him. And this time, he had stood his ground.

"I'm going, Jen."

"Jack, no. You can't."

"I'm going, Jen, because if I don't go, I'll die here. I have to get away, if only to regain my sanity."

But what about her sanity? she'd thought. What about us?

She remembered how Jack had just stared at her, and the lifelessness in his eyes had frightened her. Because it was then she'd realized that he'd stopped *seeing* her altogether.

He had stopped seeing *us*.

She should have just let him go, but she hadn't. Instead she'd gotten emotional—they were going to have another baby and he was only interested in going off to play at being single with the boys.

So she'd pushed.

And he only pulled away.

The more she tried to get into his head, to make him see reason and maturity, the more he refused to let her in.

Until, finally, he'd pulled away completely.

Standing there between her warring parents, Cassie had begun to cry, as if sensing the brewing tension that was threatening her little world. Jenna left to put her in her room, asking her to nap while Sam went to his friend Billy's apartment down the hall. Jenna had hoped it would give Jack time to calm down, so when she came back, they could sit together and talk it all through.

Then she would tell him about the baby.

But when she returned, Jack had already gone.

He'd left her.

Jenna had been so wrapped up in his departure, she hadn't seen that the dodgy latch on their apartment door hadn't caught properly when he'd gone.

She'd thought Cassie was napping.

So Jenna gave herself over to a good, hard, well-deserved cry.

She had no idea that the little girl had slipped out of her room and had followed her father out the door.

Somehow, at some point, Jenna remembered. She didn't know why. She just realized that something wasn't right. And her first thought had been Cassie. She'd gone to check on her, only to find the toddler-sized Barbie bed lying empty.

Fifteen minutes later, she'd found her daughter facedown in the near-frozen retention pond that had been dug out in an empty lot beside the apartment building. In the flash of an instant, what had begun as a domestic squabble became the worst nightmare of her life.

The sudden strident *buzz* of the alarm clock wrenched Jenna back from the horrible memory. She blinked and pushed the thoughts back where she usually kept them, locked deep away in the cellar of her mind.

The present, and its responsibilities, beckoned.

"Sam, Cassie," she called. "Six thirty!"

Jenna got up, stretched the kink from her neck, and flipped on the shower. As she waited for the water to warm and ping its way up through two floors of ancient plumbing, she slipped out into the hall.

She rapped a second reveille on each child's bedroom door, then threw them open wide, one then the other. "Let's go, troops. Up and at 'em!"

Sam's "bunker," a mound of blankets and pillows, responded with a groan. "Why do they have to have school anyway?"

Jenna grabbed the nearest corner of his Boston Bruins comforter and gave it a good yank. "So you can grow up and become smart enough to take over for Principal Edwards one day. And then you can have school start at noon instead of eight so that everyone, yourself included, can sleep in. Just think how all the kids will love you . . ."

Jenna threw open the folding shutters on his window, letting in the day.

"Mom!"

Sam covered his eyes with his forearm to block out the sudden sunlight. "I'm not going to be a stupid principal. They torture kids like making them clean gum off the bottom of chairs and gross stuff like that."

Jenna stood, hands on hips. "So then what are you going to do with yourself, Sam Gabriele?"

He pulled his arm away and grinned at her through squinted eyes. "I'm going to take over for Bill Gates instead."

"From your mouth to heaven's ears," Jenna said, tugging on the toe that was sticking through yet another hole in his sock. "But even Bill Gates had to go to school, so get yourself out of bed. Now!"

Cassie, bless her heart, was already up and dressed and brushing her teeth in the bathroom.

"Hi, princess," Jenna said as she grabbed a towel from the linen closet for her shower. After the unhappy reminiscing from that morning, she found herself stopping for a moment to bury her face in her daughter's soft hair, breathing in the lavender scented curls as she hugged her.

"Hi, Mommy."

Blinking back emotions, primarily a deep thankfulness for still having that precious gift in her life, Jenna headed for her bedroom.

"Mommy?"

She peered back into the bathroom. "Hmm?"

"Can I invite Marcy Waterhouse to my birthday party?"

"Sure, Cassie."

"And Kaleigh Lansky?"

"Of course."

You can invite the queen of England, if you so desire, my little miracle. . . .

It didn't hit Jenna until she got under the now steaming shower, bringing her fully awake, that Cassie's birthday was just two weeks away.

And Jenna hadn't yet made a single plan for the party.

Kid's birthday parties, and most especially little girls' birthday parties, were no longer just the cake-and-ice-cream-in-the-garage sort of occasion from Jenna's childhood. Suddenly they were all about *themes,* and twenty-first century mothers outdid one another in their efforts to try to maintain the par of birthday party originality.

Last year, when Cassie had turned seven, she'd invited a half dozen girls and Jenna had opened up the salon to them for the day, giving them all movie star makeovers and ending it with a do-it-yourself sundae bar. It had been a huge hit and Jenna knew it was going to be difficult to top.

Especially with less than two weeks to plan.

Think, Jen, she said to herself as she did a quick shave of her legs. *If I were an eight-year-old girl, what would I want for my birthday party?*

She hadn't been blessed with any epiphany by the time she stepped from the shower to towel off.

An hour later, Jenna was still trying to come up with something brilliant as she walked the kids to school.

She first sensed something when she kissed the kids good-bye; Cassie on the forehead, Sam with a simple nod and a smile because it was just too *uncool* for a mom to kiss a sixth grader. A trio of the other mothers, Patsy Lansky, Kathleen Spencer-Brown, and Alice Rogers, were standing together in the school yard chatting.

They were the *Mothers,* the ones who organized every extracurricular class event, who chaperoned the field trips, and brought perfectly iced cupcakes to class, which they'd just happened to "pick up" from the Magnolia Bakery during their weekend shopping jaunt to Manhattan. They'd moved from Boston "out to the country" in Ipswich-by-the-Sea, buying one of Blair Pritchett's ultra-modern, 3600-plus square foot homes in the most exclusive subdivisions, ones called *Wildewoode* or *Valhalla.* Only the "warriors" who came home to rest in this place were six-figure financiers who took the commuter rail to State Street while their wives dressed in their best designer sportswear, perfect faces, perfect hair, just to drop their kids at school.

The Mothers' chatter quieted the moment they saw Jenna walking up the sidewalk. As she checked

Cassie's backpack and handed her daughter her lunch, they just stood there, staring queerly at Jenna as if she'd just danced a polka across the sidewalk.

And then Jenna realized why they were looking at her.

The town meeting the night before.

Her declaration about Rachael Hathaway.

Jenna wondered whether she should have worn her pointed hat and dashed in on her broomstick.

"Hi, Patsy, Kathleen, Alice," Jenna said, and simply smiled in greeting as she walked by.

"Jen-na . . ." they chorused in perfect unison.

And then Jenna heard one of them whisper, "Oh, fine, I'll just go and ask her."

It was Patsy Lansky who had apparently drawn the short straw. She trotted to a stop in a pair of chic, gleaming white Mephistos when she reached Jenna.

"Jenna."

Jenna turned. "Patsy."

"I, uh, *we* were wondering."

"Yes?"

"What you said last night at the town meeting . . . about Rachael Hathaway . . ."

"Yes?"

"Is it true?"

"Do you mean was she really my great-great-great-great-great-great-great-grandmother?" Jenna smiled assuredly. "Yes. Yes, she was."

"And you weren't just saying that to help Betty Petwith halt the sale of the island?"

Jenna shook her head.

"And the stuff you have, in the salon, the lotions and potio—" She stopped herself. "Your mother with her baking and her preserves, all the herbs and such. Is that . . . ?"

Jenna lifted one brow. "Witchcraft?"

Patsy looked at her, obviously embarrassed. "Well, yes." When Jenna didn't expound, she asked, "Is it?"

"What do you think, Patsy?"

The question made Patsy's Botox-tightened forehead furrow. "Well, I guess, no. I mean there's no such thing as magic anyway. Is there? It's not like we're living in the world of Harry Potter or anything."

Jenna smiled. "I guess that would depend on your definition of magic. I see magic every day. In the faces of both my kids."

And with that, she turned, leaving Patsy Lansky staring after her.

The curious stares and whispers persisted.

On her way back home from the school, Jenna stopped in at the market to pick up some milk and fabric softener. When she walked in, Mildred Cartwright was standing at the counter, talking to the clerk, Mary Whittendon. They both fell mute at the sight of Jenna, staring as if they expected she'd sprout a second head.

As she strolled the aisles, filling her basket, Jenna glanced now and then out of the corner of her eye.

She picked up a carton of milk.

Mildred and Mary were still watching.

She got a brick of fresh Colby cheese to cut up for after-school snacks.

No second head yet, ladies . . .

She chose several apples from the basket of McIntoshes, added a half carton of eggs. Neither of them moved, not even when Jenna brought her basket to the cash register.

"Good morning, Mary. Mildred, how is your brother Pete doing? I heard he got into a fender bender the other day with the Wilsons' fence post."

Mildred didn't so much as blink as she continued that same stare. "He's fine."

Jenna smiled. "Glad to hear it." She took her purchases out of the basket and waited while Mary rang them up.

"Will that be all?" Mary asked before hitting the TOTAL button.

For a split second, Jenna considered asking if they had any eye of newt, but decided the joke probably wouldn't go over too well. "Yes, I think that's it."

She drew the necessary money out of her pocket, then took her change and the bags to leave.

"Have a nice day, ladies," she said, and left them staring as she slipped through the door.

When she went to open the salon for her nine o'clock, there were messages waiting on voice mail canceling her first two appointments of the day. One of them was the same Mildred Cartwright she'd just seen at the market. Apparently her morning gossip was going to keep her a little too busy to come in for her nine forty-five facial.

By ten thirty, Jenna had a very bad feeling in her stomach.

Other than a new client from Peabody and a regular from Marblehead, all of her appointments—all local residents, too—had called in either to cancel or reschedule for another day, and with one of the other stylists. As soon as she finished with her last client, Jenna shucked off her smock and headed for the door.

She needed to get some air.

"Becca, my schedule has unexpectedly cleared. I'm going to be out the rest of the afternoon. Would you mind locking up today?"

When Becca nodded, Jenna grabbed her keys and stopped by her mother's on the way to the car.

"Mother, can you get the kids from school for me? And just check that Becca locked everything up after closing?"

Eudora immediately sensed the trouble. "What's wrong, baby girl?"

Jenna gave a tight frown. "Apparently the people of this town aren't willing to have their personal needs seen to by a witch. Every local I had scheduled for today called in to cancel. So it looks like my afternoon is free. I'm going for a drive. I don't get to do that very often. I have my cell if you need to reach me."

Jenna drove her sensible sedan along the coast road, windows down despite the autumn chill while Shania Twain sang "I Ain't No Quitter" as loud as her car stereo would play it.

In fact, it was playing so loudly, she didn't hear the sound of the siren, nor did she notice the squad car that swerved from behind Morgan's farm stand to pursue her as she zipped by.

She did notice his lights, though, about the time he sped up to drive alongside of her.

"Well, hell . . ." Jenna muttered.

She eased off the gas pedal, coasting to a roll as she pulled onto the shoulder to stop. The black-and-white turned in front of her and at an angle, boxing her in as if he expected she might try to run.

Good grief, she thought. *This is Ipswich-by-the-Sea, not L.A.*

She looked at the uniformed officer who came to her door, cliché mirrored shades in place, and wondered if the day could get any worse.

"Ms. Wren," he said as Jenna rolled down the window.

She frowned. "Officer Faraday."

He was the newest cop on the local force, hired just the summer before. He already had made a name for himself around town for being overzealous when he dragged her friend Flora in for questioning on the very day she arrived in town from Scotland.

But that was another story.

"License and registration please."

Jenna couldn't wait to see what this was going to cost her. She dug her license from her wallet and pulled the requested registration from the glove box, handing both to him.

"Do you have any idea how fast you were going back there?"

She looked at him and felt the unwelcome stinging of tears at her eyes.

Don't cry!

Jenna just shook her head, trying to stem the waterworks. "No idea."

"I clocked you at fifty-seven. The posted limit on this road is forty. It's for your own safety, ma'am. This road has a lot of curves and hugs tightly to the coast."

Jenna nodded, and the tears began to fall despite her attempts to stem them.

"Something wrong, Ms. Wren?"

She worked to take hold of herself. "Just a colossally bad day. Ever had one of those, Officer Faraday?" She shook her head. "And it started out so nicely, too."

Faraday just looked at her. "Yes, ma'am." He wrote something on the clipboard he'd carried with him from the car. "Sit tight for a minute. I'll be right back."

So much for her unblemished driving record. She'd driven all of twice in the past three months. Now she'd have to pay some ridiculously huge fine and her insurance rates would go up and—

Well, crap.

Officer Faraday was walking back to her car. He returned her license and registration. "I'm going to cut you a break, Ms. Wren. We've all had bad days. But let this serve as a warning. Keep the driving at the posted limit from here on out, okay?"

Jenna looked at him and nodded contritely. She immediately took back all the ungracious things she'd been thinking to herself about him. "Thank you, Officer Faraday."

Jenna waited until he'd gone before turning the key in the ignition. As she pulled back onto the road, she lowered the music, switched it to a less rebellious Faith Hill song, and drove a good deal more slowly till she reached the turn into the drive at Thar Muir.

Flora's SUV was parked on the gravel drive that circled in front of the sprawling blue sea captain's house. Flowers exploded from boxes beneath every window and dripped from baskets hanging on the porch. Flora had arrived in Ipswich-by-the-Sea just the previous May, coming to open the house for its inaugural season as a B-and-B. A widowed mother of three, she'd only intended to stay the summer, but then she met Gavin Matheson, a brilliant composer who had lost his muse. She never would have dreamed that they both would be given a second chance at life . . . and at love.

But they had.

And now they were married and expecting a child, and Flora had decided to stay on, managing the inn for the winter.

With Hallie handling the bookkeeping, the technical side of the reservations, and managing the Web site, Flora was left free to explore the more creative aspects of innkeeping. And the B-and-B had enjoyed a triumphant first season, receiving very favorable write-ups in the Boston magazines and newspapers. Just recently, Hallie had come up with a new promotional idea that would offer a packaged "Spa Weekend" for out-of-towners, including the services of both Jenna's salon and the inn. She'd been after Jenna and Flora for weeks to get together to discuss it; Jenna figured today was as good a time as any.

Rather than go directly up to the house, Jenna decided to take a short detour. She circled around to the back of the house, past the newly painted trellis thickly twined with rich green ivy, around the carriage house, and through a garden that in summer was heavy with the perfume of brilliant pink beach roses. Across the sweeping expanse of clipped lawn lay a sea cliff of Massachusetts coast that stood far above where the Atlantic churned, washing its salty waters onto a small sliver of beach. The boathouse, which had been recently renovated, was tucked away from the main house behind an orchard of fruit trees and perched near the edge of the cliff. Jenna knew that Declan would be there, but that wasn't where her heart was calling her, especially since he'd been at the meeting the night before and Lord knew what he must now be thinking. It certainly wasn't something she was up to facing just then.

Jenna headed for the ancient woods on the far side of the house that stretched inland from the shore.

Earlier that summer, an unidentified grave had been discovered by Flora's children when they'd been out exploring in these same woods. Previously unknown to most, the marker stone they uncovered was simply carved with the initials *R* and *H* and a year, *1753*. When it was found, there was speculation that it must have belonged to some long forgotten relative of the house's original owners, the Hutchinson family.

But Jenna knew better.

For as long as she could remember, back to when she had been just a girl, even younger than Cassie, she and her mother and her sister had been coming to that secluded wooded spot, unbeknownst to anyone. The Wren women would come to sit, to remember, and to honor the woman buried beneath the blanket of wintergreen.

It was the final resting place of Rachael Hathaway.

It had showered earlier that day and the leaves were heavy and wet beneath her feet as Jenna kicked her way along the pathway. The grave lay in a small clearing beneath a stand of silver birch trees, their stark white trunks tilting at odd angles around it. It was a peaceful spot, with birds flitting overhead, the mingling smells of the forest and the rain filling the air while the sound of the sea hushed softly in the distance.

Jenna knelt and placed her hand gently against the moss-covered stone.

"I guess I should have learned from your example," she whispered. "Even three hundred years later, we're still misunderstood."

A gust of wind swept through the woods, circling around Jenna in a swirl of fallen leaves. She smiled, comforted by the reassurance of her ancestor's embrace.

Jenna spent a little time clearing away the autumn leaves and brushing off the moss that had grown to cover the small inconspicuous stone. Just coming to that place had given her a renewed sense of peace, of acceptance in herself, and a confidence of knowing where she had come from. It had helped to renew the strength that had been passed down to her from the woman who lay beneath that thick layer of earth.

"You're right," Jenna said to the stone. "We've never let anything defeat us before. Not even being banished to an island. I guess I just needed a little reminding."

Jenna finally stood, taking a deep breath as she brushed the dirt from her hands.

Minutes later, she heard the sound of leaves rustling and knew someone approached through the woods behind her.

"Heya. Saw your car in the drive," said a lilting Scottish voice. "When you dinna come up to the house, I wondered where you'd gone. Wasna much of a stretch to think I'd find you out here."

Jenna turned and smiled at the woman she had befriended just the summer before.

Flora MacCallum Matheson was the very image of the beautiful and mysterious Scotswoman, with fiery red hair, soft green eyes, and a gentle sort of air. She was one of the wisest people Jenna had ever met. A mother of three, with a fourth now on the way, although to look at her, you'd hardly know it. Lithe and graceful, even walking through an autumn wood, she looked more like a forest fairy than a living, breathing woman.

"Salon close early today?" Flora asked.

And suddenly Jenna's reasons for coming there returned in all its starkness.

"For me, it did." Jenna went on to explain. "Seems my neighbors are a little uncomfortable with the idea of having their hair done by someone who is descended from a witch."

The need to talk, to unburden her churning emotions, was burning in Jenna.

And wise Flora immediately sensed it.

"Why dinna you come up to the house, have a cup of tea with me? I've just taken some shortbread out of the oven. It's still warm."

Minutes later, they were settled at a small table in the sunny kitchen.

"I shouldn't be taking you from your guests," Jenna said as Flora measured out leaves, spooning them into a flowery china pot.

"Don't be silly. It's the off-season. We've only one room let right now, other than Mr. Cavanaugh down in the boathouse, but he keeps mostly to himself. The others are off antiquing in Rockport for the day. The kids are at school, due back any minute, and Gavin is with Alec working on the final arrangements for the recording. We go to the studio next month."

It had taken some effort, but Gavin had convinced Flora to let him record her beautiful singing voice. And the moment she'd agreed, he and his partner, Alec Grayson, had begun compiling an eclectic collection of songs to be recorded as modern lullabies. They'd spent most of the summer selecting songs that varied from Flora's native Gaelic airs to classic Eric Clapton, and one very special composition that Gavin had written especially for his new wife. It would be the first recording the Grammy-winning composer had done in nearly three years.

"So," Flora said then, breaking Jenna from her thoughts, "I hear you've been seeing something of my new boathouse tenant."

Jenna shook her head. "Hallie has a mouth like a dripping faucet. Always running."

Flora smiled. "No, actually, it was Declan who was inquiring after you. I'd 'say you've definitely intrigued the man."

"After the meeting last night, and the way the rest of the town is reacting, I wouldn't be surprised if he should suddenly change his mind."

"Just because your ancestor was accused of being a witch? Goodness, it's not like she was Lucrezia Borgia, was she?"

Jenna shook her head. "No one would deny that Rachael Hathaway was peculiar for her time. But evil? No. Rachael Hathaway was above all else a healer. She grew odd plants in her garden, plants that did remarkable things. What I know of her was passed down through the generations, but even that is rather vague. She was a widow when she came to this village, back in the late sixteen hundreds, although no one could truly say who her husband had been. She dressed boldly in bright colors and striped stockings, much to the dismay of her dour and somber Puritan sisters. Some said she'd even smoked a pipe. She'd lived alone on the outskirts of the town, arriving, some had claimed, on the crest of the New England fog."

Flora smiled. Her kids had just come in the door from school, and while the boys, Robbie and Seamus from her first marriage, and Gavin's son, Gabriel, all ran out to the back of the house to burn off their after-school enthusiasm, Flora's daughter, Annie, came to join them at tea. The same age as Cassie, the little strawberry blonde was fascinated by Jenna's tale, no matter how many times she'd heard it before.

"You know," Flora said, "one of my ancestors was supposed to have been descended from a mermaid. Dinna stop me from enjoying my fish 'n' chips."

She was trying to lighten the mood, Jenna knew. "Unfortunately when Salem started locking up their witches, it gave the good governing men of Ipswich-by-the-Sea reason to go knocking on Rachael Hathaway's door. They took her into custody and locked her away in a prison cell to await trial. But, somehow, that cell wouldn't hold her. Rachael would escape, would return to her farm, only to be taken into custody again. Further proof, they said, of her magical practices. So they decided to stick her out on the lonely island in the harbor until they could decide what to do with her. A fair exchange, the townsfolk insisted, that whole island for the arable acres of Rachael's rich farmland."

"Hmm. Sounds more as if a few of those 'good governing men' had their eye on Rachael's lands." Flora refilled Jenna's teacup from the pot of steaming Earl Grey. "And this is the document Betty Petwith discovered?"

"Yes, apparently so. But Rachael's trial date never came to be, which is probably a good thing. If it had, they most likely would have hanged her, like they did those in Salem. But, fortunately, the hysteria in Salem began to die down, and The Ipswitch, as Rachael was known, was simply left on her own out on the isle. Forsaken, but never quite forgotten.

"But that doesn't explain how she came to be here, on the mainland, and why she was eventually buried here at Thar Muir," Flora said.

Jenna smiled. "Do you want to know the real story?"

Annie's eyes grew wide.

Flora grinned. "I hope you don't think you're leaving this kitchen without telling us."

"Well, I am told that Rachael cast a spell, sending a bird, a tiny wren, to the mainland. Whoever the bird encountered first would become enchanted, and would sail out to the island to rescue Rachael from her prison. The bird flew here to Thar Muir, and the one who became enchanted was a man who lived here."

"Hiram Hutchinson," Annie said. "He lived here then."

"Yes, Annie. That's right. He was a farmer and a bachelor. A bit of a loner. He preferred to keep to himself. He brought Rachael here and they lived together for the rest of their lives. They never 'officially' married—they couldn't with the townspeople still believing Rachael to be dangerous. But still they pledged their lives to one another. And they had two children, a son and a daughter. The son took the Hutchinson name and went on to inherit this house. And the daughter, they named simply 'Wren.' "

"For the bird that had brought them together," Flora finished.

"Is that how you got your name: Jenna Wren?" Annie asked.

"Yes, sweetie. And it's why every daughter born to my family since bears the name of Wren. In honor of Rachael and the struggles she went through. So we would never forget her."

Flora sighed. "It's as beautiful a tale as any Scottish legend."

"Only it's not any fairy tale," Jenna finished. "That's the thing. It's history. It's the story of how my family came to be. Rachael tutored little Wren in the ways of nature as she grew, teaching her the knowledge of herbs, instructing her in all her spells and enchantments. Those people who claimed they'd seen Rachael Hathaway haunting their gardens? It was just Rachael gathering her herbs, which she did at night when she could hide behind the cloak of darkness. Rachael always warned her daughter never to tell anyone of their craft, because she knew people could not understand that which seemed so mysterious, so powerful. And every generation since has kept the secret faithfully. . . ."

"Until you," Flora finished.

"Until me. I just couldn't stand there and let them sell that island. I couldn't imagine someone putting up a slew of condos on it, or making it so no one could ever go there again. I guess, much as I hate the way she is remembered in this town, with that island as it is, Rachael is at least remembered. And maybe someday people will come to realize that she was not the demon they've painted her, but a living, breathing woman who was really just misunderstood. That is my hope anyway. But now, after that town meeting, I can't help but feel a little as if I've just opened Pandora's box."

"You did what you had to, what your heart told you to do." Flora looked at Jenna. "And if I've learned anything in the past six months it's that sometimes you just have to take that leap, and trust that things will work out as they should."

Chapter Ten

Jenna left Thar Muir feeling much better than she had when she arrived. Flora seemed to have that way about her, a way of putting things into the simplest perspective, seeing through the muddle to the very heart of things.

Sometimes you just have to take that leap, and trust that things will work out as they should.

Daylight was fading fast as Jenna drove along the coast on her way back to town. Everything around her was tinged with the silvery haze of twilight. She checked her watch. It was nearing six. She hadn't meant to be gone so long, but she knew she'd needed to have some time with a friend, to let go of her troubles instead of continuing to bear them all on her shoulders alone.

But now it was time to return to being Jenna Wren, single working mother, again.

So she flipped open her cell phone and dialed her mother's number as the Atlantic Ocean broke on the shore beside her.

Eudora answered the kitchen phone on the third ring.

"Hellooo?"

"Mother, it's me."

Eudora already knew that from the caller ID, yet still she acted pleasantly surprised. "Oh, Jenna, dear. How are you?"

"I'm fine. I just had a visit with Flora and—"

"Lovely! Such a sweet girl, that Flora. How is she feeling? How are the kids? Is the baby doing well?"

"They are all doing very well. Dr. O'Leary says she's right on schedule, seventeen weeks and due at the spring equinox."

"A baby conceived at the solstice," Eudora realized. "She'll be a special child, indeed."

"You just said 'she.' Does that mean . . . ?"

Eudora smiled. She had a certain sense for these things, and didn't need a needle hanging from the end of a thread or any of the other superstitious rituals to tell her. She just had to look at a woman and she knew. "You should know better than to ask, dear. I never tell. Besides, I'm sure Flora will be thrilled no matter."

"How are things there?" Jenna asked. "How are the kids?"

"Sam is on the computer and Cassie is here in the kitchen with me." Eudora winked at her granddaughter, and put a finger to her mouth in a *shh* gesture. "She's, uh, helping me to cook something up."

Well, technically they were *cooking*. They'd spent the past few hours preparing an infusion with various herbs and ingredients steeped in rainwater. And now Eudora's ancient cast-iron cauldron stood in the center of the kitchen table. She and Cassie had placed several branches of heather and bracken, which they'd gathered from the garden, into the cauldron and then enchanted it all with a spell. A candle flickered in the waning light of day on the table beside the cauldron.

"Where are you, dear?" Eudora asked Jenna then, even though she already knew. All she'd had to do was gaze into the reflection of the water in her cauldron, and she'd seen the image of Jenna driving along . . .

"The coast road," Jenna answered. "I just left Thar Muir."

Eudora motioned Cassie to take the branches from the pot, and carry them outside to the garden where they'd already cast a circle using a knotted cord. "Have you passed Siren's Cove yet, then?"

Eudora already knew she hadn't.

"No. I'm nearly there, though. Do you need me to stop for anything?"

"If you wouldn't mind, dear, I could use some . . ." There was Morgan's farm stand, and if Jenna stopped, it would give Eudora and Cassie time to set the spell fully into action. She made a quick motion with her arm, demonstrating for Cassie the way to swing the branches upward so that that water they'd soaked in sprayed out in a wide arc, showering around her.

". . . currants," Eudora finished. "Yes, see if they have any currants for me, would you, dear? I've a mind to make a new preserve."

"Sure, I'll be there shortly and—Goodness!" Jenna gasped into the phone.

"What's the matter, dear?"

"A flash of lightning just split the sky, right above the car. Five minutes ago, it was clear and calm. Are they predicting a storm tonight?"

Eudora then took up some branches of bladderwrack and yellow-flowering broom that she'd also cut from the garden, and held them out to Cassie, who was still standing in the middle of the corded circle. With her free hand, Eudora demonstrated to her how to make the same sweeping motion she had with the other branches.

"I'm afraid I haven't heard the weather report, dear."

Cassie swept her arms outward, and the branches made a soft *hiss*.

"Mother, I better go. The wind just came out of nowhere and now it's pulling at the car. I need to concentrate on the road. I'll stop at Morgan's for the currants and then I'll be on my way. I hope I can get home before this storm hits."

"Okay, dear. But please, don't rush. A little rain is nothing to fret over. Just drive safely now."

As she disconnected the call and set the phone back in its cradle, Eudora smiled to herself. She glanced at Cassie again, who was still waving the branches about. "That's very good, Cassie dear. Now, why don't you keep holding out the branches, but spin about a bit while you're in the circle? That's it, my sweet girl. We need that storm to be as strong as it can be."

Back in the kitchen, Eudora checked the water in her cauldron. Very soon, Jenna would be drawing near the road that wound up the hill.

The same hill that led to Jack's place.

Eudora joined Cassie inside the circle and sprinkled a bit of comfrey in the air, blowing on it to send it swirling on the wind while Cassie went on waving the branches. To the east, over the sea, storm clouds darkened, quickly swelling and surging. The wind blew in off the harbor, sweeping through the garden as together, grandmother and granddaughter recited the closing words to the spell.

As I will it, so mote it be. . . .

Jenna felt the car lurch, and then suddenly it lost all power, at almost the very moment she rounded Siren's Cove.

Her headlights dimmed and the car simply rolled, slowing quickly. She managed to pull off the road onto a wide shoulder clearing just before it stopped dead altogether.

She turned the ignition, but it didn't catch. It didn't even make a sound.

Great.

Jenna opened the door to check under the hood, but as soon as she did, rain began to fall. It wasn't just falling; it was peppering the windshield and the hood of the car with what sounded like buckshot.

Jenna closed the door and quickly grabbed her cell phone from its cradle. Thank heavens for AAA.

And then she noticed the display on her phone read NO SIGNAL.

How could that be, when she'd just been talking to her mother?

Jenna tried to call anyway, but after thirty seconds of silence, the display read CALL COULD NOT CONNECT.

Outside, the wind was howling and the rain was washing down the windows in sheets. Somehow, in the time it took to travel the space of about four miles, the temperature outside had dropped. Jenna frowned when she realized she hadn't brought a jacket. From the way it sounded as it hit the car, the rain seemed almost to be freezing.

Jenna waited a while to see if any cars might drive by to help her, but the road was deserted. She tried the phone again, but still couldn't get a signal. After fifteen minutes or so, during which a noticeable chill crept inside the car, she decided she'd better seek more adequate shelter. The sky was getting darker by the second and she certainly didn't want to be stranded in the middle of the night alone.

Jenna peered through the blurred windshield and saw the turnoff for another road. She realized then that she was within running distance of Jack's place.

She reached for the umbrella she kept under the driver's seat and on the count of three, grabbed her keys and purse before making a dash for it.

The moment she opened the door, the umbrella blew inside out and then completely pulled out of her hands. It flew down the road, a twisting and turning beacon of red, until finally it disappeared altogether. Jenna tried to push her wet hair from her eyes so she could see. The rain was showering down in fat drops, leaving her no choice but to run for it up the hill. She just hoped the trees would offer some little protection.

Jenna wondered if Jack would be there, and then decided if he wasn't, she'd just have to break in. She was sure he'd understand.

Very soon she was freezing. Her breath was coming in a fog and her blouse clung to her skin. Soaked from the rain, her teeth began to chatter. Her fingers cramped from the cold as she struggled to shield her face. She had nothing to cover herself with and the dirt and water washing down the hill was sloshing around her ankles, ruining her favorite pair of clogs.

By the time she saw the lights at Jack's cottage, she was gasping from the run and soaked completely through.

Jenna stumbled up the porch steps and pounded on the door. When he didn't immediately answer, she tried the knob, nearly crying out in joy when it turned.

She lurched inside just as Jack was coming to the door.

"Jen! What the hell is going on?"

She fell against him, trying to catch her breath. Her teeth were chattering uncontrollably. "The car—it died—my phone—it died, too. Had—nowhere else—to go—"

Jack grabbed a blanket and yanked it around her. "Get over here by the fire. Geez, you're soaked."

Jenna sloshed over to where he already had a fire blazing in the hearth. The warmth hit her, tingling on her chilled skin. Without hesitation, Jack reached for the waistband of her jeans.

Jenna stared at him. "What are you doing?"

"You need to get out of those clothes before you catch pneumonia. Your skin is like ice."

Jenna pushed his hands away. "I can do it."

But her hands were shaking so badly, and her fingers were so stiff from the cold, she couldn't seem to grasp the button.

Jack covered her fingers, warming them as he eased her hands away. "It's not like I haven't done this before," he said and quickly undid the button and zipper, then helped her to shuck off the wet and heavy denim. Then he went to work on the front of her blouse.

When she was left standing in just her sopping socks and underwear, Jack wrapped the blanket around her again, setting her in the chair by the fire. He tossed another couple of logs in the hearth, poking at them to goad the flame.

"There."

When Jack turned to look at Jenna, his breath caught in his throat.

She looked so delicate, so small, eclipsed by that heavy blanket with her teeth chattering and her hair plastered to her face. He grabbed a towel from the laundry he'd been folding when she arrived and tossed it to her. "Here, dry your hair. I'll get those socks off."

He knelt before her and took one foot and then the other into his hands, peeling back the dripping, muddy socks. He wrapped his hands around each foot, rubbing the circulation back into her toes. When he was done, he tucked her bare feet beneath the cover of the blanket.

As he stood, he noticed that his hands had gone hot, just from touching her. He wanted nothing more than to take her into his arms and warm her with his own body, but knew he couldn't.

"Tea?" he managed.

She nodded, her teeth still chattering. "P-please . . ."

While he waited for the water to boil, Jack went up to his bedroom where he got a set of thermals and his heaviest flannel shirt from the dresser, along with a pair of thick socks. He brought them to her. "When you've warmed up enough, put these on."

"My mother. The kids. I'd just talked to her, before the storm broke. I told her I was coming home. They'll be worried when I don't arrive."

Jack grabbed the phone just as the tea kettle began to scream.

"Eudora? It's Jack. Yeah, nice to talk to you, too. Listen, Jen had some car trouble. No, she's fine. She's just sort of stranded out here at my place, at least until this storm lets up and I can go see to it. I'm sure it's nothing. Probably just stalled from the rain. She didn't want you and the kids to be worried. Okay. I'll tell her. Yeah. Tell the kids to be good for me now. Okay. Thanks. See ya."

He plopped a tea bag into the "World's Best Dad" mug the kids had given him for his last birthday and filled it with the steaming water. Then he took out the bottle of Glenfiddich Flora and Gavin had brought back for him from their last trip to Scotland. He added a healthy splash of the whisky to the tea to help warm where the fire couldn't reach.

When he returned to the living room, Jen had already put on the clothes he'd given her. The first thing Jack noticed was her lacy panties and matching bra hanging on the crooked handle of the fire poker, drying by the fire. She'd been wearing them when he peeled off her wet clothes, but then he'd been intent on getting her dry and warm. It wasn't until he saw them drying in the fire's glow that it struck him.

He was instantly taken back to the days when they'd been married and he'd walk into their shared bathroom to find her lingerie drying in the shower. His own temperature warmed just at the thought of it, and he certainly didn't need any help from the whisky. Even wearing oversized socks, grey thermals, and a baggy red and black flannel shirt that fell to her knees, Jen could still give his pulse a lurch.

"I, uh, called your mom. I told them you'd be here for the time being. They're all fine. They've already had dinner. Eudora said she'll stay with the kids at your house till you get home."

He handed her the tea. "Have you had anything to eat? I'm afraid I don't have much. Just brought home a pizza from Pop's place. It's warming in the oven."

Jenna smiled. "Sounds great. You know I've always loved your father's pizza."

It was a good thing he'd already warmed it, too. Because as soon as Jack took the pie out of the oven, a shock of thunder shuddered overhead, so close to the house, it sounded as if it had touched ground right outside the door.

A moment later, the power went out.

"This storm is sure gearing up to be a bad one."

Jack got candles from the drawer in the kitchen and lit them, setting them about the room. The soft light glowed on Jenna's face. "So much for the weatherman. The report on the radio earlier said it was going to be a calm, clear night."

He noticed that Jen had finished the tea, so he took up the bottle of Chianti he'd uncorked only a few minutes before she had come pounding on the door. He poured a second glass, setting it before her. Jack reached for his own glass and sat on the floor, plate of pizza on his lap, watching the fire.

Jen slid down to join him a few moments later.

"So, what were you doing out this way tonight?" he asked.

Jenna snatched one of his pepperonis. "I was up at Thar Muir."

"Oh." Jack frowned, already knowing that Declan Cavanaugh had taken an extended stay at the B-and-B. Just the thought of Jen with him soured the wine in his mouth.

"I had a nice visit with Flora and the kids. We're

planning to offer a spa weekend package together starting with the new year." And then Jenna frowned. "Of course, after the day I had today, I could be in need of the new business."

"What do you mean?"

Jenna told Jack about the cancellations at the salon, and the peculiar way the people in town were behaving toward her.

"I don't see what the big deal is," Jack said, his mouth quirking just slightly. "I mean, I always knew you were a witch."

"You did?" Jenna said, then realized his joke. "Oh!" She threw her pizza crust at him.

They laughed together for a moment and then Jenna grew quiet. She passed several minutes just staring into the fire. Finally she asked, "Would it surprise you if I were to tell you that I really am a witch?"

Jack looked at her. Her hair had mostly dried and was curling around her face with a few strands falling into her blue eyes. It shimmered in the light of the fire like liquid black, filling him with the urge to touch it. Her face had pinked from the warmth of the fire and her eyes had a lazy look to them, probably from the whisky. And as he stared at her, lost in those eyes, Jack asked himself how he ever could have let her go.

He could have said something sarcastic or funny in response to her, but instead he said, "I wouldn't be surprised at all, Jenna Wren. You had me under your spell from the moment I first laid eyes on you."

He meant it.

And knowing that he meant it brought tears to Jenna's eyes.

This time, when they kissed, it was Jenna who

reached for Jack. She curled her fingers into his hair and pulled his mouth down to hers. Emotions swirled through his consciousness with the force of the storm raging outside, the soft heat of her body, the sweet taste of the wine on her tongue, the rain-washed smell of her skin. He eased her back, laying her on the soft carpet that stretched before the fire.

They kissed with a familiarity that the past four years couldn't erase. He knew how she would sigh when he touched her face, how she would run her hands slowly over his shoulders. Suddenly the clothes he'd given her for warmth were a barrier between them. Jack needed to feel her, every inch of her, against him. He fought to free the buttons on the flannel shirt, dragging his mouth along her neck. He felt her breath against his forehead as she pressed her lips to him, felt her fingers raking through his hair. Finally, he freed the last button and pushed at the heavy fabric. Then he lifted his head to stare at her in the firelight.

She regarded him through half-closed eyes. Her mouth was still moist from their kiss. Her breasts were rising and falling softly. Jenna was so beautiful, so unbelievably beautiful, and Jack committed the sight of her to memory just in case he should wake and find this all nothing but a dream.

Please don't let it be a dream.

His breathing was ragged. He wanted to feast on her with his eyes and his mouth and his hands. He somehow found the strength of will to pull off his T-shirt, then gently lifted her so that he could slide her free of the flannel shirt.

Jenna sat before him, bare to the waist, limned in feminine perfection by the firelight. Jack reached for her, tracing his fingers along the curve of one breast. He watched the dusky nipple tighten, saw

Jenna blink at him breathlessly, arching just slightly against his touch.

"Do you have any idea how incredible you are?" he whispered, and then before she could answer, he covered her mouth with his, cupping her face with his hands.

He needed to memorize every inch of her, the elegant curve of her shoulder, the soft skin behind her ear.

Jack touched her with his hands, with his eyes, with his mouth, and when he found her breasts, he suckled her as he laid her back before the fire.

When he lifted his head, her eyes were closed and she caught her breath, just waiting . . .

Waiting for him.

Jack slid off the thermals, pulling the socks with them, and then shucked his jeans until they were both naked and glowing in the firelight. As he kissed her again, he rolled her above him, mouth to mouth, relishing the weight of her while her breasts filled his hands.

"God, I've missed you," he breathed into her hair and fell back as she straddled him. He slid his hands along her thighs, spanning her waist.

"Jenna . . ."

"Shh," she whispered. "No more talking. No more thinking. Just love me, Jack. *Love me.*"

Jack gathered Jenna up and stood, carrying her across the room to the stairs. He kissed her neck as she nibbled his shoulder and locked her legs around his waist. She smelled so incredible, like flowers and rain and wind and fire. He wanted to breathe in every inch of her. He laid her on the bed, and fused his mouth to hers.

Hunger for each other and desire long denied surged through them both. They couldn't get enough of each other. His hands slid over her belly, parted her legs, and delved to the moist center of her. And when he found her, Jenna gasped and arched against his touch. She raked her hands through his hair. He broke from the kiss and followed the path of his hands, kissing her breasts, her belly. He nibbled at her side and then he took her hips into his hands and lifted her, loving her with his mouth, knowing just how to stroke her so that she lost herself to the promise of her climax.

And when her body rocked, when her breath hitched, Jack knew true fulfillment.

He pulled Jen into his arms and held her, basking in the moment, having her there, with him, in his bed. In his arms. Jenna stirred, and her hands gently drifted down his torso. She caressed him, taking him into the warmth of her hands.

Jack tensed in response.

Jenna slid over him with a seductive light in her eyes. She kissed him—tasted him, nibbling his bottom lip as she played her fingers against his chest. Jack filled his hands with her breasts, sucking in a hard breath when he felt her reach for him, lift her hips over him and slide the hard length of him fully inside of her.

"Oh, God . . . Jen . . ."

Jenna slowly rocked her hips.

Jack gasped.

Jenna moved over him, rolling in a rhythm as ancient as time.

She took him deeply, loving him with a passion and a heat equal to the roar of the storm. They rode its thunderous wave, locked together soul to soul.

And when he came, Jack grabbed her hips, pulling her over him so he could empty himself within her.

She was his. Once again, Jenna was truly his.

Jack eased her to lie against his chest. He never wanted to let her go. He let the tremors of his release rock her just as strongly as they did him.

Jack traced his hands over her back, lifted her head from his shoulder, and kissed her.

She was there.

His Jen.

No longer the girl, but now the woman.

And she had bewitched him all over again.

The sun was shining when Jenna awoke.

She was alone, lying on Jack's bed. She didn't have a stitch of clothing on, her hair was a nest of tangles, and she felt absolutely wonderful.

The storm had passed overnight, and the daylight was fresh and sparkling with renewed hope. Jenna slid from the bed and crossed the room to the window where she stared out to sea as it glimmered and stretched into the sky.

She had told Jack her secret.

All through their courtship and marriage Jenna had feared what would happen if Jack should ever learn the truth about her family and their history. Would he shun her? Would he stop loving her? When she'd given Cassie the Wren name, he hadn't understood. He'd thought it some sort of feminist gesture and his Italian pride had been stung. Back then, he could never understand and Jenna had convinced herself she must never tell him.

But she had. And he hadn't reacted oddly or treated her differently like everyone else had. He had simply shrugged. And then he'd loved her, accepting her for who she was. A witch.

Jenna was still standing at the window when Jack kneed the door open a few minutes later.

She was in profile as she leaned against the glass,

one hand resting on the sash, the curve of her back flaring to her bottom. The picture of her, basking naked in brilliant sunlight, left him blinking.

"God, if I could have that image on a canvas . . ." he said, and she turned, smiling at him.

He carried the tray he'd prepared in the kitchen, setting it on the bed while she grabbed one of his shirts from the closet.

What was it about the sight of a naked, just-loved woman wearing a man's shirt that could make a guy instantly hard?

Jenna slid onto the mattress, lying on her stomach with her knees bent and her feet crossed behind her. She grabbed a pancake from the stack he'd built, folding it in half before taking a healthy bite.

"These look incredible," she said and then her eyes went wide and she moaned a sound of pure pleasure. "Jack, either I'm half-starved or these *are* incredible!" She took another bite. "How . . . or better yet, where did you learn to make these?"

He grinned. "Thought you might wake up hungry. Making love all night tends to build the appetite." He poured a cup of steaming coffee, prepared just the way he remembered she liked it, no sugar, extra cream. "So, I was thinking about what you told me last night while I was making these *incredible*—if I do say so myself—pancakes downstairs. Let me ask you something. When you say you're a witch . . . does that mean you're the wiggle your nose *à la* Samantha on *Bewitched* sort of witch who can, oh, say . . . get the Patriots into the Super Bowl again this year?"

Jenna smiled at him and swallowed her breakfast. "What? The Red Sox winning a World Series after eighty-six years wasn't enough?"

Jack stared at her. "You?" He shook his head. "No . . ." And then he narrowed his eyes. "Are you seriously saying you . . . did that?"

Jenna lifted her chin. "Well, someone had to do something to stop all that whining at the end of every season about that ridiculous 'Curse of the Bambino.' Mother and I decided enough was enough. All it took was a little counterspell, and well, the rest is history."

"So the eighty-six years before that was . . . ?"

"A spell?" she finished.

He nodded.

"Yep. Come on, Jack. There's no such thing as an eighty-six-year coincidence. Didn't I ever tell you that my great-grandmother, Constance Wren, was a huge fan of Babe Ruth? She was really upset when the Red Sox traded him back in 1920—and all so the team owner at the time could finance a stage musical. She decided to teach them a lesson. I'd say she sure did."

Jack just stared at her, dumbfounded. "Well, that certainly shoots my incredible pancakes all to hell, now doesn't it? So what else can you do? Can you spin gold out of straw? Predict the lottery numbers? Make a broom sweep the floor all by itself?"

Smiling, Jenna shook her head. "You've got to forget all about what you've seen in books and movies. Well, most of it anyway. Real witches do not float in bubbles like in *The Wizard of Oz,* or keep a squadron of flying monkeys. I am what is called a 'hedge witch.' I come from a long line of hedge witches."

"Your mother, obviously."

Jenna nodded.

"Hallie?"

Jenna nodded. "And Rachael Hathaway."

Jenna told Jack the story she'd shared with Flora the day before about Rachael Hathaway and what had become of her. "But it goes back even further, generations before her. Back in the oldest days of history, my ancestors were village wise women, medieval-age herbalists who used nature to cure sickness, give advice, do what they could to provide aid to those in need. The difference is then they were revered for their knowledge, and respected. It's what some today would consider folk medicine. This revival lately of all-natural products and botanicals . . ." Jenna laughed. "It's nothing new to us. It's what we've been doing for centuries."

Jack shook his head. "And all these years I've known you, I had no clue."

"Because I never let anyone see that part of me. We're no different than other people, really. We are just more in tune with nature. And there are different paths we each take, all based on our own intuition. Me, I follow the path to the garden. I'm what some would call a green witch. Mother is more of a kitchen witch. She focuses her magic on hearth and the home with her baking. Hallie is more a modern witch. A techni-witch. She studies the stars and uses calculations and formulas."

Jack took it in, nodding. "And Cassie, does she . . . ?"

"Not yet," Jenna answered. "But she knows about it, and I will teach her, as my mother taught me, about the garden, of our tradition. And then we will see which way the wind takes her."

"But why hide it all this time? Why especially didn't you ever feel you could tell me?"

Jenna reached to touch Jack's face. "It wasn't because I didn't trust you, Jack. It was, just, I guess, what we did. I grew up being told that it was never to be spoken of. You must remember that the last time anyone in my family came close to being found out, she was forsaken to an island to die. That alone has been enough to keep us silent ever since. You know how Rachael Hathaway is regarded in this town. She's 'The Ipswitch,' remember? Do you have any idea what it's like to grow up with friends who dress up as your great-great-whatever-grandmother for Halloween?''

Jack looked at her. "No. I can't say that I do."

The phone rang and as Jack took the call, Jenna retrieved her clothes from where they had dried by the fire the previous night. She headed for the bathroom to dress, hoping to do something to tame her hair. As she walked past Jack's computer, she spotted some drawings spread out across the desktop. They were drawings of a house, a beautiful Victorian. It was the sort of house she had always dreamed of, complete with a turret.

Jenna was still looking at the drawings when Jack hung up the phone.

"This house," she said when he came to join her. "It's incredible. Whose is it?"

Jack looked at her. "Well, actually, it's mine."

"Yours? But . . ."

"Jen, perhaps you better sit down for this."

She let Jack lead her across the room to a chair. He hunkered down before her and took her hands.

"I went back to school, Jen. The times I've been late coming to get the kids, when I've had to cancel, that's what I was doing. Studying. Learning my craft. You only knew that I had quit working for Blair Pritchett. You thought I'd just gone to work for my father at the shop, that I had no real ambition. But I was actually doing an apprenticeship under Jimmy O'Connell while I went back to school to get my degree. In fact, we just finished the boathouse up at Thar Muir." He looked at her and grinned. "I even did some of the work at your place."

"What?"

He nodded. "I told Jimmy not to tell you and I made sure to be there only when you were busy working. But there's more. I've started a new business, with Brian O'Connell and his dad. It's called O'Connell and Gabriele, and we're doing architectural restoration. In fact that phone call just now was Brian calling to tell me we've got a potential new client. We're going to continue O'Connell's work but we're also going to offer more. I'll do the design work while Brian handles the architectural end. We are going to specialize in reclaimed materials, salvaging parts of older houses that are being torn down or dismantled, and incorporating them into the new. I'm going to build houses with souls, Jen. No more of Blair Pritchett's cookie-cutter LEGO blocks."

"But all this time, Jack. Why didn't you ever tell me what you were doing?"

"Because I didn't want to see the disappointment in your eyes." Before she could deny it, Jack went on. "Jen, it's okay. I know I was a disappointment. To you. To the kids. I was a disappointment to myself, too. I was selfish. I got lost in thinking about all I had given up. Youth. Freedom. I completely ignored what I had with you and the kids. The day I came back to that house and found all of you gone, I felt like I died. To know we almost lost Cassie nearly killed me. To know that I hadn't been there for you when you'd needed me to be, that I'd been off seeing to my own entertainment, refusing to even turn on the cell phone so you couldn't reach me. You must have been frantic that weekend, Jen."

She shook her head. She didn't want to revisit that time of her life now. "You had no way of knowing."

"No, Jen. Don't make excuses for me. I should have been there for you and for Cassie, and I wasn't. Unfortunately, it took your leaving for me to realize that. I wanted, no, I needed to change. But I knew, after all that happened, you weren't going to just give me another chance. I'd spent all my chances with you. I had to prove something to you. But first, I had to prove it to myself."

Jenna had tears brimming in her eyes. "Oh, Jack. For a second, when you first told me I'd better sit down, I thought you were going to tell me you were in love with Double D—I mean, Diana De-Nunzio, and that the house was . . ." She shook her head. "I saw her here, the other morning. Wearing your shirt. I jumped to conclusions. I sound like such a jealous idiot, don't I?"

Jack looked at her. "Jen, last night you shared something with me, something that you had kept locked away from everyone. I understand about keeping confidences because I kept one for someone else, even at the peril of hurting you. There never was anything between Diana and me. I know I have told you this before, but you never believed me. And how could you have? I defended her our senior year because someone had learned something about her that could have hurt her very much. Ten, twelve years ago, people weren't as tolerant as they are today, and Diana already had a tough enough time dealing with her home life, her parents. Jen, there never was anything between Diana and me because there never could be anything between us. All the makeup, the tight clothing, the bombshell blonde act that she puts on is really just that, an act. Diana isn't, uh, *inclined* toward the male gender."

"You mean she's—"

Jack nodded. "And that idiot, Pritchett Junior, thought he had found out about it—he had found out by stealing her diary, where she wrote all the things she could never say out loud. You know how her mother is, how she was after Diana's father left. Pritchett was going to tell everyone about what he'd read at the senior prom, to get back at Diana for kicking him a swift one in the balls when he tried to pull her behind the bleachers. Diana would have been an outcast, every bit as much as your Rachael Hathaway was all those years ago. For being misunderstood. So I defended her. I had to. She was suicidal. I got the diary back—I won't go into how—and I told everyone she and I had been together. I swore to her that I wouldn't tell anyone the truth. Not even you." He looked into her eyes. "I had no idea at the time that you were already pregnant with Sam. I know I hurt you, Jen. It was the first of many times I hurt you. And I want you to know that I will never ever hurt you again."

He took her hands, covering them with his own. "I love you, Jenna Wren. I have always loved you. I don't know where things stand with you and this Cavanaugh, but after last night, I have to believe there is still a chance for us. To be *us*. Again. Come back to me, Jen."

For several moments, Jenna just stared at Jack. She was trying to take in all he'd just told her, struggling to realize the misconceptions she had made about him. Those times when she had chastised him for being late, thinking he was just irresponsible, immature . . . and even her belief that there had been something between him and Diana DeNunzio. All of it was wrong. And as she looked at Jack now, she wondered what else she might have been mistaken about.

Above all else, a man must have honor. . . .

Jenna remembered that night she and Hallie had been complaining to one another about men, when they'd played at creating a recipe for the Perfect Man.

Jack had had that last "ingredient" all along. He had honor. Jenna had just been so determined never to forget what had happened in the past, that she'd never allowed herself to see anything else.

She'd been so unfair to him. Yet here he stood, asking her to give him her heart once again. To give him another chance.

Dare she risk it?

Sometimes you just have to take that leap, and trust that things will work out.

With Flora's words echoing through her thoughts, Jenna looked into Jack's eyes.

And she leapt.

Chapter Eleven

By the time Jenna returned home from Jack's cottage that morning, the kids had both gone off to their friends', Sam to Timmy's and Cassie out to see Annie at Thar Muir.

Jenna stood in a kitchen that was empty and bathed in autumn light, with only the ticking of the wall clock to measure off each moment. It was too quiet when they were away, she thought. The house felt almost hollow without all the noise and chaos of their getting ready in the morning, the stomping of feet down the stairs, the brother-sister bickering. Jenna had begun her day to it for so long that it had become her every morning song. Without that song, her day just didn't seem right.

Still, in a way Jenna was relieved the kids had already gone, if only for one reason. She couldn't help but wonder that they would take one look at her and would know.

Would know that she and Jack were together, and because of that would hope, too.

It was no mystery that Sam and Cassie both clung to the dream that their parents would find a way back to one another. In fact, it had been Cassie's wish over her last birthday cake, seven candles

of a child's most heartfelt dream. And Sam . . .
well, Sam idolized his father. He brooded every
time Jack had to leave after their weekends together. It was for this reason Jenna and Jack had
both agreed that they wouldn't rush back into a
reconciliation. They would take it slow, keeping to
their separate routines for the time being, seeing
each other when they could, so not to confuse Sam
and Cassie, or risk their tender feelings. They
needed to make sure that they did things right
this time.

Surprisingly, it had been Jack's suggestion.

"We hurried into things the first time," he'd said
to Jenna. "Circumstances . . . youth . . . impending
parenthood. Our choices were made for us. This
time, I want you to be sure."

Being with Jack again after having spent the past
four years telling herself—*convincing* herself—that
she didn't need him, or *anyone* for that matter, had
been a bit like swearing off an indulgence—like
molten chocolate lava cake—and then in a moment
of weakness, giving in to it.

Twice.

But the question Jenna had niggling at her now
when her head had cleared and reason had returned was whether molten chocolate lava cake was
truly good for her . . .

 . . . or whether she'd step on the scale of conse-
quences, and come to regret it.

The night before, while she'd been caught up in
the intensity of the raging storm, the boundlessness
and secrecy of the night, it had all felt so . . .
breathtaking.

She had let down her defenses, just once had let
herself go wherever destiny would take her.

It had felt so good.

Jenna had been wounded after the town meeting by the sudden and unjustified turning away of people she had known all her life. She had been left feeling vulnerable. Being with Jack had made her feel wanted again. Even needed. And the fire she'd seen burning in his eyes, along with the touch of his hands, had made her remember what it was to be desired.

It had been so long since she'd known that feeling.

Even that morning when Jack had brought her breakfast in bed and then had loved her again, slowly, tenderly, and with the sunlight pouring down on them through the windows, Jenna had felt cherished. But even more so than that, she had been accepted for who she truly was.

Jack was the one man who knew her. The one man she'd ever let get *that* close. But he was also the one who had caused her to lock that part of herself away, hiding the key from anyone else who might happen to come to her heart's door.

Could she open herself to him again?

As soon as Jenna had reached the center of town and saw the playground with kids playing on the swings and jungle gyms, the magic of the night had started to dim. Her priorities—Sam and Cassie— came rushing to the forefront like the tide roaring in to shore, washing away the moonlight under the echo of the mantra she had sworn to for the past four years.

I am a mother first.
I am their mother before all else.

From the day—no, the moment—she had brought Cassie home from the hospital, three weeks and four days after she'd fallen in that pond, Jenna had pledged the rest of her life to her children. If she had learned one thing it was that marriages faltered, coming to an end with a constancy that was almost blinding.

But she was the most important person those two little people had in the world. She was their protector.

She was their *mother*.

She had vowed she would never put herself, or them, in a place where danger might sneak in and taint them again because she was too distracted, too caught up in a conflict of emotions with someone else.

It was a lesson Jenna had learned the hard way, very nearly at the expense of her daughter's life.

Jenna dropped her purse, setting her keys on their hook above the counter. The car had started immediately that morning, of course, when Jack took her to check on it. But he'd still made her promise she'd have it looked at when she returned to town.

True to her word, Jenna grabbed the "Things To Do" notepad and wrote under #1:

Call Mac @ the garage

She noticed three messages blinking on the machine and pushed the button to listen to them. Betty Petwith's soft voice murmured first from the PhoneMate.

"Jenna, dear. It's Betty Petwith here. Will you please give me a call at your earliest convenience? 978-480 . . ."

Jenna scribbled the number and the initials *B.P.* on line #2 of her notepad, then hit ERASE to queue the next message.

She doodled a daisy as a deep voice spoke to her from the machine.

"Jenna, it's Declan. Been"—he paused, breathed softly—"thinking about you. Give me a call."

Jenna stared at the blinking red 2 on the machine.

Declan.

He would have to be faced. She would have to talk to him. But not today. After the night with Jack, Jenna realized now that the giddiness she had been feeling whenever she was with Declan was purely in response to his open appreciation and profuse flattery toward her. He was interesting, and yes, handsome and charming, too. But there was something missing, she realized now. A spirit. A soul.

She didn't feel anything like the connection she had always felt with Jack.

Jenna pushed the ERASE button again.

The last message clicked on.

"Jen. Hey. It's Becca. I wanted to let you know you had, um, two more cancellations for tomorrow morning. But, hey, looks like you're free till after noon. So . . . sleep in for once. Watch some tv. Paint your toenails red, too. I'll open up for the morning. All right? Talk to you later . . ."

Jenna punched the ERASE button a third time, frowning.

She was just boiling water for tea when she heard a familiar scratching at the back door. She opened it, and Ogre came scampering inside.

"Good morning, monster," she said as he made himself at home, sniffing his wet little nose at the bowl she kept waiting for him by the stove. He looked at her, onyx marble eyes shining in expectation. She tossed a piece of cheese to him as Eudora followed him in.

"Good morning, Mother." Jenna smiled. "Tea?"

Eudora stopped, studied her daughter closely. After what seemed an interminable amount of time, she said, "Well, it's about time. I was beginning to worry that my daughter was going to spend the rest of her life living as a nun."

Jenna hated that her mother always knew. She also knew better than to try to deny it. When she was twelve and Brian O'Connell had kissed her under the very teeter-totter she'd watched the children playing on that morning, Eudora had taken one look at her and had known. "You had your first kiss today," she'd said. And then she had told Jenna if he tried it again to punch him in the nose.

Brian had—and so Jenna had, leaving the oldest O'Connell son with a nosebleed that earned Jenna a trip to Principal Edwards' office for a stern lecture on ladylike behavior.

Even now, all these years later, Brian still sometimes looked at her funny.

"Mother, I do not want to be standing here talking to you about my sex life."

Eudora cocked her ample hip. "Well, then what do you want to talk about? The weather?"

Jenna completely missed her jest. Instead, she frowned. "No. The salon. Mother, I'm scared."

Eudora sobered. "Of what, dear?"

"That this business with the island and the town and now Rachael Hathaway is going to be the ruin of everything I've worked for. All these cancellations. I don't want to lose the salon, Mother. I can't."

"And so you won't."

Eudora covered Jenna's hands with her own. "Come on with me and we'll just make sure of it."

She led the way out the back door.

They went through the garden to Eudora's kitchen where the jars of herbs and colored powders stood like soldiers at attention, waiting and ready on her shelves. Together, they cast spells both to protect IpSnips from failure and to bring it renewed fortune. They burned an incense of frankincense to smudge the salon of all negative energies, and then they fashioned an autumn wreath made with balsam and clove and bayberry to hang on the door. Mother and daughter crafted together, strewing herbs, burning green candles that they'd anointed in almond oil, and then swept the salon with a "broom" made of juniper branches to dispel any residual pesky cobwebs. To conclude their work, they used an infusion of yellow dock to wash the doorknobs, a sure thing to attract new customers.

Afterward, Eudora gave Jenna an amulet she'd made for her that combined rosemary for luck and basil for success.

"There," she said as she fastened the satin cord that held it around Jenna's neck. It settled gently against her breastbone. "That should do it. Now may your phone begin ringing off the hook with new appointments."

As we will it, they recited together, *so mote it be. . . .*

Jenna smiled. She felt better, and gave her mother a tight hug. "Thanks, Mother. Once again, I don't know what I'd do without you."

"You needn't worry, dear. Just remember that no matter where you are, I am always there for you."

Neither of them were surprised when the phone started ringing a moment later.

"Jenna, dear, it's Betty Petwith."

"Betty, hi. I got your message. I—"

"I'm sorry to bother you so early, but"—Betty paused—"I think you'd better come."

"Come where? What's the matter?"

Betty sighed. "Lou Pritchett and the Board of Selectmen have retained the services of a lawyer, a big name from Boston." Her voice broke. "Oh, Jenna, they've already filed a petition with the Land Court to request that the title for Hathaway Island be registered under ownership of the town. Their argument is that since there is no confirmed heir to Rachael Hathaway, the land has been legally abandoned and therefore should revert to the town, who were the prior custodians of the island before it was deeded to her. They say unless you can prove you're really descended from Rachael Hathaway, they mean to go through with the sale of the island. I've already called James Dugan. He's asked us to come down to his office as soon as possible. I know it's terribly inconvenient, but do you think you could . . . perhaps, come meet with us?"

Jenna was shown into Dugan's office less than an hour later.

Betty Petwith was already there and she and the lawyer were paging through a volume of very old-looking documents that was spread out across a conference table. A box of doughnuts stood alongside, with a thermal coffee pot and cups. There were photographs and survey maps of Hathaway Island displayed on an easel in the corner.

"Jenna." Dugan motioned for her to sit. "Thanks for coming so quickly."

James Dugan had been a lawyer in Ipswich-by-the-Sea for as long as anyone could remember. The son of a cod fisherman, he had been born and raised in the village, and had broken a four generation tradition by pursuing the law instead of the sea. Rather than join an established firm in Boston, his ambition had always been to set up his own practice right in his hometown, which he'd done immediately upon passing the bar and taking his Attorney's Oath.

Where he had once been a high school quarterback, as strapping and sunny-haired as his Irish ancestors, he now had thinning hair and a nose that was perpetually reddened from his nightly dram of Irish whisky. Closing in on his mid-fifties, he had acquired a paunch from a weakness for Maria Capone's muffins, and looked more like a middle school geography teacher than an agent of the law. Still, there was a calm but able air about him that somehow, immediately put one at ease.

Despite his younger good looks, Dugan had, oddly, never married. As she took her seat, Jenna recalled what her mother had told her, how he'd cornered Eudora that long ago day against the kitchen sink. It made Jenna wonder how long he'd been carrying a torch for her. His next question made Jenna suspect it had been for quite some time.

"I'm sorry your mother couldn't come with you."

Jenna shook her head. "I wasn't certain how long this meeting would take, so she's going to stay home, in case she needs to meet the kids from school."

"She is well?"

Jenna smiled. "Yes. She asked me to give you her regards."

He nodded, hiding his disappointment at not seeing Eudora behind the business at hand. He eased back with a weighty creak in his office chair.

"So Betty told you what Lou Pritchett and the selectmen mean to do?"

"Yes, and I don't quite understand it. How can they petition the Land Court and simply demand that ownership of the island be given over to the town? Particularly since their intent is to then sell it for profit?"

Dugan steepled his hands on his sweater-vested girth. "Well, they can't. It was an aggressive move to be sure, meant merely to set the tone for this conflict of affairs. In other words, they wanted to see if it would scare away anyone who thought to stop them. Well, I certainly mean to do whatever I can to fight them regardless of this showboating. In order to do that, however, I am going to need your help, Jenna. Because our ability to prevent this action hinges solely on your claim of inheritance to Rachael Hathaway, I am going to need proof that you are, indeed, descended from her, as you say."

Jenna looked at him. "Unfortunately, Mr. Dugan, I have no proof. Other than the word of my mother, my grandmother, and my great-grandmother, and so on before them."

At that, Dugan frowned. "Okay . . . maybe it would be better if you told me why it is you believe you are descended from Rachael Hathaway in the first place."

Jenna accepted the cup of coffee Betty offered her, added a splash of half-and-half, and then settled in. She began telling them both the story of Rachael's rescue from her island prison and her subsequent common law marriage to Hiram Hutchinson. She left out the bit about the enchanted wren, to keep things as uncomplicated as possible.

"My next question, and I preface this by saying

I only ask it because I am certain it will be the first point presented by the opposing side whenever this comes to a hearing . . ." Dugan looked at her. "If you are indeed descended from Rachael Hathaway, why did you wait until just now, when there is a valuable piece of property at stake, to reveal it? It will, I'm sure, appear to some people to be . . . well . . . opportunistic."

Until he'd said it, Jenna hadn't considered the possibility that someone might think she was claiming her birthright out of personal gain. The idea had never even occurred to her. She had stood up at that meeting out of desperation, to protect something that should be preserved, not exploited. Jenna chose her next words carefully. "Mr. Dugan, you grew up in this town. And from the time you were a child, I'm sure you were told the stories of Rachael Hathaway."

He nodded. "The Ipswitch."

Jenna had always hated that particular moniker. "Tell me how you'd feel if your great-great-something-grandmother was held up to be the local boogeyman, the town curse. My first realization of how reviled she is even today was back when I was about five years old when a pod of pilot whales beached themselves out at Siren's Cove."

Dugan nodded. "I remember that day. My father's boat was one of those used to try to save them. It was right after a fierce nor'easter, the largest and most tragic stranding of whales in recent Massachusetts marine history. There were over a hundred of them. We worked for days to try to save them, but the whales would just keep coming back in, getting caught up on the sand ledge that runs between Hathaway Island, the islets, and the mainland. We could hear the sound of the poor things keening all the way into town. It was such a miserable sound. They couldn't save a one of them. Bodies were washing up for weeks afterward."

"Yes, well, perhaps you don't recall as I do what, or rather *who*, was purported to have been the cause of that horrible stranding?"

Dugan looked at her, his guilty expression revealing that he himself had been one such accuser. "The Ipswitch . . ."

"Would you be so willing to have all your school friends believing your relative had been responsible for killing so many innocent creatures?"

"No. I don't suppose I would."

"I even had to stand there after my own daughter nearly drowned and listen to my neighbors *tsk* and shake their heads, blaming the ghost of Rachael Hathaway for Cassie's fall into that retention pond. It has been the same every generation before me. We've just learned over the course of the past three hundred years that it's better to keep some skeletons locked securely in the family closet."

Dugan took a long moment to digest Jenna's story. "Well, while I understand your silence, this presents me with something of a dilemma. Call it legend, fairy tale, or ghost story—whichever you prefer. Even the fact that there is no official documentation for any marriage between Hiram Hutchinson and Rachael Hathaway isn't so much an issue, because you're not claiming anything through the Hutchinson line. My problem is that there is nothing documenting that they had any child, legitimate or otherwise. A birth should have, at the very least, been recorded with the church."

"But they couldn't," Jenna protested. "If they had, then the people of the town would have questioned who the mother was. Rachael's escape from the island would have been discovered and she probably would have been hanged. It's the very reason they could never legally marry. In their hearts and in their souls, they were as married as if a cleric or a judge had declared it."

Dugan agreed. "Even if they weren't married, it wouldn't matter because the documentation deeding the island to Rachael specifies that her heir is anyone *of her blood*. What we need to prove is that either you, or Eudora, or better yet both of you, share that blood. Now, along that line of thinking, Betty tells me that there is a grave up at Thar Muir."

"It's where Rachael was buried by Hiram after she died."

"This is the one that Flora's children uncovered this past summer?"

Jenna nodded. "However, it was no surprise to me when they found it. My family and I have been going to that grave all of my life."

"Forgive me for a lack of delicacy here, Jenna, but there is the possibility of an exhumation—"

"No." Jenna shook her head against the suggestion. "The poor woman was tormented enough in life by the people of this town. I will not be party to disturbing her eternal rest, too. No island is worth that."

Dugan frowned. "You realize that without something to bring before the court as proof, this situation becomes little more than our word against theirs. I've no idea which way the court will rule."

Jenna looked at him. "Well, then I guess it's the best we can hope for."

"Perhaps not," Betty suddenly spoke up. And then she shook her head. "Fiddlesticks, I can't believe I didn't think of this sooner." She looked at

Jenna. "We have something that might prove evidentiary enough and it wouldn't require that we disturb Rachael's gravesite at all. You remember in June when they were renovating the boathouse up at Thar Muir?"

"Of course. I helped Flora with the layout and the design."

"Right. Well, Jimmy O'Connell did the renovation, as you know, and when he was working the teardown, he discovered a small box of sorts that had been sealed up inside one of the walls."

"Yes," Jenna said. "It contained personal items that belonged to Rachael, some clothing, journals she'd written. But how can that help us? Because it will lend support to the theory that she lived there at Thar Muir with Hiram?"

Betty nodded. "Not only that, dear. We have her handwriting in the journals, which we can compare to other documents that Rachael signed that are in the town archives, in order to authenticate that they were indeed her belongings. And we have something more. There was a lock of hair in that box as well."

Dugan sat up in his chair with renewed energy. "Where is that box now, Betty?"

"It has been locked in the storage vault at the Historical Society since it was found. I've been planning a display at the museum, and with Flora's permission, I put it there for safekeeping."

Jenna looked at them both. "So what are you suggesting? Some sort of DNA test on the hair?"

"Precisely," Dugan agreed. "Mitochondrial DNA, to be exact. I'm something of a closet genealogist and I attended a seminar on this very topic. Mitochondrial DNA comes solely from our mothers, who inherit it from their mothers, who inherit it from theirs, and so on back through time. There is little change in it generation to generation, unlike nuclear DNA, which changes by fifty percent each generation. And, it is so plentiful in cells that traces of it can be found in human remains many thousands of years old. Or"—he centered his gaze on Jenna—"in something as simple as a three-hundred-year-old hair clipping."

"So all we have to do is test the hair sample against my DNA and there can be no doubt as to my connection to Rachael Hathaway?"

"Not exactly. Without actual documentation as to where that hair sample came from, it's still something of a long shot. In other words, the opposing side could say we got the hair from anywhere. However, I do think with testimony from Jimmy O'Connell about discovering the box, and Flora and Betty and anyone else who witnessed it, along with the items that were found inside, we might just have a chance at convincing the Land Court that the island is legally your property. All provided, of course, that the DNA test comes back a match," he concluded.

Jenna looked at him. "Well, then, I guess there's only one way to find out. Just tell me what I need to do."

Jenna awoke to Jack's mouth on hers.

It was late—or perhaps it was very early—and she had gone to bed hours before. Now the moon was high, shimmering its full light through her bedroom window in shades of soft blue and pale gray. She could see Jack's silvery outline against the moonlight as he climbed into her bed.

All at once, his hands seemed to be everywhere.

"Jack," she whispered as his mouth claimed hers

again. She pulled back. "I thought we said we were going to take it slow."

Jack grinned at her, kissing her throat. "Oh, I intend to take it slow." He released the top button on her nightshirt, pressed his lips to where the fabric parted. "Very slow."

He kissed her again and Jenna let the kiss take her, losing herself to his taste and touch, to the moonlight and stars that were their blanket. He slid off her nightshirt and every stroke of his hands against her skin left her shivering, though not from any cold.

It was a shiver of pure exhilaration.

Jack worshiped her with his mouth and his fingers, tracing soft patterns along her neck and nibbling sensations along the curve of her hip until she was trembling with anticipation. He knew just how to caress her, how to make her body sing, and he played her softly, gently, stroking her deeply, relentlessly until she was lost and pulsing around him.

Jenna reached for Jack, welcoming the weight of him over her as he touched her deeply inside, drawing her up into his arms.

And then he carried her up to the heavens.

Afterward, as they lay together with her back spooned against his chest, he rubbed his hands lazily over her shoulder and kissed her neck softly.

"I missed you," he sighed, breathing in the scents of her hair, her neck.

Jenna smiled. "It's only been a handful of hours since I left yesterday morning."

"No. I missed you, Jen. Every day of the past four years has felt like a lifetime."

Jenna turned to face Jack, placing her fingers against his mouth.

"Shh."

She looked at him, blinking in the moonlight. "No more thinking back. No more regretting. No more looking at yesterdays, Jack. I've been doing that for too long. From this moment, right now, there is only today . . .

. . . and the promise of tomorrow."

Dr. O'Leary had taken a cheek swab sample from Jenna, Eudora, and Hallie, too, just so there could be no question once the results came in comparing their genetic makeup to the hair sample found in the box hidden at Thar Muir. It would take up to two weeks to receive the results. Until then, Jenna could only sit and wait.

Word, however, had a way of getting around in a small town.

One night the next week, Jenna was lying in bed, unable to rein in her chaotic thoughts enough to allow herself to fall asleep.

She couldn't rid herself of the feeling that something just wasn't right.

Pulling her robe around her, she went down to the kitchen to brew a cup of chamomile and lavender tea, in hopes that it would help to soothe her. But as she wrapped her hands around the steaming mug, sipping quietly, she found herself wandering through the silent, shadowed house.

Inevitably that wandering led her into the salon.

Jenna was troubled. It had been a week since the town meeting, nearly that long since she and Eudora had cast their protective spells, and in that time—just seven days—the business she had spent the past three years building had nearly ground to a halt.

She thought of Rachael Hathaway, all those generations ago. While they might not be able to banish Jenna to an island, they could certainly destroy her livelihood. It was just another form of exile.

Was it worth it? She sat in the dark with the moonlight flooding the empty row of chairs, glimmering on the faucets and shining on the pristine porcelain sinks. Was the claim to that island—Rachael's prison—worth losing everything she'd worked so hard for?

Before she could begin to answer that question, that something that had kept her from falling asleep, the something that she felt just wasn't right, came sailing through the salon's front window.

Jenna didn't immediately move. She just stood for a moment, staring at the paper-wrapped missile while the last shards clinging to the window frame gave up and dropped to the floor, only to splinter into oblivion.

Surely, she was dreaming.

She was still standing there, staring at the brick, when Jack's father, Tino, came rushing in. He had the spare key he knew she kept under the mat for the kids in his hand. He flipped on the lights, illuminating the whole of the salon.

"Jenna, I was outside looking for the cat when I heard the glass breaking. I knocked on your kitchen door, but no answer. I was worried for you. So I came in. What happened? Are you all right?"

His question died in his throat when he noticed the brick lying on the floor. He looked at Jenna, who still stood frozen to the same spot. It was as if she feared should she move, she would wake and find it wasn't a nightmare after all.

Tino's wife, Rosa, clad in her housecoat and nightcap of hair rollers, arrived a few minutes later.

"I couldn't find Tino. I saw all the lights on . . ."

It wasn't until her former mother-in-law stood before her, her concern shimmering in her eyes— the same warm hazel eyes as Jack's—that Jenna realized she was shaking.

"Bella" was all the older woman had to say, and she took Jenna into her arms to quell her trembling.

Tino crossed the room and retrieved the brick from where it lay, ominous as a bloodstain, on the floor.

"Disgraziato me!" he exclaimed after he had removed the paper that was wrapped around it and read what was printed on it.

Jenna lifted her head from the soft comfort of Rosa's orange-blossom perfumed shoulder. She blinked, and realized she was crying. "What does it say?"

Tino looked at her. "Jenna, maybe you call the police first, eh?"

"Papa, what does it say?"

He handed the typewritten paper to her, shaking his graying head.

If you know what's good for you,
you'll forget about that island.

Jenna felt a chill, jagged as a razor, cut through her. "Who? Who would do this?"

"Idiots, that's who." Tino grabbed the note from where Jenna had dropped it on the floor. "They are stupid, is all. *Un pazzo imbecile!"*

"They . . ." Jenna said. "Papa, do you know who would have done this?"

He frowned. "I only know that I hear things when people are waiting for their pizzas. And Sal, he hears things at the café, too. I know that some people in this town, they think they know how things should be run. They think they have power because they have money. They threaten others, tell them to tell their wives to stay away from your place. Hurt your business. Like mafiosi, these men. But this . . ." He palmed the brick. "This is more than stupidity. This is dishonor to threaten a woman in such a way. You call the police, and you call them now, bella."

But Jenna didn't have to. Blue lights were already flashing down the street.

Officer Faraday came to the door, stopping at the threshold to assess the crime scene with the eyes of a true investigator. "Ms. Wren, we received a report from one of your neighbors of glass breaking. Are you all right?"

Jenna nodded, wiped her eyes as she summoned up the fortitude she would need to confront the situation. "Yes, Officer. Just unnerved. As you can see, someone has vandalized my salon and . . ."

She looked at the destruction around her, felt her composure begin to slip.

Jenna closed her eyes.

"Was anyone hurt?"

"No, I'm fine and the kids—"

The kids.

If someone would do something like this, who was to say they wouldn't take it a step further and try to harm Sam and Cassie?

Jenna turned without another word and ran for the stairs.

Dear God, please let them be in their beds . . .

They were, and they were completely unaware of the threat that had been visited upon them while they'd slept.

"Mommy?"

Cassie blinked against the glare of the hall light as she lifted her head from her pillow.

Jenna went to her, sitting on the edge of her bed. "Cassie, honey, there's been . . . a bit of a problem in the salon. I need you and Sam to go over to Nanny Wren's for the rest of the night, okay? Tell her I'll be over to explain just as soon as I can."

Cassie looked toward her window where the flickering of the blue police light shone through her lacy curtain. "What happened, Mommy? Why are the police here?"

"I'll tell you about it later, okay? I have to get back downstairs. Please now, go with Sam. And tell Nanny not to worry, okay?"

Jenna squeezed Rosa's hand in gratitude when the older woman appeared, and took over the task of ushering the kids to Eudora's.

She was answering questions for Faraday's report when Jack arrived some time later.

"Jen, Sofia called me. I got here as fast as I could. Are you, the kids, is everyone all right?"

As soon as she saw him, it was as if the hold Jenna had been forced to maintain on her emotions was passed immediately over to Jack. She could even feel the weight of it leaving her shoulders, freeing her to contend with the anger, the icy outrage, that had followed the initial shock of the assault.

"Who the hell did this?" Jack asked no one in particular. He looked around at the broken glass until he saw the note the brick had been wrapped in sitting on the reception desk. "Never mind. I have a pretty good idea who."

Before Jen could respond, Officer Faraday spoke up.

"You have a suspicion of who might have done this, Mr. Gabriele?"

"My first guess would be either Lou or Blair Pritchett. Take your pick. Although something this gutless . . . has more the flavor of Blair than Lou."

Faraday cleared his throat, glancing at Jenna. "I'll, uh, certainly look into the possibility, Ms. Wren, although, I'm sure you're aware I can't just go off making accusations without some sort of evidence. . . ."

"Of course."

Jack took up the brick. "Bricks are used to build houses, aren't they, officer? Especially big colonial boxes with the same chimney design on every cookie-cutter blueprint." He left it at that, handed the brick to Faraday. "There are roughly eighty or so brick manufacturers in the United States today. Perhaps one of them can tell you if this one is theirs, and who, locally, might be one of their clients."

"I'll look into it," Faraday said. "In the meantime, I would suggest that no one"—he looked at Jack, then repeated—"*no one* go seeking retribution. Leave the meting out of justice to those who have the legal authority to do so. I would also suggest, Ms. Wren, that you spend the rest of the night somewhere else. At your mother's, or maybe the Gabrieles' next door. Just in case whoever did this decides to pay another call."

Tino, who was still there, standing, Jenna suddenly realized, in a pair of red striped pajamas, agreed. "Of course, bella. You come home with me. Mama and I will—"

But Jenna squared her gaze on Faraday. "I'm not leaving."

"Ms. Wren . . ."

"Jen . . ." Jack joined in.

Jenna stood her ground. "This is my home. I have worked damn hard for it and for my business. Too hard to just abandon it because someone is trying to put a scare into me. Whoever did this . . . Getting me to leave is exactly what they want. Well, they should have realized a long time ago, the women in my family don't scare that easily. I'm staying right here."

Jack just stared at her. He already knew how stubborn Jenna could be when she set her mind to something. He conceded. "But I'm staying here with you."

"Fine."

Jenna turned then, took up the broom from the supply closet and began sweeping up the pieces of broken glass.

When she was finished, and when Officer Faraday and Tino had finally gone, Jenna waited while Jack nailed a piece of plywood over the broken window. It had been a long time since she had felt this sort of despair, and this came at a time when she should be filled with such bliss.

Jenna felt very tired. It seemed as if she had been working for so long, staunchly following the path she had mapped out, fighting to prove herself, to prove *to* herself that she could do it all. But suddenly, now, she didn't want to be strong, independent, resilient. She didn't want to be alone.

When Jack came up to her, drew her against him and held her, she let him. And when he slid his arm beneath her knees and lifted her up, she dropped her head against his shoulder and closed her eyes. He carried her up to her bed, laying her gently on the featherbed, and she felt him cover her with the comforting sea-salted wool of her grandmother's afghan. As she closed her eyes, Jenna saw Jack lower into the chair by her window, the one that faced onto the street.

Where he could watch.

For the first time in a long time, Jenna turned off that ever watchful part of her that never quite seemed to relax.

That night, Jenna Wren let someone else watch over her.

Chapter Twelve

When Jenna awoke the next morning, it was to the sound of her children's laughter.

First there was Cassie's high-pitched squeal. Then came Sam's subdued chuckle, rich and warm. The music of them both in harmony together rushed over her like a playful sea breeze, leaving her tingling with goose bumps.

And then another sound.

A yip.

More laughter.

A yip again.

Ogre.

Cassie now, giggling solo, the kind of deep belly laugh that made Jenna's mother's heart swell.

Jenna smiled, remembering how, just days earlier, the house had been too quiet. She loved hearing the sounds she'd been blessed with.

Jenna sat up, stretched, glanced toward the clock. Ten o'clock? She blinked. She hadn't slept till ten since . . .

She couldn't remember when she'd last slept so late.

Sliding her feet into her well-worn slippers,

Jenna shuffled out of her bedroom, and headed for the stairs.

The laughter beckoned from the kitchen like a siren's song.

"Do it again! Do it again!"

Cassie's enthusiasm even seemed to bring the sun out from behind the morning clouds, splashing it in brilliant abandon through the windows. Jenna stopped at the front door, grabbed the log of a Sunday newspaper, and then turned for the kitchen. She hesitated just outside the doorway.

There was Jack standing at the stove, wearing her red and white checkered apron over a rumpled T-shirt and jeans. His hair was mussed from having spent the night in that chair by her bedroom window. He had a griddle pan with one of his "incredible" pancakes browning inside, and he was tossing it in the air, only to catch it behind his back with a waiting plate that he held in his free hand.

Cassie was beside him in her nightgown and bare feet, her own hair a tangled nest from sleep. She was clapping her hands and laughing while Ogre danced on hind legs beside her, hoping he might grab anything that Jack dropped. Sam was sitting at the table. His pajama-bottomed legs were propped on a nearby chair and he was leaning back with a smile on his face that Jenna hadn't seen in what seemed like forever.

All the turmoil of the night before with the salon, that dreadful threatening note, seemed to vanish like the clearing of a fog as Jenna stood and watched her family.

Her family.

Just standing there, thinking the words to herself made her feel warm all the way to her toes.

"Mommy!"

Cassie had caught sight of her mother. Her out-burst jarred Jack's concentration and the pancake he was about to catch landed with a slap on the floor.

Cassie gasped, covering her mouth with her hands.

Sam laughed, applauding the effort, and almost toppled over backward in his chair.

Ogre pounced before anyone might try to re-trieve the pancake. It was almost as big as his whole head.

Jack looked over at Jenna and just smiled.

"Good morning."

"Morning yourself," she said and set the paper on the table with a thud. Sam immediately launched forward for the comics while Cassie bus-ied herself with pouring a steady dripping stream of syrup in a perfectly round corkscrew pattern on her pancake.

Before Jenna could grab a cup for herself, Jack had coffee and a small carton of half-and-half wait-ing before her.

"Thanks."

"Pancakes?" he asked. And then he shrugged. "Sorry, they're about all I can do. Eggs are just too much of a challenge, unless of course you like them scrambled. No matter how they start out, mine all end up that way anyway."

"Anything is fine," she said, and sipped the cof-fee. "You really didn't have to go to the trouble and . . . oh! Mmm . . ." She closed her eyes and savored the wake-up shot the coffee gave her. "There's no way this is from my coffeemaker," she said when she tasted Sal's familiar, fantastic brew.

"*Zio* stopped by to check on you a little while ago. Brought a couple of to-go espressos along with him. Just gave it a quick nuke in the microwave to rewarm it."

Minutes later, Jack set a plate in front of her with a huge, heavenly-scented pancake. "Hope you don't mind, but I snatched the last few blackberries from your garden."

Jenna smiled as she took a bite. "Delicious . . ."

Jack replied, untying the apron from around his waist, "Okay, well, I guess I'm off."

Sam and Cassie chorused a groan.

"Why so soon, Daddy?" the little girl asked. "It's still just morning."

Jenna was also disappointed to see him go though she hid it behind the cover of her coffee cup.

"I'll be back," he told the kids. Then he looked at Jenna. "I, uh, called in a favor to a friend who owns an architectural salvage yard north of Nashua. He's not usually open today but he said he'll let me come in to see if I can find an old window to replace the broken panes in the salon."

"That's all the way in New Hampshire, Jack. Please don't trouble yourself. I could just call in for a repair . . ."

"Jen, we both know you don't just put twenty-first century commercial glass in a seventeenth-century window frame. I know people who know how to find things that seem impossible to find. So how about you let me help. Okay?"

Jenna looked at him, then conceded. "Thanks, Jack. Just make sure you tell me what it costs so I can reimburse you."

"Can we come, too, Daddy?" Cassie asked. "We can help you look!"

Sam echoed the request, although he cleverly

made sure not to mention that Sunday was his day to clean his bedroom.

Jack looked at Jenna. "That's up to your mom, guys."

"Sure you can go," she said, knowing they would never forgive her if she refused. "But dress in old jeans and sweatshirts and don't forget your jackets. It's sunny, but it's also October out there."

The kids ran off to change and grab their sneakers.

"What are you going to do today then?" Jack asked as he stood at the sink and started to wash the breakfast dishes.

Jenna joined him to dry.

"Oh, I don't know. Maybe I'll read a book, or clean out the pantry, or something . . ."

Jack went to hand her a cup, but grabbed her hand instead. "I have a better idea. Come with us. It'll be messy work, digging through piles of old doors and stuff, but it's the perfect time of year for a drive up north. The trees are incredible right now and I know the best back roads. We could even bring a picnic, if you'd like. I know a great place where the kids can run and climb and hang from trees. What do you say?"

Jenna looked at him. She couldn't think of a single reason why she should refuse.

They invited Eudora, who only cried off. She was already at work in her kitchen, where she intended to spend the day over iron pots filled with peculiar and mysterious mixtures. She did suggest they take Ogre, though, to give the beast some freedom to run and stretch his legs with the kids.

As they bid her farewell, closing the kitchen door behind them, Jack glanced at Jenna. "Is she . . . ?"

"We call it casting," Jenna replied. She watched Jack, wondering how he'd react.

But he just grinned. Raising a brow, he said, "Hmm, you know, the Bruins lost again the other night and dropped to one and seven. Wonder if I should ask her about a Stanley Cup spell now, or wait till after the All-Star break . . ."

Jenna punched him playfully on the arm.

They couldn't have asked for a more perfect day. Although mid- to late-October was typically the close of the fall foliage season in New England, this year they'd had a warm, wet, and particularly long summer, which only served to stretch the season closer to Halloween.

The leaves with their concert of colors were simply breath-stealing, Mother Nature's own fireworks display. As Jenna peered out the window of Jack's monster of a truck, the rolling mountains looked as if Monet himself had come through, stippling in the fiery reds, shocking yellows, and bright brilliant oranges across the landscape.

They were in no rush and simply let the spirit of the day direct their route, turning off whenever the mood struck, or wherever another splash of incredible color beckoned. White-steepled churches peeked from the trees while century-old covered bridges drew them over meandering rivers. On they went, passing through a succession of sleepy New England villages with names like Happy Valley, Box Corner, and Chase Village. They savored every new sight, stopping at the roadside to feed horses through a fence line while Jenna purchased a bushel of tart McIntoshes to take home to Eudora from the farmer's stand.

They reached the salvage yard around one and

spent the next couple of hours scavenging and ex-
claiming over the treasures they uncovered. Jack
and Jenna dusted off panes of wavy and bubbled
glass set in ramshackle window frames, searching
for just the right ones to replace those broken the
night before. All around them lay long forgotten
pieces of former lives. There were doors still hung
in their original casings, just waiting to welcome
visitors home once again. Whole paneled walls,
fireplace mantels, even a complete spiral staircase,
all of them orphaned by demolition and progress.

As they searched, Jack would stop every so often
to point out certain pieces to Jenna, sharing with
her his appreciation, his *passion,* for the craft-
manship of generations past.

"Look at this, Jen," he said, running his hands
over an eighteenth-century stair newel. It was
carved in an elaborate corkscrew design with a leaf
motif trailing around it in a vine. "This is mahog-
any. Probably cut from the Indies. You don't find
anything like this at Home Depot."

Jack explained to her why old wood, even wood
that looked as if it had come from some dirty,
abandoned barn was actually more stable than the
new and "green" lumber that filled the aisles at
every DIY superstore.

"The lumber being cut today comes from trees
that are young in comparison to the timber used
two, three hundred years ago. The trees of our
forefathers had been growing wild in Native
America for centuries. With every passing century,
they grew even stronger and more dense. The
woods used for most lumber today are 'farmed'
woods. The wood is soft. It's moist and has to cure,
dry out. But they build with it anyway because they
have to. Progress can't be stopped, after all. In

doing so, the beams will move as they begin to dry out, turning in the tree's natural growth pattern. This causes spaces in walls and gaps in floors. Brian and I, we want to build homes using the strength still inherent in these old beams to make stronger homes that will last through yet another lifetime."

He turned the newel that he still held, showing her the wear pattern on its top. "Just think of the generations of kids who must have turned at the bottom of their stairs clutching this newel post. Brides who were carried past it by grooms. Grandmothers and grandfathers who clutched it for support. Their lives are a part of this piece of wood, recorded in every notch and scratch."

Just listening to him talk, Jenna could hear the enthusiasm brightening his voice. It was the same excitement she'd felt when she'd been renovating her house, how she'd celebrated each unexpected clue of those who had lived there before her, painstakingly researching every detail to make sure she did things right. During their marriage, Jack and Jenna had had their own separate interests and it had been one of the things she believed had led to their eventual divorce. All this time, she'd thought she and Jack had nothing other than the kids to hold in common. She'd had no idea he felt as deeply about history and preserving tradition as she did.

As the day moved on into afternoon, they left the salvage yard and headed back to Massachusetts, following a different but no less meandering route. A short while after crossing over the border, Jack pulled off at a secluded spot, well away from the main road. The sun was filtering down through the trees and they picnicked on a carpet of fallen leaves, sharing the cold fried chicken and cheddar wedges Jenna had packed for their late lunch, along with the apples they'd bought.

It was so peaceful there, so idyllic, it almost seemed a world unto itself. Thick trees surrounded the small clearing, echoing with the music of the songbirds that flitted overhead. A brook rambled nearby and while the kids went off to explore with Ogre, turning over rocks in search of whatever creepy crawlies they could find, Jenna sat on the blanket, leaning on her elbow, and tilted her face to the waning daylight. She took a deep breath, filling her lungs with the mingling scents of earth and nature and brisk autumn that surrounded them.

"I love this place," she said, eyes closed while a breeze teased a strand of hair across her cheek. "It's so away from it all. No roar from a multilane highway. No superstores. It is just tucked away here, safe in the hands of timelessness. How did you ever find it?"

Jack had poured them each a glass of wine from the bottle of cranberry merlot they'd picked up at a local winery along the way. It was surprisingly good, the perfect country complement to the relaxing afternoon.

"Oh, I guess you could say I just happened upon it one day."

Jenna smiled, shading her eyes. "Couldn't you just imagine an old farmhouse nestled right there, in that clearing among the trees?"

"With a porch swing for lazy summer nights . . ." Jack looked at her. "Yes, I could imagine it, Jen. Exactly where you said. Which is why I bought it."

Jenna sat up. "Bought it . . ." She looked at him. "Bought what? You mean this? Here? This place?"

He nodded. "All twelve acres of it, with my father's help. It's where I intend to build the house, from the plans you saw at the cottage."

"Do you mean you'd leave Ipswich-by-the-Sea?"

Jack shook his head. "I could never really leave it. Believe it or not, we're only thirty-five minutes away here."

He moved beside her then. "Jen, I know I said we should move slowly, but this past week, and especially after today . . ." He looked into her eyes. "We've lost so much. Four years, and even longer before that when I was blinded to what I had—to what *we* had together. The kids. Us. I don't want to miss another birthday, another holiday, another *any* day when we could spend it together like this. That house I designed, and this land. I went after it all for you. Every detail, every decision, they were all made because of you. Because of the hope of you."

Jenna felt her breath catch. Her eyes swelled with tears. "Oh, God . . . Jack . . ."

"I know you thought I wasn't listening all those years, but I was. It just seemed as if I wasn't because I couldn't stand hearing your dreams, your deepest wishes, believing I could never give them to you. I thought I couldn't because somewhere, somehow, I lost the belief in us. Remember how you used to dream of riding again, like you did with your father when you were little? We can build a barn with stables right there." He pointed across the way. "And all of this borders on conservation land so you need never worry about some housing development or strip mall coming in to ruin your view. There can be miles and miles of riding trails. You can teach Cassie to ride, too. And that tree, right there . . ." He motioned to a huge, ancient-looking oak. "That is where Sam and I can build a tree house together.

"Jen, I've been working for this ever since the day I came home to find you'd gone. I even drove to Vermont last week just to find you the perfect bathtub like you always wanted. All of it is, and has been, for you." He brushed her tears away. "I want to be there for you, Jen. I want to be with you through this thing with the town, and through whatever else comes our way. Tell me you're not lonely. Tell me you don't lie awake at night wishing things had been different. Wishing you could live it all over again. God knows I do. Well, we can live it all over again, Jen. You—me—neither of one of us has to feel alone anymore. All you have to do is say yes."

Jenna remembered how deeply she'd wished to hear something, anything like those same words years earlier, back when they'd still been married, when things had just begun feeling as if they weren't right between them.

Back when there had still been a chance for them.

But when she hadn't heard them and things had had no other direction to go but apart, she'd tried to convince herself she'd been wrong about Jack, that for whatever reason, they had never been meant for each other.

She'd tried to wipe away the love she'd had for him, steeling herself against it when in truth it had hurt so very badly to leave him. She knew now that if she hadn't truly loved him, it never would have hurt. She never would have cared as deeply as she did. But some things just couldn't be washed away by the tides of time. Some things clung no matter what tried to pull them away, like the starfish who defied the sea's pull come hurricane or peaceful waters.

And because of this, Jenna knew there was only one answer she could give Jack as he sat there, watching her, waiting for her to speak it.

Jenna looked into his eyes and whispered it to him, soft as the autumn breeze.

One single word.

"Yes."

Rather than making any significant announcement to family and friends, Jenna and Jack decided it would be better to ease their two lives back into one, quietly and discreetly. He packed some of his clothes and moved them into Jenna's place, where he could be with her and the kids, especially at night should any further threat come to call. He would continue to work at the cottage, and she at the salon. A wedding, they'd decided, would certainly come, but unlike the first one, they would wait for a time that was appropriate for them. They would celebrate with a small ceremony, without all the pomp and formality of the first one.

Since the salon was typically closed on Mondays Jack spent the day replacing the broken window panes with the ones they found at the salvage yard. Jenna sat down with Hallie to formulate a plan.

A battle plan to save her business.

First they worked out the details for the "Spa Weekend" with Thar Muir. Jenna wanted to come up with something truly different—offering those special little extras that would make the service unique. She wanted it to be something that would have customers returning, recommending it to their friends and families time and again. After brainstorming together, they came up with just the thing.

At Thar Muir, a box of chocolates and a bottle of fine champagne would await their guests' Friday night arrival. A gourmet dinner at an exclusive restaurant in the village would be followed by a jazz concert on the common in summer, or piano music performed by a certain award-winning composer by a cozy fire at Thar Muir in winter.

On Saturday their guests would wake to Flora's delicious Scottish breakfast and then head off to the salon to enjoy such delights as an herbal facial, body massage, lavender and lemon grass salt scrub, manicure, pedicure, and relaxing aromatherapy. Tea (or espresso) at the café would follow with Maria Capone's delicious *zupas* and *tramezzini* for lunch and then time for shopping in town. Afternoon yoga would be offered for those inclined, a twilight walk on the beach at Thar Muir in summer, or a relaxing evening by the fire with local wine selections and a light supper. After a parting breakfast of scones and tea Sunday morning, guests would be given a dozen roses and a care package of lotions, candles, and herbal tea to remember their special weekend by.

The package, Jenna and Hallie decided, could also be customized for couples seeking a romantic retreat, girlfriends wanting a weekend getaway, or even a very different, very refreshing alternative to the traditional bachelorette celebration. Flora was thrilled. When they finished, Hallie left to spend the rest of her day putting together an advertisement for posting on both the salon and B-and-B Web sites, as well as for print in select publications.

It was nearly two o'clock when Jenna realized

the time. The kids would be coming home from school in less than an hour, so she decided to take a stroll down Main Street to meet them when the bell rang at two forty-five. She waved to Tino and Rosa from the pizza shop window and stopped to fill Sal in on the café details for the Spa package. She took a detour into the bookshop and asked Mrs. Evanson to set aside the latest Lemony Snicket release for Cassie's birthday, then dropped in to the market for a few essentials before heading for the school.

The routine, the normalcy of each stop she made along the way, helped Jenna feel as if perhaps— just perhaps—things were taking a turn back to where they should be. After all, hadn't Mary Whittendon even managed to smile when she rang up Jenna's purchases at the market?

Jenna, however, couldn't have been more mistaken.

The bell rang out across the schoolyard and Jenna stood back against the fence, watching for Sam and Cassie to emerge. Sam came out first, laughing and horsing around with his friends Timmy Spencer and Billy Chufford. Sam wanted to walk home with Timmy and stay for a while to do battle over PlayStation, but Jenna told him not until after he finished his homework.

They waited, debating the "worth" of having to do homework as the schoolyard slowly and methodically thinned out. When there were just a handful of children left loitering about, Jenna worried why Cassie hadn't yet come out.

"Did you see her?" Jenna asked Sam as she scanned the faces of those still standing around. "Maybe she didn't see us and we missed her while we were talking."

Sam just shrugged.

"Okay, you run on home and see if she's there. Call me on my cell. I'll go inside and see if something else is up."

Jenna waited until Sam had disappeared down the sidewalk then entered the school. She made her way down the central corridor that was papered in class art projects—abstract finger paintings, drippy watercolors, and various other macaroni-pasted-onto-construction-paper masterpieces.

As her footsteps echoed down the empty hall, she was taken back to her own school days. The same classrooms. The same homemade artwork. The same smells of cafeteria lunchroom, gymnasium, and Magic Marker. She stopped when she reached the second grade classroom and peered inside.

Cassie's teacher, Mrs. Ogilvy, was cleaning off the whiteboard. Jenna knocked on the open door to get her attention.

"Ms. Wren . . ." The twenty-something blonde looked puzzled to see her. "Did we"—she glanced at her desk calendar—"have an appointment?"

"No. Actually I was looking for Cassie. I didn't see her come out after the bell rang to dismiss school."

"I don't quite understand," the teacher said, glancing at the clock and looking suddenly concerned. "Cassie went home early today. Just before lunch."

"She did? But I've been home all day. And she didn't . . ."

Jenna and Jack had both been working in the salon. They wouldn't have known if Cassie had come home unless she'd come to tell them.

Jenna turned. "Thank you, Mrs. Ogilvy. I'll check at home."

"Ms. Wren?"

Jenna paused.

"I was going to call you anyway. Cassie's been having some difficulty lately, it seems."

"With her school work? But Cassie's always gotten excellent marks."

Mrs. Ogilvy shook her head. "It's more to do with some of the other students. You know how girls can be."

Yes . . . especially when they grow up to be women, Jenna thought, recalling Patsy Lansky and the other mothers the week before.

"When Cassie told me she felt sick today, I sort of sensed it was more to do with that than illness. It's why I let her go home, but she was supposed to stop in at the office first to have them call you. I should have checked later but Cassie is always so good, so well behaved. I just assumed she'd go right to the office like I told her."

Jenna nodded grimly. "Thank you, Mrs. Ogilvy."

As she retraced her steps down the corridor to leave, Jenna's cell phone began ringing. She flipped it open. Sam's voice spoke from the other end.

"Mom? Cassie's here. At home. She's in her room. The door's locked and she won't open it."

"I'm on my way."

Shoving the latch lock with a clang to release the exit door, Jenna ran from the school and down the street.

At the house, Jack and Sam were standing outside Cassie's bedroom, trying to talk to her through the door. Jenna moved in front of them, knocking softly.

"Cassie, honey. It's Mommy. Mrs. Ogilvy tells me you weren't feeling well today. I wish you would have told me you came home so I could have made you some tea or something."

No response.

"Will you please open the door so we can talk?" She knocked again. "Please, Cass. You're scaring Mommy now."

Jenna waited for a response. She heard the sound of small footsteps, then the click of the door latch.

Jenna turned the handle slowly.

The lilac-colored walls glowed softly in the waning daylight. Across the room, Cassie was curled upon the bed with her back to the door, in her favorite "comfort" position, a tight ball, clutching her soft blanket before her. Ever since she was a little girl, she would always lay like that when she was either very scared or very troubled.

Jenna waved Jack and Sam off, then moved across the room. She sat on the edge of the bed, smoothing Cassie's brown hair from her eyes. It was then Jenna noticed Cassie still had on her tattered sneakers and her jacket even though she'd been home for hours.

"Hey, Cassie Bear," she said softly. "What's going on today?"

Cassie sniffed, squeezed her arms more tightly around her blanket. "Nuthin'."

"Mrs. Ogilvy tells me you came home early today. Why didn't you come and tell me?"

"Dunno. Just wanted to be alone, I guess."

"Okay," Jenna said. She lay down beside her daughter, tucked Cassie's head beneath her chin, then kissed her gently above her ear. "Want to tell me what's bothering you?"

"I just don't feel so good."

Jenna reached for her forehead. "You don't feel like you've got a fever. What hurts? Your tummy?"

Cassie shook her head.

"Your head?"

She shook her head again, then mumbled into her blanket. "They hate me."

"What? Who, baby? Who hates you?"

At that, the dam broke. Cassie erupted in a flood of tears.

"Everyone! My friends at school. They all hate me! They make fun of me. They call me 'the Witch Girl' and they say that we're greedy because we want to take that island for ourselves. They say that I'm going to grow up ugly with a wart on my nose because great-grandmama Rachael was a witch. And, oh, Mommy, *no one* is coming to my birthday party either!"

Jenna pulled Cassie into her arms and just let her cry it out. It was all she could do. But with each sob that rocked her daughter's small body, a mother's outrage filled her. She simply breathed— in and out—trying to calm her anger, to show the strength, the fortitude that Cassie would need.

After a while, Cassie's sobs quieted. Jenna gently stroked her hair. "I'm so sorry, Cassie. Sometimes, people—some people—are just afraid. They are afraid of anything or anyone who might be a little different. You're special. I've always told you that. And now that other people know it, they are scared of it. You remember when I first told you about your great-grandmama Rachael?"

She felt Cassie nod against her neck.

"Well, she was special, too. And the people back in her time were so scared of her, they tried to lock her away on Hathaway Island. They wanted to leave her there to die. But you know what? Not everyone felt that way. Someone came to save her."

"Great-grandpapa Hiram?"

"Yes. So you see, not everyone is scared. Just

the silly people are. And no matter what, nobody hates you. It just feels that way because you're hurt right now. I'm sure your friend Annie doesn't feel that way."

"No." Cassie turned to face her mother. She sniffed loudly. "Annie told Kaleigh Lansky that she better watch out, or I'd turn her into a fat toad. But I don't know how to turn anyone into a toad, Mommy. You won't teach me how."

Jenna shook her head. "Because that's not what our magic is about, Cassie. We don't use it to try to harm others. We never have, even when people were terrible to us. And if we ever did, then that would be proving what all the silly people believe, now wouldn't it? And that would only give them a real reason to be scared. I know it's hard, but you just continue being the beautiful little girl you are, and things will work out. You'll see. And if the other girls don't want to come to your party, well then they're going to be the sorry ones. They are going to miss out on the best birthday party this town has ever seen."

At that, Cassie blinked. "Really? What is it?"

"It's going to be a surprise, pumpkin."

That was all Jenna had to say. Cassie absolutely loved surprises. She tightened her arms around her mother's neck and squeezed as hard as she ever had.

"Thank you, Mommy. I knew you'd know how to make it better."

Jenna smiled at her daughter. At least she'd been able to talk her through this particular catastrophe.

Now, if only she knew what in the world that *surprise* might be.

Chapter Thirteen

Jenna sat at the reception desk watching the clock tick off the seconds—

thirty-eight . . . thirty-nine . . . forty . . .

—while she waited for the minute hand to "officially" reach the twelve.

It was nearly five o'clock. Three minutes till to be exact, but even though she hadn't had a client since eleven o'clock that morning, she'd promised herself that she would keep the salon open the full business day, just so she would know in her heart that she had.

She watched the second hand move on to the next rotation. Started counting again.

One . . . two . . .

The bell above the salon door tinged.

Jenna looked up.

And blinked.

"Diana . . ."

The large-breasted blonde stepped into the salon, but kept her hand on the doorknob, as if trying to gauge whether she would be welcome.

"Hi. I know it's late, but I, uh, thought I'd stop in anyway. I wondered if I could schedule an appointment for your next available opening?"

At another time, Jenna might have thought

Diana was purposely taunting her for the downturn in her business. But there was something so patently vulnerable about her, even with all that overdone blond hair and the impermeable cosmetics. After what Jack had confided in her that day at the cottage, Jenna had begun to see a different side of the woman known so unkindly throughout the town as "Double D."

All this time, Jenna and everyone else for that matter, had believed Diana to be just a brainless, overripe pair of breasts who flaunted herself for male attention. But knowing what she knew now, Jenna could see the facade for exactly what it was.

Veneer.

Armor.

Protection.

And Jenna certainly knew firsthand what it felt like to be afraid to show your true self to the world.

She smiled. "Actually, I can take you right now, if you've got the time."

"Oh." Diana took a second or two to wrangle with the offer. Perhaps she'd worked up the courage to come in for scheduling the appointment all the while never intending to see it through. But, as if sensing some unspoken connection between them, she nodded and said, "Thanks. That would be great."

Jenna took Diana's coat and hung it on one of the hooks by the door, then led her through the salon, past the stylists' chairs and the row of sinks to the client lounge at the back.

"Wow, this place is great," Diana said as Jenna put on the kettle to boil for tea.

She knelt to stoke the fire that had nearly burned out in the hearth, adding a couple of fresh logs. "Thanks."

"I've been meaning to drop by for some time, but . . ." Diana looked at Jenna, neglecting to finish the sentence even though they both knew she had avoided the salon because of the interlude Jenna had always believed had taken place between Diana and Jack.

Jenna simply said, "I'm glad you finally found the time."

The fire was burning well now, so Jenna turned, showing Diana to a cushy armchair while she went to the adjacent counter to fix them both a cup of tea. "There's some style magazines on the table there, if you feel like taking a look."

"Oh, okay. Great."

As she searched the shelf above the small stove that was lined with glass jars of various herbs, Jenna felt herself returning to the very thing that had induced her to open the salon in the first place.

Using her magic to help people feel good about themselves.

She took down bachelor's buttons first. The herb would serve a dual purpose, first to help release Diana from the oppression and pain of her childhood but also to energize the magic of the spell Jenna intended to cast about her. Sweet laurel would help ease the conflict Jack had indicated Diana battled with, the guilt over her mother's depression, the remorse of her parents' bitter divorce, and the role they both played in her denying her true sexuality. Tetterwort would help her in letting go. Borage would bolster her courage (there was a reason Roman soldiers had drunk borage wine before going off into battle). And finally chamomile, for the comfort and peace she'd been denied so long.

Jenna spooned the herbal mixture into a tea

strainer, then poured the steaming water through the leaves, allowing it to steep for several minutes in the small teapot before pouring.

While they sipped the tea, Jenna guided Diana through some of her own favorite style books while asking her specific questions about what she did or didn't prefer. Jenna listened carefully to what Diana said, and more importantly, to what she didn't say, too. Just as she'd suspected, the images Diana seemed most drawn to were in direct contrast to the extreme look she had adopted for so long.

It was nearly forty minutes later when Jenna finally led Diana over to her chair.

"So, do you have any thoughts about what you'd like for your hair?"

Diana looked at herself in the mirror's reflection. "Well, to be honest, when I first came in, I was just going to ask you for a quick trim, maybe a color if you had time. But now . . ."

Her voice thickened and Jenna noticed the sheen of tears in her eyes.

Diana was clearly struggling.

Jenna kept it casual. "You're not so sure anymore?"

Diana shook her head. "I just know I want a change. I *need* a change."

Jenna knew she was talking about more—much more—than just her hair.

"Okay. I think I have an idea of what you might like. But I'm going to have to ask that you trust me. Do you think you can do that?"

Diana thought a moment, then nodded. "Yes. Yes, I do." She blinked back the tears as if relieved that Jenna had stepped in to make the decision for her. "Jenna? Thanks."

"Of course."

Jenna went to work. First she washed Diana's overprocessed hair with a shampoo of nettle, jojoba, and nasturtium, working it through carefully so not to cause any further breakage. She followed it up with a rich watercress conditioning treatment that would help soften her hair and restore some of its lost flexibility.

Any number of other salons would have just slathered on whatever harsh cleanser or coloring treatment they had, but Jenna had listened to what Diana had said, the small, subtle comments murmured almost unconsciously. And because of it, she had something else in mind.

Now she needed to meet the *real* Diana DeNunzio.

Wrapping her conditioned hair in a warm towel, Jenna began first by cleansing away the layers of heavy makeup using one of her exfoliating almond and oatmeal soaps. The skin underneath showed signs of fatigue, as it would from having to hold all that powder and pore-clogging foundation every day. But Diana was young, which meant there was still time to show her the error of her ways.

As she worked, the two women continued to talk. Jenna noticed that Diana purposely avoided the subject of Jack, instead keeping to commonplace discussion like the weather, recent movies, the escalating price of gasoline.

Next, Jenna mixed a clay-based mask containing lavender and rosemary to help soothe the skin and remove any last trace of impurities. Jenna smoothed the mask on gently, then covered Diana's eyes with a soft towel that she'd soaked in an infusion of chamomile and eyebright. It would help reduce the puffiness and lighten the dark circles that Diana usually covered with heavy concealer.

While her face absorbed the benefits of Jenna's attention, Jenna worked a lotion of almond and comfrey into Diana's hands, more as a means for relaxing her than anything else. Twenty minutes later, she washed the mask away to reveal skin that was much brighter and softer, and now that it was revealed, a face that was naturally striking.

Jenna had had no idea how beautiful Diana truly was.

After rinsing the conditioning treatment from her hair, Jenna led Diana back to the chair. There she set to work with her shears, taming the typically teased tresses into a softer, much less vivacious style. She'd only intended to shorten the length by a couple of inches, removing some of the dead weight, but Diana insisted on a more radical change. And in truth, with all the processing it had endured, a good deal of Diana's hair was beyond repair.

So Jenna cut, and then cut some more, each time checking with Diana, inch by inch, until finally what remained barely brushed her nape.

Jenna kept the length a little longer in back but layered it to add depth and softness around Diana's face. Other than her admittedly large breasts, Diana's most striking feature was her eyes, so Jenna wanted to draw attention up to them, and away from that which swelled beneath her neck. She took advantage of the hair's natural curl, fluffing it into soft waves while lifting it away from her forehead with a sweeping side part.

From what Jenna could remember, Diana's natural color was more a rich caramel, much better suited to her turquoise eyes than the platinum near-white she'd armored herself with. When she finished with the cut, Jenna led Diana back to the sinks for a second round of rinses.

"Okay, this may seem odd, but rather than recoloring your hair and risking more damage, I'm going to apply an herbal paste that will help subdue that leftover tint."

As Jenna mixed and then started pouring the sludgish-looking mixture over her hair, Diana recognized the smell.

"Is that . . . coffee?"

Jenna nodded. "Along with some black tea, sage, walnut, and even clove. It's not going to drastically change the color, but I'll give you a container to take home with you. If you continue to use it, eventually it will help get your hair closer to its natural color and continue to improve its overall health as well."

Jenna worked the paste through with gloved hands so that her fingers wouldn't end up looking as if she'd been digging through the garden all day.

Sometime later, she rinsed the molasses-like glop away.

"There. Every time you treat it, the color will darken a little more, while the herbs will help keep your hair soft and moisturized. That's the key. Now we'll use a cold air dryer and bring out the new and improved you."

Jenna blew Diana's hair into a style of graceful waves that softened her face and really showed off her eyes to advantage. Afterward, she showed Diana how to apply just a few slight cosmetic touches, a light dusting of subtle shadow and then kohl liner on her eyes and a sheer sweep of lip color.

"That's all," Jenna said. "It's perfect."

"But what about—"

"No foundation," Jenna scolded her. "Honestly, Diana, you don't need it. You've got naturally great skin. Just let it breathe and keep it moisturized and Mother Nature will do the rest."

She finished with a yarrow styling spritz before finally turning Diana to face her new reflection in the mirror.

"What do you think?"

For the first few moments, Diana didn't speak. She just stared at the face that was staring back at her as if she were looking into the eyes of a stranger.

"I . . . I don't know how I can possibly ever thank you. It's miraculous. It's unbelievable. It's—"

"It's you," Jenna said, smiling. "I just took the time to uncover the real you. That's all."

Jenna pulled something out of her smock pocket and handed it to Diana. "Whenever you feel your confidence start to slip, just wear this." It was a small silver pomander pendant that she'd filled with rosemary and primrose, before enchanting it with an empowerment spell. "This will guard you against frailty of spirit and self-doubt."

Diana looked at Jenna as if seeing her for the very first time. "You're . . . different than I thought. I was mistaken about you. I'm sorry for that."

Jenna smiled. "That makes two of us."

By the time they were finished, night had fallen. Still feeling the "high" of accomplishment for her efforts, Jenna found herself reluctant to part with her "new" old friend. Somehow they had found a kinship in the knowledge that both of them had spent most of their lives hiding a certain aspect of herself from the rest of the world.

"Feel up to sharing a pizza and some wine? Sammy's spending the night at Timmy's, Cassie's at my mother's, and Jack had to drive up to Maine on business. I'm pretty much on my own tonight."

Diana smiled, and agreed.

By the time Hallie arrived home from work about an hour later, Jenna and Diana had scarfed down all but two slices of the pizza and were just opening their second bottle of wine.

"Hey!" Hallie dropped her purse on the kitchen counter. "Who said you could start the party without m—"

She froze when she recognized the newcomer. "Is that you, Double—I mean, Diana? Oh my God . . . it is you!"

Diana, relaxed from the wine and Jenna's company, simply beamed.

"What did you—? I mean, God! It's just incredible!"

"Well, quit standing there gawking like an idiot and join us," Jenna said and poured Hallie a glass. She slid a plate with the last two slices of pizza in front of her. "Here, you need to catch up with us. I'm calling over to Tino's for another pie. . . . What'll it be this time, ladies?"

Jenna delighted in coming up with new and seemingly incompatible combinations of toppings. It drove her former father-in-law *fuori di testa*— out of his mind. She laughed. "How about strawberry and ricotta?"

When Jenna failed to pick the pizza up, Jack's sister, Sofia, brought the pie the three doors over from the pizzeria. And then, at the urging of the others, she agreed to join the impromptu get-together.

Sofia Gabriele was a sociable, slightly tomboyish

signorina who spent most of her time in the shadow of her oftentimes overbearing Italian parents. They told her how to dress, what to eat, and kept a close watch on her by insisting she work at the pizzeria until the day she would take on her expected role as wife (preferably to an Italian) and mother (hopefully to many *bambini*). She had her father's natural dark hair (although Tino's had gone to gray) and typically kept it clipped back in a serviceable ponytail.

Jenna had been itching for years to get her hands on Jack's little sister, to transform her in much the same way she'd transformed Diana, but had never had the opportunity. Since the divorce, there had been a sort of unspoken but implied barrier between the two, a distant cordiality that prevented anything more intimate.

So Jenna was glad for the addition of Sofia's company that evening.

The four women spent the next couple hours talking, drinking, laughing, drinking more, and eating. The faster the wine flowed, the more deeply personal the conversation turned. Eventually nothing seemed to be out of bounds: menstrual periods, losing their virginity, even the confession by Sofia that she'd once, on a dare, thrown a pair of her panties on the stage at a Bon Jovi concert.

"And it got stuck on one of those knobby-looking thingies on his guitar," she said. "There were my Victoria Secrets, dangling from the handle like a purple flag of surrender while he played on. . . ."

As they chorused a raucous laugh about men and their instruments, Diana suddenly grew serious.

"I have something I need to say," she said. She toyed with the stem of her wineglass.

The other three silenced, and waited.

"I'm . . . gay."

Diana immediately covered her mouth as if she couldn't believe she'd spoken the words she'd yearned to say for so long out loud.

For a moment, no one spoke. Hallie glanced at Jenna, who merely sat. She didn't reveal that she already knew.

And then Hallie, bless her heart, merely picked up the wine bottle and refilled Diana's empty glass.

"God, I thought you were going to tell us you had polio or something!"

Leave it to Hallie to put things into the proper perspective.

"Here's to the new and definitely improved Diana DeNunzio!" she said, raising her glass in a toast of congratulations.

"Hear, hear," the other two echoed, and all four women clinked their glasses in a celebration of female unity.

Bolstered by Diana's show of courage, Jenna felt herself wishing she could lay her own soul bare. She looked at Diana, her new friend.

"How did it feel," she asked quietly, "letting that out?"

Diana smiled. "As if a fifty-pound weight was lifted off my shoulders." She glanced down at her burgeoning bosom then. "Or, as I would imagine a much needed breast reduction surgery would feel, too!"

The other two laughed along with Diana.

Jenna, however, remained thoughtful.

Should she?

Shouldn't she?

Finally, she just said it.

"I'm a witch."

Hallie went wide eyed, then added, "So am I. . . . We're both witches."

Jenna looked to Diana and Sofia and couldn't help but grin. "Damn, but you're right, Diana. It felt good to finally say that. *I . . . am . . . a . . . witch.* There, I said it again. Come on, Hallie. You, too. *We . . . are . . . witches.*"

After a barrage of questions that lasted nearly a half hour, stretching from how the sisters had gotten involved in their craft to the not unexpected comparisons to Sandra Bullock and Nicole Kidman in *Practical Magic,* Diana smiled, raising her glass in a second toast. "Well, here's to refusing to hide anymore."

They joined each other in a sip of wine over another "Hear, hear!"

And then all three women turned to Sofia, awaiting her revelation, thinking it only fair. "Well, I don't think even my panties getting stuck on Jon Bon Jovi's guitar come close to topping either one of those," she said.

But Hallie wasn't about to let her off that easily. "Come on, Sofia Gabriele. You have to have some other secret, some dream or wish that you've never told anyone, ever. Now, spill it!"

"Fine." She hesitated, blinking her huge dark eyes, then blurted out, "I hate pizza."

The other three women burst out laughing.

"No . . . I wasn't joking. I'm serious. I don't want to spend the rest of my life working in a pizzeria or, worse, getting married and living above a pizzeria with babies clinging to my skirts all day."

She glanced at Jenna then, suddenly worrying she'd said too much. "Sorry."

Jenna grinned. "You know I keep telling Sammy he's going to have to let go of my skirts and soon,

at least by his wedding day, but he just won't." She
threw up her hands. "What's a mother to do?"

Sofia giggled.

"What do you want to do, Sofia?" Hallie asked,
turning the subject back to her.

"You won't laugh?"

"Sofia," Hallie said. "In case you weren't paying
attention, a lesbian and two witches just came out
of the closet." She looked at Jenna and asked,
"You know, I've always wondered . . . do witches
come out of the *broom* closet?" Then, without
missing a beat, she went back to Sofia. "I'm sure
whatever your secret is, it isn't going to be *that*
shocking."

Sofia gave a small smile. "I want to race cars.
Professionally."

Jenna looked at her, pleasantly surprised. "Then
do it."

Sofia breathed out heavily. "How? You know my
family. Papa would be so upset if I didn't stay at
the shop, and Mama, she's already despairing that
I haven't found a husband yet. After all, I'm
twenty-five years old and—"

"And yada yada yada," Hallie interrupted. "You
know what? I'll bet you can write a laundry list of
reasons that will serve to convince you why you
can't do it. Now, how about giving us just one reason why you *can*?"

Sofia shook her head. "I . . . I don't know."

"Fine," Diana said. "Then I will. *Because you
can.*"

Sofia thought about it, furrowing her brow as she
took a bolstering swallow from her wineglass. Then
she smiled and said, "You know what? You're
right. I can. And I'm going to. Mama will have a

fit, but she just doesn't understand that every Italian girl doesn't share the dream of getting married and having copious numbers of Italian babies."

"Mama Rosa will just have to get over it," Jenna said. "Besides, once she finds out your brother and I are planning to get married again—"

"*What!?*"

Jenna put her hand over her mouth. "Oops. Did I say that out loud?"

The other three women shrieked. Within four seconds, maybe five, they had surrounded Jenna, and were giving her a clumsy, drunken, hysterical group hug.

And at that very moment, Jack opened the kitchen door.

Before he could even say "Boo" they were on him. He was inundated by a trio of squealing, slightly inebriated females. Well, probably *completely* inebriated. It took him a full minute to figure out that they weren't dying or that the world hadn't somehow slipped off its axis, but that they were actually celebrating.

For him and Jenna.

But he soon found out that Jenna's inadvertent declaration about their reconciliation wasn't the most shocking admission of the night.

"You want to what?" he asked when Sofia revealed her secret dream.

"I want to race cars, Jack. I've always wanted to. You might have thought I hung all those pictures of Max Papis and Jarno Trulli on my walls because they were Italian and hot—and they are—but that wasn't the reason why. I wanted to *be* Jarno Trulli. I just didn't think a middle-class Italian girl from some forgotten Massachusetts town could be."

Jack smiled at his little sister, pinching her chin. "And why not? You're a Gabriele, aren't you? And Gabrieles can do anything."

It was past midnight when the girls decided they should probably call it a night and head off for bed. Jenna offered to have Diana stay in one of the kids' rooms, until Mama Rosa (in her housecoat and curlers) came looking for Sofia. She dragged both Sofia and Diana back over to the pizzeria, but not without first *tsk*ing at Jenna and Hallie for letting them drink too much. Jack offered to see Hallie over to Eudora's while Jenna rinsed the dishes and wineglasses, tossing the empty bottles in the trash.

When Jack returned, the lights in the kitchen were out. In fact all the lights were out except for the beckoning glow of candles that Jen had lit, starting in the hall, up the stairs, and leading to the bedroom. As he reached the stairs, he could smell the scented candles and could hear the soft sounds of Norah Jones slinking from the Bose on Jenna's bedside table.

When he got to the doorway, Jack froze. His pulse surely jumped a full beat. There was Jenna sitting on the bedcover, stretched out like an artist's model, waiting.

Waiting for him.

She wore nothing, nothing at all, except a sleepy, seductive smile.

Jack felt his throat tighten and found himself struggling to swallow the lump that had formed there.

"I guess I should go to Maine more oft—"

He never finished his sentence.

Jenna slid off the bed and walked straight for him with her body curving, silhouetted in liquid perfection by the flickering candlelight. She stood before him, her breasts just brushing his chest, her blue eyes sparking with a fire as bright as the flames that danced around them.

"I missed you today," she said. Her voice was husky with desire. She slid one hand up his denim-clad thigh, slowly bringing it to rest on his erection. She smiled, an enchantress's smile. "Looks like you might have missed me just a little bit, too."

She raised up on her toes and snaked a manicured hand around his neck, pulling Jack's mouth down to hers. She kissed him hot and wet and sweet as she worked to free the waistband of his jeans, dragging the zipper down while Jack reached to help her, sliding the jeans off.

Then she started on his shirt buttons.

Jack grinned against her mouth. "A little patience, madam."

But Jenna Wren wasn't in a patient mood.

She grabbed the front of his shirt and yanked it open, scattering the buttons across the pumpkin pine floor. Her eagerness only fueled his own sexual appetite, making him hungry for more, setting their kiss on fire with an almost desperate intensity.

Jack couldn't get enough of her, couldn't smell, couldn't taste enough of her.

He wanted her.

He *needed* her.

Now.

When Jack was finally naked and standing before her, the two of them limned by the candlelight, Jenna pushed him back, leading him toward the bed. She lay him on the soft mattress and then slid over him with a delicious and deliberate restraint. She smelled like heaven. Her skin was hot and smooth; her hands and mouth ran all over his body.

And after a failed attempt at participation, Jack simply surrendered and let her have her way with him.

And she did.

Oh, did she.

He'd never seen Jenna so free, so confident of her own sexuality. She loved him with her eyes and her hands and her kiss in complete abandon, until he felt himself begin to lose his hold over his imminent climax.

Jack decided it was time to turn the tide on their lovemaking.

He took Jenna up into his arms and flipped her onto her back. He seized her, kissing her hard and ran his hands over her, caressing, teasing, as he parted her legs.

He drove into her with a single thrust.

Jenna gasped, arched against him, locking her legs around his hips. She tightened her fingers around his arms, digging in, and rocked with him, thrust for thrust, over and again until suddenly, finally, together, they climaxed.

Jack called out her name, emptying himself deeply inside of her. He buried his face against her neck and clutched her pulsing body tightly to his as wave after wave of their orgasm carried them away to a lover's deepest fulfillment.

Later, they lay in the bed, arms and legs wrapped together as they watched the moonbeams through the window.

Jenna stroked her fingers lightly over Jack's hands while Jack pressed his mouth against her neck, kissing her behind her ear.

"I received some good news today," he said.

Eyes closed, Jenna smiled, shivering with the tingle his kiss gave her. "Oh yeah?"

"Yeah. Brian called. That job he was working on . . . it's looking good that we'll get it. It's a substantial one, too. A custom home, minimum seven thousand square feet. The guy must be a millionaire or something. We're meeting him tomorrow."

Jenna turned to face him, taking his face with her hands, her eyes bright. "Oh, Jack. That's wonderful news. I can't wait to see your design. I know it will be just incredible."

Jack drank in her enthusiasm. It was so good to see her smile again. "Don't get too excited. We don't have the job yet."

"But you will. Whoever this millionaire is, he'd be a fool not to hire O'Connell and Gabriele to build his dream house."

Jack grinned at her, touching a finger to her nose.

"Well, maybe you could cast a little get-the-job-done spell for me anyway, just to be sure."

Jack gathered Jenna into his arms and held her. They stayed together the rest of the night, wrapped in one another, heart to beating heart.

Chapter Fourteen

"Is that all, Ms. Wren? *Ms. Wren?*"

Jenna snapped out of her musings and saw that Mary Whittendon had finished ringing up her market purchases.

"Oh, sorry. Guess I was daydreaming." She sighed. "Cassie's birthday is coming up and I'm trying to think of a special party idea." She looked to the cashier, wondering if the elder woman of the perpetual *hmph* might have some insight to offer. "Any ideas?"

Mary just looked at her, giving her standard response—"hmph"—then she glanced at the cash register. "Twenty-seven forty-five."

Jenna simply smiled, remembering the days when she would stand at that same counter and chat with Mary endlessly and pleasantly. She wondered wistfully if those days would ever return as she counted out the cash and paid for her groceries.

As she left the market and started back for the salon, Jenna went back over the list of possibilities she had to consider.

Tino had offered to give Cassie free rein in the pizzeria for an afternoon, where she and her friends could make up their own pizzas, playing with the dough and coming up with their own unique creations. It would have been a fun idea any other time, but with Kaleigh Lansky and the other girls promising not to attend, it held the potential for far too much heartache.

No, it had to be something more intimate, with just their family.

Horseback riding? Perhaps.

A day in Boston walking the Freedom Trail and riding the Swan Boats on Boston Common? It was a possibility. Maybe even an amusement park.

But nothing Jenna came up with provided that special something she had promised Cassie the day she'd come home so upset from school. There just had to be *something*. Jenna felt it in her heart. The only problem was the clock was ticking on the time she had left to prepare and she just hadn't found it yet.

On the subject of time, Jenna glanced at her watch and frowned. Nearly quarter to ten. The market had taken longer than she'd expected. She quickened her pace so not to be late for her ten o'clock appointment. She crossed the street, trying not to jostle the eggs. She certainly didn't want them scrambled before they reached the frying pan. She speed-walked past the bookshop just as Mrs. Evanson was opening for business, called out a "Good Morning" without stopping. She turned the corner onto Elm . . .

. . . and nearly ran head-on into Declan Cavanaugh.

"Oh!"

"Jenna."

Declan leaned an arm against the café wall, blocking her way. "I just stopped by the salon to see you, but they said you'd gone out on an errand."

He was dressed in tailored trousers and a blazer over a fitted black cashmere V-neck, the color and the autumn sun setting off his golden hair. He smiled at her in that California way, easy as a drive down the Pacific Coast Highway.

She returned a tentative smile and adjusted her grocery bags. "Yes, the market. Hi, Declan. How nice to see you again."

"It's been a while. I heard you came by Thar Muir last week. I was sorry you didn't stop by the boathouse."

"Yes, well, I'd actually come to see Flora. We had to discuss some business. It went later than I'd expected and then there was that storm that blew in so suddenly and . . ."

Why did she feel so uncomfortable with him?

At first, she thought it was probably because she knew she needed to tell him she was back with Jack. But then she realized there was something in the way he was staring at her, as if she'd just run into him stark naked. His eyes seemed to consume her and left her feeling *exposed*.

"I left you a message a few days ago. Perhaps you didn't get it. . . ."

She had, but she'd completely forgotten about it. In fact, the truth was, since Jack had moved back in with them, she hadn't given Declan much of a second thought.

"Feel like taking a little walk?" he asked. "I was hoping we could talk."

Jenna glanced at her watch.

9:48.

"I've got an appointment at ten and—"

"Good." He smiled, ignoring her excuses. "It will only take a minute or two."

She had little choice but to go with him. "Sure, Declan. I'd like to talk to you as well."

She allowed him to help her with the groceries, handing him one bag while she carried the other. Together they walked down the sidewalk, crossing Main to stroll along the town common. The grass was still green, though going winter dormant in places, and it was littered with fallen leaves from the oaks that circled the park. Further on, the harbor stretched in a half circle beneath the town, where summer sailors and fishermen alike were now busy preparing their boats for the winter.

They stopped at the whitewashed bandstand, empty now. In summer, the local musical society hosted concerts there on weekend evenings. Parents would stretch out on picnic blankets and lawn chairs, socializing with friends and strangers alike while the kids played ball on the lawn or hunted fireflies. And on the Fourth of July, fireworks would fill the whole of the harbor with dazzling displays of magical lights.

But now the breeze was brisk, rustling the leaves around them, and Jenna was glad for the jeans and heavy fisherman's sweater she'd put on that morning. In another month, maybe two, snow would blanket the common and the huge blue spruce that stood in its center would be lit with a thousand twinkling lights while the kids pulled each other on sleds all around it.

Jenna took a seat on the steps of the bandstand. She tried to think of what to say first.

"Declan—"

"Jenna, I have a proposition for you."

She looked at him, startled, and pushed the

strand of hair that blew across her face from her eyes.

"I have some business coming up. In Venice. I remember you telling me how you'd always dreamed of going there someday. I'd love to be the one to make that dream come true for you."

He might as well have said he wanted to take her to the moon for as unexpected as his offer was.

"Venice?"

Had she been another woman, living another life, she might just have said yes.

But she was Jenna Wren, and she was in love with Jack Gabriele. He and her kids and their family was everything to her.

"I'm afraid that's not going to be possible, Declan."

He looked momentarily confused, as if her refusal had come completely unexpected.

"Is it the kids? I understand if you don't want to leave them. So we'll bring them along. I don't mind."

He didn't *mind* her kids. . . .

Jenna shook her head. "It's not just the kids."

"What then? School? The salon?"

"No, not school or the salon either, although they are both things that should be taken into consideration." She looked at him. "Something else has come up, Declan. Something . . . *unexpected*."

He stared at her and she realized he already knew.

"Jack."

She nodded. "I've been wanting to talk to you about it. Declan, I really enjoyed meeting you, getting to know you these past weeks. And I want you to know that I appreciate the time we had together, but . . ."

He smiled but it was a smile that never quite reached his eyes. "You don't have to explain, Jenna. It's written all over your face. You're still in love with Jack."

She nodded. "We're reconciling."

"Let me ask you this, and I hope you don't think I'm being too personal. What makes you think it will work this time?"

It seemed an innocent question, but there was something—derisive—underlying his words.

It gave Declan an unappealing arrogance.

Jenna felt a sudden urge to put some space between them. She got up from the step, alarmed when he reached out and closed his hand around her arm. She felt a sharp, dangerous tingling that sizzled from where he held her. It coursed throughout her entire arm, not unlike an electrical shock.

She pulled away.

"Declan . . ."

"Okay, fine. Forget Venice. You probably never would have gone anyway. Women like you are more into your kids than having a good time."

Women like you . . .

He was clearly growing agitated about something, something other than Venice.

She was about to find out what that something was.

"I want that island, Jenna."

Island?

"You mean Hathaway Island?" And then she realized it, even before he answered her. "You? You are the one who offered to buy the island from the town?"

Suddenly it all started falling into place. His arrival there. His interest in her. The questions about the town and the island's history.

"Yes, Jenna, I offered to buy the island and I'm

willing to pay handsomely for it. If it ends up being that the town cannot sell it to me because of that ridiculous deed, I'll just buy it from you."

Jenna didn't care for the way he simply *assumed* she would be willing to sell the island to him. "Why do you want it so badly?"

He merely glanced at her. "One man's deserted island is another man's treasure."

Treasure.

"You can't seriously believe that there really is treasure buried out there. I told you people have scoured that island for years. Nothing has ever been found."

"Perhaps. But they don't have my resources—or my determination." And then he shrugged. "If it's found not to exist, then I'll just sell the island to someone else when I'm through with it."

As if it were some disposable, unwanted *thing*.

Jenna crossed her arms. "The island isn't for sale."

Declan simply smiled. "Everybody has a price, Jenna Wren. It's just a matter of finding out what yours is."

"The island," she repeated, "is *not* for sale."

That assured smile faltered. "I'm not a man who takes kindly to being denied, Jenna. You would do well to remember that."

With that, Declan dropped her grocery bag to the pavement and turned, walking away without another word.

Jenna stood for several moments, breathing slowly. She couldn't help but feel as if she'd just come face-to-face with something . . .

Evil.

She tried to shake it off, taking up her grocery bags, hoping the one she'd given him hadn't contained the eggs. She hurried back for home.

When she arrived at the salon, a phone call was waiting.

It was James Dugan.

"Jenna, I just received the results of the DNA test from the lab. I knew you'd want to know."

Jenna held her breath, and waited.

"It's a match."

Jack ducked into Common Grounds, nodding at his uncle from across the counter.

"Hey, *Zio*! *Buon giorno . . . come stá?*"

Sal grinned. "*Bene, grazie.* What can I fix for you, *nipote*?"

"Espresso . . . and how about one of *Zia's* sweet *sfogliatelle,* too?"

Jack dropped into a chair at the farthest table, drumming his fingers on the red and white checkered tabletop.

He was early, but he'd deliberately come a half hour before he and Brian were due to meet with their prospective client. He wanted a coffee to calm his nerves and time to gather his thoughts.

Brian had called Jack early that morning to brief him on a few details, but until they met with the client and heard what he had in mind, there really wasn't much Jack could do to prepare. Brian was the figurehead, the salesman of the partnership. Jack preferred to work in the wings.

He was up at the counter, picking up his espresso and pastry when he heard the café door open behind him.

In a moment, it felt as if all the air in the room had been sucked away by a vacuum. A big, arrogant vacuum wearing a Blair Pritchett Homes ball cap and Tommy Hilfiger jeans.

Blair Pritchett the younger walked around the

town of Ipswich-by-the-Sea as if he owned every blade of grass and stone, a manner he'd adopted after having watched his father carry himself that same way all his life. He had hands that hadn't worked an honest day in his life, a limitless expense account that he loved to flaunt by buying rounds for all the locals at the Pub, and a tan that he'd acquired from spending his days out sailing instead of actually working the job his father had given him solely for the tax deduction.

He got women when he wanted them, not because of his looks, which were a bad combination of his mother's close-set eyes and his father's overlarge chin. He got them because he *bought* them, with high-priced dinners and flashy trinkets, discarding them just as soon as they lost his interest.

He was, in Jack's estimation, a consummate ass, and as he came to the counter, Jack gave him the barest of glances.

"Gabriele."

"Blair Junior."

Jack had always called the heir to the Blair Pritchett empire by that name simply because he knew how much the son of the tyrant detested it. He didn't, however, detest having access to his father's millions.

Outside the café, a sleek silver Hummer H2, a near-match to his father's black tank, took up any view the front window might have offered of the harbor.

Jack went back to his table, less than pleased when Pritchett decided to follow him.

"What do you want?" Jack finally said. He glanced at his watch and frowned. He certainly didn't need this asshole causing a scene minutes before Brian and their client were due to arrive.

"Oh, hey, just wondering . . . how's business at

your wife's salon these days?" And then he laughed, correcting himself. "I mean, your ex-wife's salon . . ."

God, if this wasn't just like back in high school. Back then, Jack would have simply planted his fist into that deserving set of perfectly bleached and straightened teeth, and had done so on more than one occasion. But now, twelve years on, Jack was glad at least one of them had acquired the maturity of adulthood.

Jack stared at the wall behind Pritchett and started counting—*one . . . two . . . three*—anything to keep a lid on his simmering Italian temper.

"I don't see how that's any of your business, Junior, unless of course you've been doing a little after hours brickwork."

Pritchett's smile spread across his overfed mouth.

Jack stood from his chair, then took a step forward until mere inches stood between them. He dropped his voice to a whisper.

"Do something gutless like that again, Pritchett, and I'll wipe that shitty grin right off your inbred face."

Sal Capone, sensing trouble, stepped between the two men. "Unless you want to order something off the menu, Mr. Pritchett, I'll ask you to leave."

Pritchett looked down at the shorter Italian as if he were lowlier than one of their house maids. "I'll go where I damned well—"

The café door opened behind them. A voice, flat with the local New England accent, barked across the café.

"Blai*h* Pritchett, let's go. You've got a job to do. . . ."

Blair Sr. stood at the door, arriving just in time to prevent his hotheaded son from taking that last confrontational step.

Jack just stared at him. "Daddy's calling, Junior."

Pritchett seethed. "We're not through, Gabriele."

"Name the place and time," Jack countered as Pritchett Sr. came forward, taking his son by the arm. "Just be prepared to go running home with your tail between your legs. *Again.*"

The father gave his son a shove. "I said let's go. Now."

Jack stood until they were both gone, rumbling away in twin clouds of Hummer dust.

"Bastard . . ." he muttered under his breath.

"That one. He's *faccia di culo,* Jack," Sal said. "One day, he'll get what he deserves, eh? But not today. It isn't the time."

Jack looked at his uncle, nodded. "You're right, *Zio.* Not today."

Jack refused to let the encounter darken his mood. He went back to drinking his espresso and watched the harbor in the distance. Little did he know his mood was about to get a great deal darker.

He spotted Brian making his way across the street and waved at him from the café window.

Brian O'Connell was the very image of his Irish father. He had a strong Celtic nose that Jack knew had been broken more than once playing hockey, heathery green eyes the color of the Killarney hills, and a smile that sparkled a little more brightly with each successive Guinness he drank. But he was also shrewd and had an uncanny mind for business, handling the public side of the partnership that Jack just didn't have the flair or inclination for.

And Brian was a good friend, standing with Jack during more than one school-yard brawl. Had he

been there moments earlier, he would have stood
beside Jack against Blair Jr., too. It was just one
of the many reasons why Jack had agreed to go
into business with him.

"Hey," Brian said, dropping into the chair across
from him. "Sorry I'm late. Colleen lost the pendant
her mother gave her for her birthday and she's been
tearing the house apart, hysterical, looking for it."

He motioned to Sal for a cup, then flipped
through some papers in his file. "Okay, we've only
got a few minutes before he gets here."

"Speaking of which, who exactly is 'he?' "

"The client?" Brian looked at him. "His name
is Cavanaugh."

Jack nearly choked on his coffee. "Declan
Cavanaugh?"

"Yeah, that's the guy. New in town, staying up
at—"

"Thar Muir."

Brian stared at Jack. "Something I don't know
about you and this guy that I should?"

"He was dating Jen for a little while, that's all."

Brian frowned. "Shit."

Jack shook his head. "Don't worry about it. It's
nothing to worry over now."

"I hope not, Jack. I know I don't need to remind
you that we need this job, especially after Newburyport fell through. Colleen's none too happy
that I quit the firm in Boston in the first place.
Weekending it with my father was one thing, but
starting over when we've got two kids to feed is
another. If I don't get some action going soon, she's
going to forget all about losing her pendant and
kick my sorry butt out the door."

Jack looked at Brian. "I said I can handle it."

A few minutes later, Cavanaugh came into the

café, filling it with his presence the moment he came through the door. Everyone turned to look at him and Jack was taken back to the first time he'd seen the man, when he'd assumed he was the waiter the night he'd taken Jen out to dinner. Hopefully, the guy didn't hold a grudge.

Cavanaugh and Brian exchanged handshakes, and then the Californian turned to Jack.

"You must be Jack Gabriele," he said, giving a smile that didn't convey so much as an ounce of warmth. "Declan Cavanaugh. I've heard good things about you and your ideas from Brian here."

"Mr. Cavanaugh," Jack said and shook his hand.

The men sat at the table and Jack studied the newcomer. Blond hair. Gold watch. Good clothes. He was older than Jack had thought, but he obviously took care of himself.

They waited while Maria brought a fresh round of coffees, then got down to business.

Declan began. "I contacted Brian because I am looking for a firm to design and build a house for me. The concept is a unique one and I think your firm has exactly the philosophy I'm looking for."

"This is a house?" Jack asked. "For you?"

A house, he knew, would mean the Californian intended to relocate, at least on a semipermanent basis. Otherwise, he could have just rented.

Considering his interest in Jen, that wasn't particularly welcome news.

"For the time being, yes. I am negotiating the purchase of a piece of property right now and once the acquisition goes through, I intend to build straight away. Brian tells me you're the designer of the two of you, so I'd really like to give you my vision of the property, and then see where you can take it from there."

Jack nodded. "Sure. What do you have in mind?"

A person's taste in a living place generally reflected their personality, and with someone like Cavanaugh, Jack expected to hear words like "contemporary" and "state of the art," a design concept that was "minimalist" with "clean, precise lines." For a guy like him, bigger typically was better. What Jack hadn't expected to hear was—

"Victorian. Farmhouse. Queen Anne style, I think."

Jack looked up from the legal pad he'd begun to use for note taking and stared across the table.

Cavanaugh simply stared back. "Gabled roof. And a turret. Definitely a turret . . ."

As he went on, listing the features he desired, Jack could see the house clearly in his mind. The wraparound porch, five bedrooms, maybe six. In the tower, a first floor office for him to design in, with windows on every side. A second, bridal stair that led off the kitchen to the upper floors. And the master suite, complete with a claw-foot tub.

"But the tub has to be six feet at least," Cavanaugh said, smiling just slightly. "Big enough for two. Might be a bit of a challenge, but I'm sure you'll find one somewhere, Jack. I hear Vermont has some good antique yards . . ."

Jack slammed down his pen. "What the f—"

"Jack." Brian eyed him cautiously.

"This is bullshit, Brian."

It was as if Cavanaugh had simply taken a stroll into the most private corners of Jack's mind, stealing every detail of the house that he'd spent the past two years designing.

Only Cavanaugh wanted Jack to build it for him.

Jack noticed something, a gleam in the Californian's eyes. He asked, "This piece of property you're negotiating—where is it located?"

"It's here. In Ipswich-by-the-Sea."

"Where, exactly?"

Cavanaugh smiled. "As a matter of fact, it's Hathaway Island."

Now it was Jack's turn to smile. He sat back in his seat.

"Considering that the town can't legally sell the island to you at this point, I don't see this house ever happening. I don't know what you think you're doing, but this meeting is nothing more than some kind of demented joke." Jack closed his notebook. "Thanks, but we're not interested in the job."

Brian glared at him. "Jack . . ."

"Brian, we don't need *this* job."

"Funny," Cavanaugh said. "It was my understanding that you *did* need this job, Jack. That it would give your firm the experience you need. Otherwise, without an extensive résumé, how do you expect projects like the Newburyport deal ever to go through?"

"Newburyport?" Now it was Brian's turn to stare. "How the hell did you find out about—"

Jack just watched Cavanaugh from across the table. It was as if he were some sort of demon conjured up from hell.

"When I see something I want, Jack, I generally get it. No, the truth is I *always* get it. And I have seen something I want here in Ipswich-by-the-Sea." He lowered his voice. "I intend to get it."

Jack wondered if he meant the island or Jen.

Or both.

Cavanaugh got up to leave. He obviously had finished toying with them. "By the way," he said, "my condolences."

Jack felt a chill. "On what?"

"Jenna's miscarriage."

And with that, he turned and walked out of the café.

Jenna clicked off the television and checked the clock again.

8:45.

Where in the world could Jack have gone?

She'd been calling his cell phone most of the day, every half hour since five o'clock, first to check if he'd be back in time for dinner, then later because she was growing more and more worried the longer she went without reaching him.

She stopped in at the café, but Sal told her he hadn't seen Jack since earlier that day.

Tino and Rosa hadn't heard from him either.

She called Brian who merely told her the meeting hadn't gone well and he had absolutely no idea where Jack might have gone to.

Finally, at nine, Jenna decided to take a drive out to the cottage to see if he was there. Maybe he was working, she thought hopefully, and for whatever reason, he couldn't get a signal on his phone. She told herself not to panic. She called over to her mother asking her to come sit at the house. The kids were already in bed but if they should happen to wake, she wanted someone to be there.

Jenna grabbed her keys, slung her purse over her shoulder, and reached for the back door to leave.

She opened it . . .

. . . and found Jack.

He was standing, staring at her, his hair damp from the rain.

"I need to talk to you," he said, and his face looked almost as if he'd seen a ghost.

Jenna couldn't know that in some respects he had.

"Jack, what's wrong?"

Jack pushed past her and walked into the kitchen, pacing the floor.

After several moments, he turned to face her. "Why didn't you tell me?"

"Tell you what? Jack, you're scaring me."

"I saw Cavanaugh today."

"Oh . . ." Jenna realized that Jack must have learned of Declan's unexpected proposal. "Jack, you can't think I would have had any intention of going with him. I mean, sure, it's always been my dream to go to Venice, but—"

Jack turned. "What the *fuck* are you talking about?"

"Jack!"

He stared at her. The dark look on his face made her think back to the early years of their marriage, nights when he'd come home angry, how easily provoked he'd been.

Jenna pushed the thoughts away.

"Jack, Declan came to see me today." She spoke calmly, trying to keep the conversation reasonable. "It was all very . . . odd. He invited me to go to Venice with him, and when I refused, he asked about—"

"You know what? I don't even care what the fuck you're talking about."

And then he stepped toward her, closing in. His face came inches from hers. "What I want to know is why I had to hear that you had a miscarriage from that asshole Cavanaugh?"

Chapter Fifteen

Jenna saw her vision blur. "What did you say?"

"You heard me. What miscarriage is Cavanaugh talking about, Jenna? Whose baby was it?"

Jenna felt herself begin to tremble. She wrapped her arms around herself, suddenly feeling cold, as if she stood in the midst of the deepest winter.

"It was your baby, Jack." She closed her eyes as the soul-deep ache she'd locked tightly away those years before brutally burst free. *"Our baby."*

"What? When?"

"Four years ago, Jack. In fact on that very day when you left, before Cassie . . ." Jenna choked back a sob. "I had just found out I was pregnant. I was so excited to tell you but when you came home that night, you were in such a horrible mood."

"I'd just been laid off."

Jenna nodded. "And we had that fight, and when I went to put Cassie in her room, you left. Without a word, you just left us. And then, somehow, Cassie got out and . . ."

Jenna felt herself losing the fight against her tears.

Jack's voice grew quiet. "You never told me there was a baby."

"I know that. But it was the reason I didn't want you to go away that weekend. Not because I wanted to tie you down, or be the sort of wife who nagged her husband or forbid him all his freedoms." She blinked. "I didn't want you to go away that weekend because I was pregnant. And I didn't want to be left alone, again."

Jack didn't say anything, didn't move, barely breathed for several long moments. "And you . . ."

"Miscarried. About a week after Cassie regained consciousness."

"All that time in the hospital, you never said anything." Jack closed his eyes, battling with his own emotions. "I killed our child. Oh, my God, Jen. You must hate me."

"I could never hate you. . . ."

Jenna came before him, taking his face into her hands. She looked deeply into his tortured hazel eyes. "Jack, losing the baby wasn't because of you. And it wasn't because of me. It just wasn't meant to be. Back then, I saw no point in telling you because we were already broken apart. The only purpose it would have served would have been to hurt you even more. I didn't want that. But now, we're together again. I was going to tell you about it, Jack. You have to know that. I didn't want us to begin another *us* with anything left unspoken. But in all that's gone on in the past weeks, with the salon and Hathaway Island, the timing, the opportunity just hasn't been right."

Jenna wrapped her arms around his waist and pressed her cheek to his chest. She could hear his pulse drumming steadily.

"I love you, Jack. I love you now. And I loved

you then. With everything a woman can have. What happened . . . with the baby . . . it just happened. There are things we have to get through in life, painful things that are somehow, inexplicably *necessary* to take us to where we need to be. It's over, and we're through it now. We need to look forward, not back. We need to start again."

She felt Jack's breath hitch against her cheek. "Yet you told Cavanaugh about it."

She looked up at him. "No, Jack. I didn't tell him. I have never told anyone else about losing the baby, ever. Not even my mother."

"But I knew."

Both Jack and Jenna turned to see Eudora standing in the kitchen doorway. They'd been so caught up in the tumult of Jack's arrival, neither of them had noticed her arrive.

"Mother . . ." And then Jenna closed her eyes, nodding. "Of course you would have known."

Eudora always knew.

Eudora came into the kitchen, going to her daughter. "I never said anything to you about it, because I felt if you needed to, you would talk to me about it. There are some things a woman must endure alone. I understood your need to close the door on that broken piece of your heart. It was already too late and we had only just gotten Cassie back. And you'd decided to leave Jack. I saw no need in revisiting more heartache."

Eudora touched a hand to her daughter's cheek. "But I was and still am so very sorry, my child."

Jenna reached for her mother. "I just don't understand how Declan could have known about the baby."

"But it wasn't just the miscarriage he knew about, Jen," Jack said. "He knew about the house

I designed and the Newburyport deal that fell through. He even knew about the bathtub I went to get up in Vermont for you. It's like he's *supernatural* or something. All day I've been trying to think how Cavanaugh could have known about all this. I even went to the cottage to see if he might have gone there at sometime to riot through my things when I wasn't around. But everything was there. My notes, the drawings I made of the house, all my files were where they should be. Not a single sheet of paper was out of place. And then I even went to Thar Muir tonight to confront him, but he was gone."

"Gone?"

"Hallie said he just suddenly checked out. Paid his bill and left without any notice."

Jenna shook her head. "None of this makes any sense."

Eudora frowned. "Declan Cavanaugh doesn't make any sense."

"And it's all because of me!"

The three of them turned toward the stairs and the desperate child's voice that had spoken. They hadn't noticed that Cassie had awoken and was now standing in the hall.

"I heard you fighting with Daddy, Mommy. It scared me."

Jenna closed her eyes, wondering how much the little girl had overheard. "Cassie, honey, everything is all right now. Mommy and Daddy are fine. Please go on back to bed."

"No, Mama . . ." She shook her head, her eyes wide. "It's not all right. Don't you see? It's all my fault."

Jenna knelt before her. "Cassie, I don't understand. How is any of this your fault?"

Cassie glanced at Eudora. "Ask Nanny. She knows."

"Nanny knows what?"

Eudora looked at Jenna, then said, "It was . . . a spell."

"A spell?"

"Cassie's spell."

Jenna felt herself growing only more confused. "Are you saying Cassie performed a spell? When?"

"Oh, Mommy . . . I just wanted you to be happy again! I heard you and Aunt Hallie talking one night about conjuring up the perfect man for her."

Jenna remembered that night, the bottle of wine, she and Hallie writing that silly, stupid recipe.

"I just wanted to make him come true. So I took the paper you'd been writing and I performed a spell."

"Where?"

"Out in your garden. I thought if I could make you happy again, you would see I was old enough to learn to cast. But the Toothpaste Man was supposed to be for Aunt Hallie, not for you. You and Daddy were just supposed to fall in love again, too. But something went wrong. Ogre ate Aunt Hallie's poppet, and then the next day, the Toothpaste Man was there. Only he's Declan and now everything is a mess and it's *all . . . my . . . fault!*"

Utterly and truly at sea, Jenna looked at Eudora.

Eudora explained. "She cast a spell, only it got crossed somehow. She told me about it shortly after it happened and I've been trying to break it, but nothing I do seems to succeed. There's something else at work here, something that is undermining my efforts. It's got a power all its own, a presence I just can't seem to banish."

While they were talking, Jack went to the desk in the corner where Jen's computer stood. He slid the mouse forward, and clicked the monitor out of hibernation.

As the Google home page brightened on the screen, he started typing: D-E-C-L-A-N C-A-V-A-N-A-U-G-H. He hit ENTER.

One of the first results he found was an obituary notice.

> Declan Cavanaugh, born in Cape Charles, Virginia, to Patrick and Madeline Cavanaugh, and who last resided in Monterey, California, died on September 30 in a tragic car accident on the Pacific Coast Highway near Carmel . . . Mr. Cavanaugh had recent success in print-ad modeling . . . He leaves no other family. . . .

Jack clicked the photograph link on the obituary. The pixilated image came slowly into view, revealing the blond hair, the tanned face, the same arrogant smile that had mocked him from across the café table that morning.

Jack drew a slow breath. "Jen, you'd better come and have a look at this."

Jenna stood beside Jack, reading the screen. She turned to Cassie. "Honey, do you remember what day it was when you cast your spell?"

"Are you mad at me for casting, Mommy?"

Jenna looked into her daughter's eyes and smiled. "No, Cassie. I'm not mad at all. I understand, more than you will ever know, about wanting to learn to cast. Now can you tell me when you cast the spell?"

Cassie nodded. "It was the day after you and Aunt Hallie were talking in the kitchen that night, about Mrs. Greer and how Mr. Greer had painted all over her grandma's quilt."

The night after they'd written that silly recipe . . .

Jenna reached for the mouse, double clicking the program that archived all her salon appointments. She did a search for Hannah Greer's most recent entry.

September 29.

Which meant Cassie must have cast the spell on September 30.

The same day that Declan Cavanaugh—the real Declan Cavanaugh—had been killed in an automobile accident.

Jenna stood, staring at the computer screen.

Eudora came to join them. She looked at Jenna. "Call your sister. We've got work to do."

"Jenna, you're not going without me."

Jenna was on her hands and knees, searching under the bed.

Where the heck had she put that crystal?

She got up, blew her hair out of her eyes, and turned to face Jack. "Jack, this is something you don't understand. It's something you'll never really understand."

He frowned at her. "You are not going out to that godforsaken island alone."

She went to her closet and started rooting around inside, looking through boxes and neat containers of her belongings. "I won't be alone. Mother and Hallie will be with me. And I'm taking Cassie with us, too."

"Cassie? Are you nuts? She's just a little girl. You are going to be performing some sort of crazy exorcism spell . . ."

"*Banishment* spell," Jenna corrected, looking through a stack of boxes.

Still nothing.

"Banishment. Exorcism. Whatever. What if something goes wrong? From what you tell me, as fantastical as it sounds, this guy is supposed to be some sort of malevolent wandering spirit who, according to you, just happened to take up residence in the most convenient dead body he could find."

Jenna sighed. "I explained all of this to you, Jack. When Cassie called him forth—that is Declan Cavanaugh, toothpaste model—this other *entity*, whatever or whoever he really is, decided to seize the opportunity to wreak a little havoc. So now we just have to shove him back into the slimy abyss where he belongs."

"Oh, you mean the underworld," Jack said sarcastically. "The raging chasm of death. The afterlife gutter of the wicked and depraved."

"Something like that." Jenna tapped her chin with her finger then looked up at her shelf. "Aha!"

She took down a box and opened it, revealing a fat, jagged hunk of stone that was purple and white and silver intermingled. Amethyst had been used for centuries for protection, and tonight, they needed all the protection they could get . . .

. . . even if it meant Jenna had to use it to cosh Declan over the head.

"Listen to me, Jack. Do you remember how when you first learned about all of this . . ." She motioned to the bed where she had set out the tools she'd started gathering together, her cape, her casting rod, and a collection of various heavy-duty banishing herbs.

"You asked me how you'd never realized I was a witch when we were married. Well, you didn't realize it because for a time, I turned away from the craft. I turned away because, just like Cassie, I had performed a spell when I shouldn't have. I was angry at my mother because she wouldn't let me go to the end-of-year dance at school. Her reason for not letting me go was because my father was due back from sea and whenever he came home, we all had to be there. I was a teen and I was rebellious and angry and didn't realize the ramifications of wanting to have it both ways. So I conjured up a storm, thinking it would simply delay my father a day or two so I could go off to that stupid dance where Blair Pritchett Junior tried to stick his hand down my shirt."

Jack looked at her. He hadn't even registered that last thing she'd said.

Instead, he said, "Your father died in a storm."

Jenna nodded. "He died in *that* storm. Whether it was because of the spell or not, I don't know. I'll never know. But I have had to live with that possibility all of my life. It was the reason I turned away from the craft. I swore I'd never perform a spell again. And I didn't, for many years. I met you. I fell in love. We got married, had Sam and Cassie. All the while I ridiculed my mother for devoting herself to what I believed was an archaic, old crone's art."

She paused, her voice growing soft. "And then Cassie fell in that pond. Jack, I was so afraid I would lose her. You were there. She just wouldn't wake up, and the longer she slept, the less hope the doctors had of her ever recovering. So I went to my mother and I begged her to intervene. I pleaded with her to use her magic, that *archaic, old crone's art* I'd scorned, to save our daughter's life. And she did."

"And I had no idea," Jack said.

"How could you? I never let you see that part of my life. This *craft* is in my blood. It has been for centuries. And it is in Cassie's blood, too. She needs to learn its power, and most importantly, she needs to learn to respect that. Not to cast misguided love spells with toothpaste advertisements for poppets. It took me almost losing her to realize what that respect should be. I don't want her to have to wait that long. I don't want her to have to know what it is to live with the regret of a spell gone wrong."

Jenna went to Jack then, placing both hands on his chest as she looked up at him. Loving him for loving her so much.

"Please understand this. Stay here with Sam. Be here to hold us when we come home again."

Jack could only stand and watch the woman he loved more than life itself walk out the door.

They gathered in Eudora's kitchen—Hallie, Jenna, Cassie, and Eudora—three generations of Wren witches. They prepared mixtures of herbs, aromatic oils and powders, and gathered together candles, which they enchanted beneath the light of the full moon.

And then, before they were set to leave, Eudora removed a key from the chain that hung around her neck and unlocked the antique trunk that she kept so inconspicuously at the foot of her bed.

The book she removed from inside, hidden under blankets and journals and other personal mementoes, was very, very old. The brown leather cover was worn to a shine and the pages were yellowed and brittle along the edges with age. The writing that flowed across each page was faded and florid, written in the tongue of the Gael, difficult to decipher.

Cassie whispered to her mother as her nanny

tucked the book into her bag and headed for the door. "Mommy, what is that book? I've never seen it before."

"That is great-grandmama Rachael's grimoire."

Cassie's mouth fell open. "Her spell book?"

Jenna nodded. "The spell we're going to cast to banish Declan is very old and very powerful. And it can only be cast on one night of the year. We're just fortunate that one night happens to be tonight. Fortunate, or maybe fated . . ."

Cassie nodded. "Samhain."

They had passed the past several days waiting for this time, the time of the living and the dead, while preparing for the ritual they would perform. They'd spent the hours gathering herbs and tutoring Cassie in the ways of the craft, while arming themselves with the tools they would need.

Samhain, also known as Summer's End, was the traditional Celtic time of year when the barrier between the world of the living and the world of the dead stretched to gossamer-thinness. Back when she'd been a young girl, on each Samhain night, after all the trick-or-treaters had gone off to bed to dream of Snickers bars and Everlasting Gobstoppers, Jenna, her mother, and her sister had journeyed through the ancient woods of Ipswich-by-the-Sea to visit the grave site of Rachael Hathaway. It was the time at which the ancient Celts traditionally honored the memory of their dead, the end of the harvest year, and the start of the new.

But it was also one of the most powerful days of the year for performing their craft.

Night had fallen and the streets of Ipswich-by-the-Sea were already teeming with little costumed ghosts and goblins, so no one paid any particular mind to the quartet of caped figures who slipped

through the fence that surrounded the quiet bunga-
low on Elm Street. Excited to be included in this
all-important ritual, Cassie didn't mind giving up
her Halloween candy just this once.

Earlier that week, Jenna and Jack had sat down
with Sam and had explained everything to him; his
connection to Rachael Hathaway, the craft that the
women in his family performed. At first, the eleven-
year-old said it was unfair that only the girls were
allowed to participate, especially Cassie. But after
Jenna had explained, making him a part of keeping
the family secret, he began to understand and accept it.

Although he warned Cassie she'd better never
put a hex on him.

The women drove to Siren's Cove and parked
behind Morgan's farm stand on a bluff overlooking
the sea. Once there, they made their way to the
shore in silence. The wind rushed and pulled,
shrilling through the tall beach grass and whipping
their capes around them. Out over the water, shimmering on the gentle tide, the moon was full and
brilliant, beaming its light upon that distant island,
barely visible for the darkness and the mist.

Hathaway Island.

Jenna cut the engine to Jack's fishing boat and
allowed the craft to drift sluggishly on the water's
surface, skimming slowly toward the shadowy outline of the pier.

When they drew near enough, Hallie looped the
mooring rope to the pier's supporting post, securing
the boat fore and aft so the four could safely
disembark.

Jenna stepped off first, then turned to help her
mother, then Cassie, and finally Hallie from inside.

They didn't speak as they followed the moon's light along the meandering path that led to the highest point on the island. Known by the villagers as The Witch's Table, it was a flat clearing where the ground was covered in evergreen. It would provide the perfect altar for performing this all-important spell.

Once there, Hallie and Jenna started clearing away the debris, errant driftwood and dried sea kelp, and other windswept beach grasses. Cassie began setting out the candles, forming them into a precise circle just as her mother had shown her. Finally, Jenna lit them, one by one, as she chanted the verse that would secure their magical groundwork.

Standing in the circle's center, Eudora took out her walking stick. Made of enchanted rowan, she used it as a guide to call down the elements of nature.

> *"Earth . . . Fire . . . Wind . . . and Sea,*
> *Come to us, hear our plea. . . ."*

Jenna, Hallie, and Cassie repeated the summons, echoing it three times.

The four women stood inside the circle they'd cast. Eudora, the elder, was at the very center, while the others surrounded her with hands locked, clasped around her in protective unity.

She took out a large metal vessel attached to a chain in which she burned thistle for defiance against dark forces, potentilla for empowerment, and mullein for healing. She swung the vessel outward, chanting in Gaelic as she smudged the circle with the silvery smoke that billowed from within.

Eudora followed the spell that had been inscribed in the grimoire, written in the hand of her ancestress. And when she was finished, she stood and invoked the will of the Samhain moon.

"I call upon your spirit. Come and banish that which threatens us on this sacred day. . . ."

"You know," called a voice from outside the circle, "if you'd wanted to see me, ladies, all you had to do was ask."

The voice was deep, and it echoed from the shadows surrounding them.

Cassie gasped. "Mommy, it's Declan."

Jenna squeezed her daughter's hand. "It's okay, honey. Just remember he's not real. Hold tight to my hand and to Aunt Hallie's, too. Whatever you do, don't break the circle."

Declan laughed, his voice coming closer. "Do you truly think that your little kitchen magic is any match for me? Any match for this?"

He emerged from the darkness then, dressed in the black of his soul. His hair was wild and shimmering and his eyes seemed to burn. He raised his hands and thunder shuddered across the sky above them, trembling the ground beneath their feet.

Jenna squeezed Cassie's hand. "Be strong, Cassie Bear. Don't be scared. He won't come inside the circle."

"Stupid witch," he said, hearing her. "I don't have to come inside. Your circle is nothing. Nothing but puff and nonsense."

He pointed at them, toward the candles that surrounded their feet. He laughed and the ground began to shudder and shift, pushing up with the force of an earthquake.

When it separated, splitting apart right at Eudora's feet, Cassie screamed.

"Mommy!"

"Hold tight, Cassie. Nanny is safe. So long as we are one, he cannot hurt us."

Declan laughed harder. The ground rumbled more.

"You'd better run, little witch, or the ground will open up and swallow you whole!"

Having had enough of his little demonstration, Eudora took up her walking stick and pointed it at the sky.

Lightning flickered behind the clouds.

"Spirit of the earth and the moon and sun, heed my call." She whipped her arm outward, sweeping it toward Declan. "Spirit of the air, heed my call."

A great rush of wind swept across the island, swirling around their circle. Despite its force, none of the candles went out.

Eudora brandished her stick toward the water. "Spirit of the sea, heed my call."

There came a distant roar from over the rocky shore. A mist, featherlight, shimmered around them.

And then Eudora turned to face Declan, who stood unmoving, as if frozen at the edge of their circle. Eudora leveled the rod point on him. "Spirit of fire, *heed . . . my . . . call*!"

The sky split and a great beastlike shriek screamed from above.

Jenna closed her eyes, clutching Cassie and Hallie tightly, as a force blew across the isle.

The ground trembled and shuddered, rocking them. The wind howled, pulling, billowing their capes around them, but still they clung together, holding fast until, finally, it came, a bolt out of the blue.

It struck Declan down in a violent shower of fire and sparks and smoke.

Jenna heard Cassie scream as the wind suddenly

circled, sweeping the four women together. They clung to one another—mothers and daughters—as the elements converged and bellowed around them.

And then, just as swiftly as it had come, the storm was gone. The wind retreated. The sea seemed to grow still. And the earth calmed its nauseous heaving.

"It is okay, my dears," Eudora's voice murmured gently to them. "We are safe now."

They loosened the circle and turned together, staring in the moonlight at the place where Declan had been.

There was nothing now, nothing at all, except a smoking, burning patch of charred earth.

"Kitchen magic, indeed," Eudora scoffed.

Cassie had her face pressed into her mother's chest, her arms wrapped tightly around her waist as Jenna softly brushed her daughter's hair from her eyes.

Sometime later, Cassie lifted her head. "Mommy?"

"Hmm?" Jenna said, taking the deep breath of the unbeaten, of one who had come through the battle and won.

"Mommy, your tummy . . . it's buzzing."

"What?"

Jenna searched through the folds of her cape and found the pocket where Jack had tucked something inside.

Jenna laughed. "It's my cell phone!"

She noticed the display glowing HOME on the caller ID.

She flipped the phone open. "Hi, Jack. Yes, we're here. And we're all fine. Just fine."

She looked at her daughter, her sister, and her mother, all standing around her and then added: "And we're coming home."

Epilogue

Not many little girls were lucky enough to have their seven-year-old birthday wishes come true at their eighth birthday party. *And* get to be the maid of honor, too.

But Cassie Wren did.

Her party was a week late, but what a party it was.

In the morning, her mommy and daddy were married on Hathaway Island as the sun was just coming up over the sea. It was a perfect day. The air was unseasonably warm, bringing a mist that wreathed the isle with gossamer.

The people in town called it an Indian summer. Cassie's teacher, Mrs. Ogilvy, told her class that the term "Indian Summer," or "Second Summer" as it was sometimes called, meant something that blooms late, or unexpectedly.

Rather like her parents falling in love again.

The weather, however, had been strictly Eudora's doing, by way of a little "precautionary" spell, so nothing would spoil Jenna and Jack's day.

After the ceremony, there was food and music and dancing with all their family and friends. Aunt Hallie sat clapping her hands as *Zio* Sal and *Nonno*

Tino played their accordion and mandolin. They played a song they called the "Tarantella."

Zia Maria and Jules, her daughter who'd snuck away from her studies at Harvard, started pulling the other guests from their chairs with *Nonna* Rosa, forming a circle around Jack and Jenna. *Zia* Sofia went to get Aunt Hallie, who wasn't about to go without Flora, who laughed and grabbed her husband Gavin's hand, dragging him along. Cassie and Annie didn't need any invitation to dance, but between them they managed to pull in Robbie, Gabriel, Sam, and even wee Seamus, despite their stupid boy protests.

Soon everyone was turning a circle around Jenna and Jack, whirling and laughing while the music played faster and faster.

Afterward, they shared the biggest birthday-wedding cake Cassie had ever seen. Nanny had made the cake, Cassie's favorite lemon crème, and along with the bride and groom who stood proudly on its top, there was a figure of a boy and a figure of a girl standing on either side of them.

Cassie's family.

Just the day before, Jenna had learned that the town selectmen were withdrawing their petition in the Land Court to take over Hathaway Island, after having heard about the results of the DNA test. Cassie wasn't too sure what kind of test that was; she only knew she was happy because it meant that now Hathaway Island wouldn't be sold.

To make certain of that, Mommy had decided to protect the island so that it could never be threatened again. With Mr. Dugan's help, they were putting the island under something called a stewardship with something called a land trust that would allow it to remain open to the public as it

always had been. Mrs. Petwith at the Historical Society was also planning to create an exhibit for the
isle that would tell the "real" story of Rachael
Hathaway—not the made-up wicked tale that had
been passed down for generations about her.

Cassie was particularly pleased about that, because it would mean that Kaleigh Lansky would
have to eat her nasty words.

"Cassie!"

She turned and saw Annie calling to her from
up on the bluff. The little girl was waving to her,
jumping up and down.

"Come! Come quick!"

Cassie bounded along the pathway that led away
from the wedding party up to the top of the rise.
When she got there, Cassie realized they were
standing at the same place where she'd come with
her mommy, Aunt Hallie, and Nanny Wren on
Samhain night.

The night Declan Cavanaugh had been struck down.

It looked so very different in the daylight, not
nearly as eerie and sinister, even though, a short
distance away, she could still see the blackened
grass where he'd last stood.

Cassie paused when she saw Annie. Her friend
was hunched down on the ground, looking into a
hole. As soon as she saw her, Cassie realized it was
the exact same spot where Nanny Wren had stood
that night, where the ground had begun to open up
beneath her feet.

"What are you doing?" Cassie asked, reluctant
to go any closer.

"Come here!" Annie insisted. "I think I see
something."

Somewhat fearful of what it might be, Cassie
went to join her friend anyway.

"Look," Annie said, pointing down into the dank chasm. "There's something down there. At the bottom. Move a wee bit so you can see it in the sunlight. It's something shiny."

Annie started to stick her arm into the hole, to try and reach whatever it was, but Cassie pulled her back. "No, don't!"

A small part of her couldn't help but remember how Declan had taunted her that night, warning Cassie that the ground would open up and swallow her whole.

"Let's go and get my daddy and Gavin first."

Soon the entire wedding party was standing atop that sun-kissed bluff. Gavin and Jack had retrieved some tools and long poles from the boats and were chipping away at the opening, making it wider.

Jack was down on his stomach, lying on the blanket Jenna had insisted he put down so he wouldn't dirty his wedding clothes. "I can't quite reach it," he said. "It's still down about two more feet."

"What about Seamus?" Robbie suggested then. "Maybe if you hold him he can get to it?"

Seamus was more than thrilled at the idea of digging around in the sand and rocks.

"Daddy, no," Cassie said. She looked at her mother, who understood her concern.

Jenna said, "It's okay, Cass. Daddy's not going to let anything happen to Seamus. He might get a little dirty . . ." She glanced at Flora. "If that's all right."

"Wouldn't be the first time." Flora laughed. "Or the last."

Holding the three-year-old by his wiggly waist while Gavin, Robbie, Sam, and Gabriel secured his legs, Jack carefully lowered Seamus into the hole.

Cassie waited, holding her breath, until finally, she heard Seamus's little voice echo from inside.

"I got it!"

Only it wasn't an *it*.

It was a *them*.

Seamus came out with a handful of shimmery silver coins clutched in his grubby little fists.

Annie squealed as she stared at the treasure. "They look just like the one I found last summer! My piece of eight!"

"And there's a whole bunch more still there," Seamus beamed.

It took weeks and a team of professional treasure hunters to fully excavate the hole. They eventually unearthed what had once been a small wooden trunk, rotted nearly completely away but for the iron bands and lock that had once secured it. Stashed inside was a horde of coins, five hundred and thirty-five to be exact, Spanish silver dating back to the sixteenth and seventeenth centuries. Whether it was buried there by some long ago pirate, or shipwrecked and covered over by tide and erosion, no one could truly say. Nor could anyone agree with any certainty whether or not there might still be more of the treasure somewhere else on that lonely isle just waiting to be discovered.

The coins became the property of the Ipswich-by-the-Sea Historical Society and were put on display for any and all to see.

Time went on in that coastal New England village, as it had for centuries before, measured off by the seasons' change. When brilliant autumn faded into stark winter, the uproar of that October eventually faded too, much as the hysteria of 1692 more than three hundred years before.

Like the shift of the tide, business at IpSnips Salon slowly turned back. Only now, when Hannah Greer came in for her monthly pedicure, she sometimes asked Jenna, (privately, of course), if she had a spell or potion that would induce her husband, Jim, to repair the broken screen he was forever promising to fix, or some other such chore.

The stranger from California who had vanished as quickly as he had appeared was soon forgotten. Diana DeNunzio started an awareness group that met monthly at the café. And Sofia Gabriele finished racing school down in Florida, qualifying for her official competition license.

January roared out with a blizzard that brought the town to a five-day standstill. The Lanskys relocated when Kaleigh's father was transferred to Duluth. Mary Whittendon actually stopped saying "hmph," and even cracked a smile whenever Jenna went into the market.

The third week in March, as the crocuses were just pushing up yellow and purple on the snow-patched common, Flora and Gavin welcomed their new daughter, Isabelle. The very next week, Jenna stopped in at the pharmacy to buy her own home pregnancy test . . . just to be sure.

Life went on, as it did . . . as it had . . . as it always would.

The old were lost. The new were born.

Day-to-day.

Week to week.

And season to season.

But one thing remained the same.

There would always—*always*—be something magical about Ipswich-by-the-Sea.